THE EXPIRED

B.P.SMYTHE.

B.P.SMYTHE.

B.P.Smythe studied engineering at Carshalton College and eventually became a member of the Institute of Quality Assurance.

For his published crime writing short stories and novels. B.P. Smythe was inducted into the Crime Writers Association for his achievements.

Sow And You Shall Reap - http://www.amazon.co.uk/dp/145677171X is his first self- published novel. Last year B.P. secured a three book deal of short stories from Bloodhound Books http://www.bloodhoundbooks.com/. His author bio is on their website.

From a Poison Pen is his first book of short stories http://www.amazon.co.uk/Poison-Pen-collection-macabre-stories-ebook/dp/B01BKWT4EE. His second book of short stories From a *Poison Pen VOL II* has just been released and is available on: https://www.amazon.co.uk/Poison-Pen-ii-B-P-Smythe-ebook/dp/B01LFM1032

This year 2018 and 2019, B.P.Smythe is shortly to release four full length novels – *The Expired, The Medal of Purity, The Holocaust Experience, Whatsoever A Man Soweth* including two further books of short stories - *Short Tales with Long Memories VOL 1* and *VOL 2.*

B.P.SMYTHE Amazon author page: www.amazon.co.uk/-/e/B006MCGVNU

Books by B.P.Smythe For information on obtaining free complimentary PDF, Kindle or paperback copies, contact B.P.Smythe at barrysmythe@hotmail.com - Mob: 07814780856

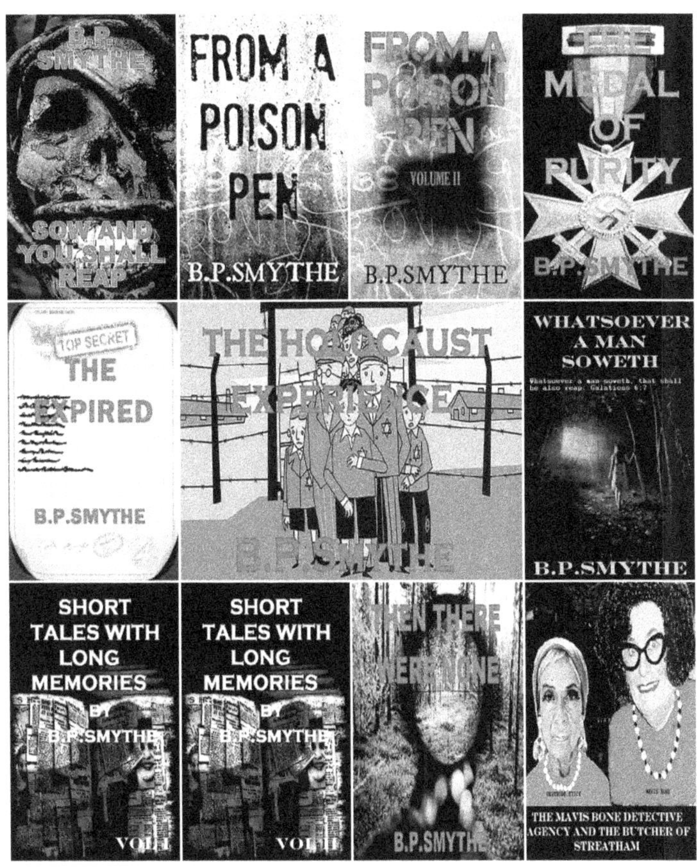

THE LETTER
BY
B.P.SMYTHE
BY B.P.SMYTHE
Girls of the BDM
by B.P.Smythe
Aunt Meg by B.P.Smythe
SOMETHING FISHY
BY B.P.SMYTHE
THE WHITE
ROOM
BY
B.P.SMYTHE
LOVER'S
LEAP
Lover's Leap
by B.P.Smythe

THE EXPIRED

B.P.SMYTHE.

CONTENTS

THE EXPIRED

B.P.SMYTHE.

Corruption, Embezzlement, Blackmail and Murder within MI5 Secret Service puts pressure on government security to find, foil and eliminate a murdering Transvestite, a cocaine drug scam and a London terrorist attack.

CHAPTER ONE

'Have you wet that bed again, you little shit?' His father took off his belt with vengeance and then strapped his backside repeatedly.

Francis cried out, 'Na please, Dada, I'm sorry.' The tears were streaming down his terrified little face.

The big man went to the draw and took out the large dressmaker scissors.

Francis watched in horror as his father came towards him with them - *snip – snip – snip.*

'The next time you do that I'm gonna lift your nightie and snip that useless thing off.' He grabbed his small arm and dragged him sobbing to his bed. 'Look at it, now smell it, you little shit.' He forced his head down and rubbed his nose into the wet sheets. 'They do that to puppies so they learn not to mess indoors.'

Francis looked up at him with pleading eyes. His long shoulder length hair clung to the sides of his face with tears and snot.

'Why, dear God, couldn't you have been a girl like your sister, Roxanne? Even your mother didn't want a boy. You're the reason she left. She wanted to take Roxanne but I wouldn't let her. I wanted her to take you.' His father raised his hands in anger and desperation. '*You made your mother run away. Boys are the curse of this family. Our first two were Mongols, now hidden away in some loonybin and then you had to come along. But I'm going to show you…believe me I'll make you into a girl before you start school if it's the last thing I do.*' He thrust the scissors into his face. '*And you dare tell anyone you're a boy and so help me.*' His father motioned with the scissors. '*Snip – snip – snip…you got that you bedwetting little shit?*'

Francis slobbered, 'Yes Dada…please don't cut it off…I won't tell. I'll be a good girl like Roxanne…'

*

In 1965 Annabel Potting had just celebrated her seventeenth birthday. One of her presents had been a large leather bound diary. Annabel was a diary person. Always had been; wrote in one religiously every day. To Annabel, a diary was important, she never went anywhere without one. Either she carried it under her arm or it was always in her shoulder bag. With one exception, on walks she let Zita her pet Golden Labrador carry it in her mouth.

Annabel put everything in her diary, thoughts, ideas, feelings, all food for a budding poet. She loved poetry it captivated her. She would read Shakespeare, Milton, Blake, Byron, Keats, Tennyson, Browning, even Greek and First World War poetry. She consumed it all with a ravenous hunger. It was her lifeblood.

As a student, it was Annabel's chosen career to teach, with a burning ambition to write a book of poems and get published. She'd done well in her final year exams and had gone to Ewell College to study A Level poetry and literature.

At this moment in time her diary was her most valued possession. It was her confidant, best friend, big sister, second mum, even substitute boyfriend. All these things rolled into one.

With this in mind and the private thoughts she would sometimes document, Annabel had to be assured it was kept in a safe place away from prying eyes.

How all this secrecy came about was due to her over protective mother. While Annabel was at college, her mother had begun searching her bedroom. After reading too many tabloids and watching too much television about the sixties sexual revolution, her mother had got it into her head that every female student was a cannabis smoking, alcohol swigging, pill-popping nymphomaniac Rolling Stones groupie. Her worry bordered on hysteria.

Looking for drugs, contraceptives, booze, even cigarettes, she rummaged through drawers, searched in the wardrobe, under the mattress; but found nothing. Of course her mother meant well. However, Annabel like all teenagers when they reach a certain age, wanted her privacy.

Annabel used to set little traps so she always knew when her mother had been nosey. Clear Sellotape was very effective when discreetly laid across doors and drawers. The problem was, hiding the bulky diary. Although she kept it with her most days, there were times when she had to keep it concealed in her bedroom. Then at last, she had a brain wave. She found the perfect hiding place. A loose airbrick in her bedroom high on the wall. Her mother would never dream of looking there.

Annabel was slim and petite with long dark hair from her mother's side. At five-foot-four-inches, she had the figure for shorts. With her model looks, she was every young lad's dream. Annabel knew she looked good. A girl gets to know from the glances. She didn't have a regular boyfriend at the moment although her interest had increased since she'd started college.

On Saturday afternoon, wearing the latest fashionable hot-pants and a skimpy top, Annabel walked down her back garden path carrying a small fold up chair with her shoulder bag swinging from the hip. Her dog Zita padded ahead with the diary in its mouth.

The weather forecast for August 1965 was warm and sunny. So, after chasing sticks and her favourite ball for an hour, Zita was quite happy to lie at Annabel's feet.

Annabel had parked herself in her favourite spot surrounded by dense hawthorn and juniper trees just out of sight from her parents back gate on the south side of Nonsuch

Park. It was a quiet place, away from the steady drone of traffic, only broken by the chatter of finches and magpies. Being some distance from the path, no one ventured here. Now she was in one of her creative moods, full of inspiration and ideas.

It had just turned 4:30 p.m. The sun was still high, the rays making short shadows on this hot afternoon. Perspiration was already forming on Annabel's forehead as she sat busily making notes in her diary. The smell of wood and dry earth filling her senses.

A lone cricket buzzed behind. Its back legs grinding together like a motor constantly revving up. Annabel's mouth was dry. Reaching for the bag she pulled out a Coca-cola. The cap hissed off as she quenched her thirst with a satisfied smile. Her dog lifted its head nonchalantly then lowered it again.

A plane faintly droned overhead leaving its fluffy trail.

She looked up. Surrounded by tall oak trees with the summer heat and the quiet, it had gradually become claustrophobic. It was as if the branches were whispering overhead. Their secrets contained in a majestic stillness, constantly exchanging what they had seen, witnessed over the long years.

Suddenly, voices. Zita's ears pricked up. Then some movement. Annabel's hand froze around her ballpoint pen. Her head jerked to the muffled cry and panting from behind. The dense bushes that partially cocooned her, gave no indication of what it was.

Annabel slowly rose. Her dog was on all fours, already in anticipation looking up wagging its tail. She quietly folded the canvas chair. Wincing as the ground crunched under her feet, she tiptoed in the direction of the sounds. Annabel wiped her forehead, the perspiration now running down her cheeks.

The odour of earth and grass had become nauseating, heavy and thick with the humidity.

The panting and moaning grew louder. She crouched down and carefully parted the hawthorn bramble, wincing as it scratched her arms and wrists. It was a couple half-naked. At first appearances it looked like a woman was sitting on top of a man having sex.

Annabel recognised the person on top even though he was dressed in female clothes. It was an 18 year old boy from her college whose name was Francis Hodder. Annabel was close enough to see the *ROXANNE* tattoo on his arm. She'd seen it before and heard rumours the tattoo was his sister's name.

Although big and burley for his age, the young man was dressed as a young woman wearing a black Cleopatra wig with green eye shadow and lipstick. A red Basque with matching suspenders and stockings finished off his transition.

Annabel watched them transfixed. Then in the heat of their buggering she heard the older man cry out, *'Roxanne'.*

After they'd finished they lay back on the blanket that was spread out on the ground. The older man lit up a cigarette and took out his wallet. Some money was exchanged.

Suddenly the younger man, Francis, stood up and snatched the wallet. The older man, shouted and grabbed his arm. With his free hand, Francis pulled out a cosh hidden under the blanket and hit him twice over the head. The man collapsed back groaning.

He looked around in case they'd been heard. Then Francis took off his wig and high heels and put on a pair of trousers and men's shoes. From a bag he took a mirror and some tissues and proceeded to wipe off his makeup.

Without a moment's hesitation, Annabel scribbled away furiously in her diary what had unfolded before her eyes. She couldn't help herself even though she was scared.

Now to get away, she thought. *Mustn't let them see me.*

Annabel turned to go but too late. Her dog started barking. She whispered, 'Shush! Zita.' Then in horror, she saw the face. The face she'd recognised. It was peering at her through the hedge and he had a look now, like a sky that could spawn a tornado at any moment. Francis recognised Annabel as well, from college.

Annabel dropped the diary and started to run, her legs were heavy with fear. The dog was ahead of her, barking. Francis stooped and picked up the diary. He saw her last entry, naming him and what he was doing. Buggering and robbery she'd written.

The dog, seeing the man with the diary, turned back and attacked him snatching the diary in its mouth, knowing that it belonged to its owner. The dog hung on and wrenched it from his hands, growling shaking its head. Francis yelled out and fell backwards to the ground in a flurry of earth and leaves. He cursed as he got up brushing himself down.

With the diary in its mouth, the dog scurried back to catch up with Annabel who was running in blind panic. Annabel ran until her temples pounded. Ran until her eyes pulsed in their sockets. Ran until she had a hot stitch in her left side from the bottom of her ribs up to her armpits. Ran until she could taste blood at the back of her throat. Then she tripped and fell sprawling, twisting her ankle. Annabel stood up. Her dog came back but she yelled at Zita to run on. The dog faltered, not wanting to leave her, still with the diary in its mouth.

Annabel started again, limping badly this time. The smell of dry earth thick in her brain.

Then the crunching of earth and twigs with heavy panting behind her. Someone shouting, 'Come here, You Bitch!'

She started to scream, *'Help me someone?—Please!'* She looked over her shoulder, the sound of running was getting nearer.

Her house was now in sight. If only she could reach it in time. Annabel was in excruciating pain dragging her left foot. *Must get to the back gate. Oh God! Please let me make it.*

Fumbling frantically for the latch, the gate swung open with Annabel falling through onto the concrete grazing her knees. Faithful Zita still with her, dropping the diary, licking her hand and then picking it up, waiting for the next command.

Annabel looked behind. Still no one in sight. With Zita ahead she limped up the garden path to the kitchen door.

Now inside, she turned the key and relaxed as the lock snapped into place.

Annabel leant with her back against the half-glazed door. Her chest moving up and down rapidly, breathing in snatches. Zita looked up at her. She patted the dog. 'Good dog,' she said. Then she stiffly bent and kissed Zita fondly on the head. Annabel took the diary from Zita and patted her again. 'Well done, Zeet.'

She looked into the garden through the window. It was all clear. The house was quiet. Her parents were out shopping. *Get up to your bedroom*, she thought. *Lock yourself in until dad gets back.*

At the rear of the house, Francis was panting hard from the running, already knowing where Annabel lived. He'd just seen them disappear behind the kitchen door, the dog still with the diary in its mouth.

The garage doors were open. There was no car. Hopefully the parents were out. At the side-entrance of the large detached house was a builder's skip sheltered by a high fence. The skip was filled with old paint tins, carpets and a three-piece suite. It looked like they had the decorators in.

The sound of breaking glass made Annabel look up from her diary. A nervous tick fluttered her cheek. She pressed her ear against the bedroom door, straining, listening.

'Ring the Police. That's it,' she mumbled nervously. Annabel picked up the extension. Hand shaking, the finger misdialled. 'Shit,' under her breadth. This time she got it right, 999.

There was a slight pause, then a voice, 'Emergency Services.'

'Police! Get me the police!' she shouted, *'I'm being—'* Annabel heard a click. Then nothing, just silence. She tapped the receiver bar frantically. Only her own breathing could be heard.

Francis stood at the bottom of the stairs. His hand clutched the pulled telephone wire. Then he called out to her, 'Oh Annabel. I know you're up there. I just want to talk. Explain things. It would be awkward if people found out, you know, my little preferences and what you put in that diary. My father can't afford a scandal you see. He's high up in government security. You know what I mean? Come on Annabel, don't make me come up there.'

He heard the sound of something being dragged. *Probably the bed? She was barricading the door with her bed.* Francis bounded up the stairs to the large balcony landing. Spotting the only bedroom door closed, he gave it a hefty kick.

Annabel started screaming. She tried pushing up the large sash window in desperation. The noise jerked him into panic; he couldn't afford her shouting out, attracting someone.

Using his shoulder, he took a flying leap and the door caved in. He went sprawling headlong onto the floor.

Annabel shrieked. As she stepped over him, he grabbed her leg and pulled her to the floor. She wrestled with him and raked his face with her nails.

He shouted at her, *'You Fucking Bitch!'* wincing with the pain.

With her foot, she shoved him back down and ran from the bedroom. Zita was in a barking frenzy ahead of her.

Annabel reached the stairs and then tripped over her dog. She screamed as she somersaulted repeatedly down the marble steps, crashing into the right-angled wall, leaving a bloody smear and then bouncing down the remaining flight. The brittle snap of her neck as she hit the bottom echoed through the quiet hall.

There was silence. Francis came out to the balcony and looked down the stairs. Zita was by the side of Annabel. She began to whine, wagging her tale, not understanding the staring eyes, the twisted head at right angles. Zita licked off some blood from Annabel's face hoping to waken her.

Francis had to act fast. He knew her parents might be back soon. That fucking diary was somewhere. He quickly rummaged through her bedroom. Nothing. 'Shit,' he whispered. Too late to look now, he couldn't afford the time.

There were two things he had to do, and quickly. Torch the house and hope the diary burnt with it. Then get rid of the body. Forensics, his hairs, his scratches, her fingernails with his skin. He was a dead man if anybody found *her* or the diary.

The dog was still pining. Francis shouted at it to shut up. He needed a clear head. And then he muttered, 'Yes, of course.'

Protected by the high fence, he made his way out of the back door to the side entrance. Francis looked into the skip and saw a big rolled up carpet. Then he heard the noise of a vehicle at the front of the house.

At that moment a skip truck with chains clunking, pulled up. *Too late now. 'Shit! Shit! Shit!'* His fist banged in desperation against the steel container. However, the driver didn't get out of his cabin. Instead, he decided to take his afternoon tea break. He opened his lunch box and started reading the newspaper.

Francis's luck was in. It was now or never. He pulled out the old carpet and unrolled it behind the skip. Then he went back for Annabel's body. He rolled the body up and then lifted the bundle with some heaving and slid it over the edge into the skip.

After fifteen minutes when the driver had finished his break, he watched from a side window as the container was lowered onto the truck. As it pulled away, he knew he had to finish the business.

Her dog was gone. It had run after the truck; still faithful to the end.

The decorators had left a two-gallon can of white spirit. Francis started upstairs shaking the fluid from room to room. Then he took one last look and flicked a match.

Twenty minutes later, Annabel's parents came home from shopping to see the fire brigade tackling the upstairs inferno. After a brief search, they reassured the hysterical mother there was nobody in the house.

A short time later, with Annabel still missing, the police were called and found the kitchen door had been forced open with down stairs drawers ransacked and furniture kicked over. Initially it looked like a robbery or vandalism, or both.

Two days later after Annabel had failed to return, the CID came to Ewell College and set up an interview room. All her known friends and acquaintances were called in one by one. With no other leads, the police turned their attention to a forty-eight year old male named Reginald Stanton.

He was a local man with a previous record of robbery with violence and had been released several months earlier after serving a seven year jail term. Annabel's parents had hired decorators shortly before her disappearance. Company records showed one of the men to be Reginald Stanton.

A neighbour had placed this man at the scene on the afternoon in question. He was picked out instantly in an identification parade. When arrested, the police had searched his rented room and found stolen items from Annabel's house. With Annabel still missing and scratches on his hands he couldn't properly account for, the case very quickly became a murder enquiry.

Eventually, after three months, even though Annabel's body had never been found, the jury at the Old Bailey took six hours to convict him of murder. In sentencing Reginald Stanton to life imprisonment, his lordship, Justice Anthony Farquason Q.C. had called him a wicked and depraved man for taking such a young life away from a loving family.

Amongst emotional scenes from the gallery with many relatives in tears, Reginald Stanton, forcibly restrained while shouting and protesting his innocence, was led away to start his life sentence.

CHAPTER TWO

'Look I've got the build and it's the top bodyguard course so I might as well put my muscles to good use. It makes sense to have me trained up to improve our security.' Francis and Isaac had just finished racing each other and were resting.

Sitting back on their bikes sweating profusely in Isaac Constantine's state of the art gym annexed to his secluded mansion, Francis added, 'You're a famous star now, you need someone close to take care of you. Even if it's just warding off over eager fans or reporters, including the paparazzi.'

Isaac reached across and put his arm affectionately around Francis's shoulder. 'I know you mean well, Sweetheart. You do the course if it pleases you.'

Francis said anxiously, 'I know you have those other minders and bodyguards around at concerts but it's just, I feel so vulnerable sometimes when we're out together in private. I'd kill myself if anything happened to you.'

Isaac hugged him affectionately. 'Nothing's going to happen to me, You Silly.'

Still sounding anxious Francis added, 'I know but you can't take chances. Look at Bobby Kennedy. If he'd had a trained bodyguard close by he might be alive today.'

'Okay–Okay,' Isaac laughed and hugged him. 'You've convinced me. So where do you go for the training?'

Francis said excitedly, 'It's a Close Protection Operations Course held at Briar Lodge Manor near Lymbridge Green in Kent. It's the most recognised establishment in the Bodyguard industry. This would lead to me obtaining the government standard SIA close protection licence.' Then he hesitated and said sheepishly, 'Only thing is, it's a whopping three-hundred pounds.' Then his face brightened. 'But it's for twenty-one days and fully residential. In fact the isolated manor it's held in has a history of training SAS and British secret service agents.'

Isaac fondly squeezed him again. 'Listen, Sweetheart, if that's what you want, to protect me, I don't care how much it cost. I'll pay for you to have the best course on offer.'

At six-foot-one and weighing a hundred and sixty-eight pounds with a full head of blonde hair and a set of features any male model would be envious of, twenty-two year-old Francis kept himself in good shape. This was using Isaac's private gym situated in the east wing of his eleven bedroom mansion set amongst the south-downs in Surrey.

It was one of the perks of being the boyfriend of Isaac Constantine who was currently the most famous black recording star Galaxy Records Inc' had ever had. Last year's record sales for 1972 had outstripped any other recording artist. This success was reflected in Isaac's other three palatial homes. Two in the UK and one in Los angles.

To keep in trim, Francis's gym favourite was the cross trainer. From here he could get an erection just looking at the black and white life size posters of his lover on the wall. Tall and shaven bald with a kind face like Harry Belafonte and the physique of a light weight boxer, the posters, taken from his European tours, showed Isaac in various stage bondage attire. From tight leather shorts and a zip up mask to being naked while on all fours. Other raunchy posters revealed him tethered by a lead and a spikey dog collar to some beautiful blonde in a figure hugging rubber suit.

His risqué stage acts that reflected his gender didn't just appeal to his huge gay following; the girls went wild over him as well.

Wanting an autograph, Francis had met Isaac at the stage door of a concert seven months ago, and it was love at first sight. Isaac Constantine at twenty-five years old and currently the most successful black soul singer in the UK and Europe with album sales increasing steadily in America, was smitten with Francis.

The singer had tried to keep their relationship under wraps, hiding from reporters and cameras when they were out together. The heavy minders had seen to it. Francis always maintained Isaac didn't need these brainless apes to look after him. He would do it.

Keeping a low profile on his love life, Isaac had kept the usual threats by telephone or mail, mostly from National Front and anti-homosexual groups, down to a minimum. His agent and secretary screened all his fan mail. If a threat looked serious it was referred to Isaac's head of security, a huge black man called Marvin. It usually finished there. Only a couple of times had they been on standby with the police, when some nutter had threatened to shoot or hurl a bomb. They'd all finished up as a hoax; sickos hiding behind their fantasies.

When Isaac Constantine first came out, the hate letters were smoking – He's not only a nigger but queer as well they'd written. Now of course with Gay Pride Rallies being held in London and Britain's first gay newspaper being launched, the racist remarks had dwindled to a trickle.

*

The Director General of MI5, Sir Geoffrey Hodder, had every reason to look worried. Recently this March 1973 there had been a cabinet reshuffle and it was known the new Home Secretary, Ruth Torrington, would be considering making changes in some top security positions.

Sir Geoffrey and the new Home Secretary had never been the best of friends since the accusations she'd made in the house while in the shadow cabinet. She had once asked for his resignation over what she called, "Lack of basic security," concerning the IRA car bombings outside The Old Baily. Since her ten month term in the new cabinet, relations had been frosty between them. Even more so now with a new kid on the block - Desmond Harrington, currently a director on the board for Northern Ireland Terrorism and tipped as a strong candidate for Sir Geoffrey's position – especially as one of his rich uncles had donated one million pounds to the party election campaign. More than once at meetings without Sir Geoffrey, she had hinted on a department reshuffle.

Sir Geoffrey knew, a strong show of senior department hands for a vote of confidence might sway her decision, perhaps curb her enthusiasm for a while. However, if he could ride out this latest MI5 reshuffle and maybe just keep his head above water on his £17,000 a year salary, he might be able to pay back some of the money on the loans he'd taken out.

Unfortunately, these were on numerous bad choice stock-exchange shares that had crashed in this year's Bear Market downturn and could force him into bankruptcy. Some of this investment money, which he vowed to pay back, he'd skimmed off the department's expenses budget and if not rectified, would show up as a deficit at the end of the year accounting period. Knowing of course, this would bring embarrassment to his department and further her call for his replacement and even prosecution. So he had to sit tight and remain squeaky clean.

Two weeks later, Sir Geoffrey received in his mail a summons for a meeting with the Home Secretary. He had expected it of course. He had five days grace to organise a vote of confidence and to make sure it was documented.

Although he was Director General, his five deputy staff that were responsible to him including, the Deputy Director

General, the Assistant Director General, the Director for Joint Terrorism Analysis, the Director of National Protection and Infrastructure and Commander Gregory Potting, former head of MI6 and the governments most senior advisor for internal affairs, constituted the management board for the MI5 service. Chaired by Sir Geoffrey, they would hold regular meetings to consider policy and strategic issues. Fortunately their next meeting was in two days' time.

Sir Geoffrey knew he could also lean on a couple of retired Director Generals he played golf with, one of whom sat in the House of Lords.

A few days later, with the ammunition tucked inside his briefcase he was shown into the Home Secretary's office. Sir Geoffrey had been a visitor here many times but was always astounded by the enormous length of the boardroom table and its thirty-two surrounding chairs. With an air of importance, Ruth Torrington sat at one end stamping her authority immediately on anyone that entered her domain.

Looking up, the pretty white face with the thin red lipstick smile beckoned him to sit. 'Ah, Sir Geoffrey, please take a seat will you.' At thirty-six years old, she was medium height and attractive with long dark wavy hair cascading down her shoulders onto a slim figure hugging lime green fashionable suit. Ruth Torrington looked as though she could be an advert for cosmetics in Vogue magazine.

On the other hand, fifty-eight year old Sir Geoffrey with his thinning silver hair and six-foot four-inch frame, engulfed the boardroom Chippendale chair.

Always with a serious expression on his lined face and wearing a dark blue pin striped suit, he cut a distinguished pose clutching his Aspinal crocodile skin attaché case.

Ruth Torrington had her notes set out. She was going to tell him tactfully, as Home Secretary she had decided changes were needed and the MI5 department required a fresh approach where its leadership was concerned.

However, before she could launch into her dismissal dialogue, Sir Geoffrey interrupted and pulled out the signed vote of confidence the department had in him. 'If this meeting is for my yearly appraisal, Home Secretary?' He knew the coming Monday would be the anniversary of his third year in office. 'I would just like to add, I wasn't happy with the department's current strategy to counteract terrorism. So I've been re-evaluating the overall structure of mainland security and wanted to make sure the senior board of MI5 were behind me on this.'

Sir Geoffrey had done his homework and produced an initial 6 page report for his proposals. He explained to her, 'This report shows the threat of the IRA and Black September attacks require two major changes in counter-terrorism. The first is to set up offices closer to the regional centres of extremist UK activity and the second, to improve collaboration with local police forces.' He passed her the buff folder. 'You will see the list of signatures endorsing my proposals including two of our most senior advisors, Lord Pendleton and Lord Manning.'

Ruth Torrington listened with a stunned look on her face. It wasn't so much the signatures from his department but the one from the former Director General, Lord Manning. He just so happened to be her husband's current boss. Ruth Torrington had to back pedal and quickly find an excuse for the meeting.

Sir Geoffrey even helped her with this. 'Do you want to discuss further actions that need addressing on this year's appraisal, Home Secretary?'

Her face lit up at the get-out and without hesitation she went into her usual summing up speech of the department's efforts and how satisfied she was. The same speech she used before the house and in front of the cameras. 'I'm pleased with the department's performance and their response to terrorist situations.' She quickly flicked through a folder in front of her and began reading from it. 'We must address the whole spectrum of terrorism and that applies to our communications response as much as anything else. It also means that the response isn't just about delivering a 'counter-narrative'. It's about promoting a whole set of positive values that define who we are and what the security service stands for. We only have to look back a few years to the threats we faced before the emergence of Black September - just imagine what could happen in the next few years if we don't act now. Imagine how the IRA and Black September threat may yet transform into something even more grotesque and inhumane - or more powerful with greater capability and reach, if we don't take action. In fact it is vital that our response is clear and consistent at home and abroad, because there is no longer any distinction between domestic and international terrorism when it comes to radicalisation, which is the communications methods used by the terrorists and the threats we all face.' Ruth Torrington carried on for another full minute and then glanced at her watch.

Sir Geoffrey yawned mentally and thanked her for her time.

At the door she shook his hand with a pleasant smile but very much aware, Sir Geoffrey had won the day and they both knew it.

*

Sir Geoffrey could relax a little even though he still had his investment problems. Then as if matters couldn't get any worse, the following day his son Francis dropped a bombshell. Sitting in his spacious Director General's office, Sir Geoffrey's telephone rang and he was asked if he would like to take a call from his son.

'It's me, Father.'

'Oh, hello.'

'Don't sound too excited. Will you.'

Sir Geoffrey matched his sarcasm. 'What is it, Francis? Phoned to tell me you found yourself an honest job at last instead of sponging off that pop idol bitch of yours?'

'No father, on the contrary. Myself and that pop idol bitch, as you call him, will be organising the annual London Gay Pride March this coming June. As you know it's for the anniversary of the Stonewall riots of 1969. It's important to us. Many of those people gave their lives for what they believed in.'

Sir Geoffrey replied sarcastically, 'So what are you telling me for?'

'I'm telling you because there will be over two-thousand people at the march this year going from Trafalgar Square to Hyde Park and they want to be assured of a friendly police presence, as opposed to their aggressive intimidation to the marchers last year. Also we want guaranteed police protection against anti-gay campaigners. It will be a great march and we're determined to have a fun time and make our point that gay is good. As usual it'll be a carnival-style parade with lots of extravagant costumes and cheeky banners poking fun at homophobes like the morality campaigner Mary Whitehouse.'

Sir Geoffrey was not amused, he told his son, 'To police the march costs a lot of money and this year with the extra security needed in place against another IRA attack, we can ill afford to keep an eye on a bunch of queers and those druggy friends of Isaac Constantine.'

'My friends aren't druggy and Isaacs been clean now for over six months.'

'Oh yes? As clean as the inside of a tramps underpants I bet,' Sir Geoffrey scoffed.

'It's up to you, Father. Be it on your head if there's any trouble.' With that, Francis terminated the call.

He'd known of course for some time his son's gender leaning. It hadn't mattered then. Francis, his fourth child had been the black sheep of the family. With two Mongol sons hidden away in an institution and a dead daughter who had drowned at seven years old, Francis had been a disappointment to him. Sir Geoffrey would have preferred a daughter. His mother would still be here if he'd been a girl.

After the mother's first two boys, the thought of Francis turning out to be mentally handicapped as well had made her run off at the outset before she could be convinced he was normal. However, Sir Geoffrey had always thought she'd produced a muscular poof whose physique could have been put to better use instead of being a lapdog to a rich nigger.

Sir Geoffrey replaced the receiver slowly. It suddenly dawned on him, the Gay Pride March publicity involving pictures of Isaac Constantine and his son could be damaging to his career. It could create an awkward situation. He'd just hoped this rich doped-up gay nigger singer would tire of his son and move on.

Ironically, he couldn't have given a monkey's toss about his son. They hardly ever spoke, and for Francis, lack of money was not an issue. Francis had all the money he could ever wish for being shacked up with a famous singer.

Everyone had read, including Sir Geoffrey, the newspaper stories surrounding Isaac Constantine's coke addiction. They'd seen the pictures from endless paparazzi vigils outside rehab clinics of him coming and going while being snapped with a hand hiding his face. Then there were the two prison sentences; one for drugs and the other for drink driving while twice over the legal requirement and injuring a motor cyclist. MI5 already had a file on Isaac Constantine because of death threats to him from The National Front.

However, most damaging was the property deal linking Sir Geoffrey with Isaacs Constantine.

Sir Geoffrey, already with a blossoming property portfolio and not backwards in spotting an opportunity to make a killing, had before his rise to Director General acquired at a rock bottom price a private residential care home. This eleven bedroomed property for the elderly situated in a picturesque secluded part of the South Downs in Surrey, was purchased by him as an anonymous buyer three-years ago. The owners, a family that had inherited the business, had not spent money on its upkeep. Consequently it was looking run down and needed major investment spent on decorating the outside and inside.

With redecorating costs taken into consideration, Sir Geoffrey had worked out an initial payback exercise before purchasing. The declared business profits, if he kept it as a care home, would show it would take seven years to break even. He decided the care home business was a nonrunner.

However, greasing the palm of a surveyor friend, Sir Geoffrey had a dodgy building society survey submitted to show the property to be a health risk. When the owners called for a second survey, Sir Geoffrey greased further palms and had that survey nobbled as well.

On purchasing the property for £15,000 below the asking price, the residents were given notice of eviction. Therefore their relations along with local authorities had to find alternative accommodation for them. Sir Geoffrey, still keeping his anonymity, spent the next five months having the property refurbished into a very desirable luxury residence and sold it to pop star Isaac Constantine, making a £25,000 handsome profit

A local member of parliament at the time started asking questions after a half-hearted petition was submitted to him by residents and staff following the eviction. However nothing came of the enquiry and the matter was soon forgotten, so Sir Geoffrey had hoped. Now the deal had come back to haunt him.

The autobiography of Isaac Constantine was soon to be published. Preview snippets had been released in newspapers, music and book magazines. The rags to riches story of Isaac Constantine. From his humble beginnings as a kid brought up in a council flat in Hackney to the fabulous pop star mansion he'd acquired deep in the heart of the Surrey downs, with pictures included. However, all it needed was that MP to see the pictures of the mansion in the autobiography soon to be released and contact the owner.

For a while he stroked his chin deep in thought going through the alternatives. Then he decided, there was no other way. It would be best if Isaac Constantine were removed; that is, removed for good. It would have to look like an accident. He couldn't afford any comebacks. He'd be the first in the frame if anything went wrong. However, who would do it?

Sir Geoffrey looked across to the filing cabinet. Sliding his director's chair along the deep piled carpet he pulled the second drawer down. He thumbed through some buff folders and then pulled the file stamped *Martin Lavender.*

About to get engaged to his wealthy girlfriend Victoria Buxton while still having an affair with the Home Secretary Ruth Torrington; thirty-three year old agent Martin Lavender still liked the company of expensive call girls. And MI5 were aware of Martin Lavender's colourful life style.

Sir Geoffrey sifted through photos of the agent caught by telephoto lens coming and going from expensive hotels with a beautiful screw at his side. He couldn't help himself. There was even one of him in bed with a well-endowed mature woman, taken by a maid who was cleaning and forgot to knock. She was paid £100 to snap them with a small hidden camera mounted on her work cart.

These photos were for insurance, in case the agent got out of order or threatened the department in some way. They were probably never going to be used – but now? Sir Geoffrey smiled to himself.

Martin Lavender also ran a very successful nightclub in London. It had recently been refurbished with no expense spared. MI5 knew the club was financed with drug money as with the agent's life style. However, the club was useful for department entertaining and a discreet place to collect information from snouts and pay them off. Even the Police had been advised to keep a low profile, which sat well with the Commissioner who used the club for the odd night out with his young mistress knowing that questions wouldn't be asked.

They'd let Martin Lavender have his fun for as long as he was useful.

Sir Geoffrey would leave it up to Lavender to devise a plan to kill Constantine. The least he knew about it the better.

Agent Lavender would be pleased. His secrets of expensive call girls and his affair with the Home Secretary would be safe from prying eyes and his wealthy girlfriend. And there was the code red contract bonus of five-hundred pounds to wet his appetite.

Sir Geoffrey picked up his telephone and dialled the number for the Vincent Hotel, Shepherds Bush. He asked reception to put him through to room thirteen.

*

'Of course I love you. Look you know the setup, Ruth. We're having fun aren't we? Let's just enjoy it while we can.'

'So what do I do, Martin? Wait ten years until my daughters are grown up and left home while I'm greying up with more wrinkles.'

'You've got too much to lose, Ruth, at the moment. Your position as Home Secretary. Your husband?'

'My husband,' she scoffed. 'I don't give a damn about him. And I'm sure the feeling is mutual.'

He stroked her chin. Their legs were still entwined after going at it for a full twenty minutes. Both of them were still sweating and her mascara had run.

The busy Shepherds Bush road outside had drowned out some of her wailing during the heat of it all. The double bed took up most of the basic room and the cracked wardrobe mirror reflected a tatty modest hotel tucked away from prying eyes.

'You haven't got wrinkles, My Love.' His hand moved down and cupped her breast affectionately.

'I suppose your right,' she said. 'I'll wait until the youngest has finished her GCSE's, that'll be later this August. It wouldn't be fair on her, be too disruptive if I filed for divorce now. But next year?' She leaned across to the bedside table and lit a cigarette. Ruth Torrington lay back and inhaled deeply. 'So what am I supposed to do in the meantime? Play the tart going from one hotel room to the other?'

'Look, it's only for a few more months, my Love. And then you can divorce him and we'll always be together.'

'Oh I know, Martin, I'm a grumbling bitch, but it's been over a year now and *you* don't have to go in disguise like me. Wearing that silly wig with sunglasses and a scarf wrapped around my face. I look a sad Greta Garbo instead of a ...'

Martin interrupted. 'Listen, I've got some leave coming up. Perhaps we could rendezvous somewhere for a week. You could tell your husband it's a business trip and you're taking a secretary. We could meet somewhere remote where you're not recognised.'

Her eyes lit up as he kissed her and she responded by climbing on again.

At that moment the bedside telephone rang. Martin picked up the receiver.

After the downstairs desk had put him through, Sir Geoffrey Hodder came on the line. 'Sir Geoffrey here. Is that Martin Lavender?'

'Yes.' Martin gulped and thought. *How on earth had he traced me to this hotel room? They must be watching my every move.*

'Martin, I want to see you first thing tomorrow in the office. I have a job for you. It's code red.'

'Code red? Okay, Sir.'

Martin replaced the receiver. 'Reception just reminding us we have to vacate the room by mid-day.'

Ruth Torrington rolled her eyes.

Sir Geoffrey sat back in his office chair and relaxed. Isaac Constantine would be one embarrassment out of the way. All that remained was to make good the deficit in his department funds.

CHAPTER THREE

Following her meeting with Sir Geoffrey, Ruth Torrington called a meeting with Commander Gregory Potting, a former head of MI6. He was a tall intellectual looking man with glasses who was middle-aged and slim with it. Sporting a full head of grey hair and her most trusted Senior Advisor for Government Internal Affairs, she wanted his advice on how to handle Sir Geoffrey's removal. She informed her personal secretary they were strictly not to be disturbed.

Sitting across the desk from her, he told the minister, 'Home Secretary, you must remember, his vote of confidence has put him in a strong position. And the press, knowing your accusations against him concerning his lack of security at the time of the IRA bombings, would see his removal as a personal vendetta - a politician using her position to settle old scores. Let's be honest, Home Secretary, the anti-Conservative press would have a field day; even more so with your proposed new appointment, who just so happens to be related to someone that donated a large sum of money to the last party election campaign.'

The Commander hesitated, he was about to continue and then thought better of it.

She asked him, 'What is it, Commander?'

He reluctantly told her, 'Internal affairs have been preparing a financial audit trace on Sir Geoffrey. I was going to let you know once they had completed the report.'

'So what's this audit trace for?'

The Commander explained slightly embarrassed, 'Sir Geoffrey's investment problems. He's been using money from the department's budget to play the stock-market. We got a tip-off from a market trader who wanted Sir Geoffrey's boss to confirm a salary twice as much as he was earning. He'd lied to them to get more loans. The stock-exchange shares he bought have crashed in this year's Bear Market downturn.'

'My, God!' Ruth Torrington put a hand to her mouth in shock.

'Having lied to them, Sir Geoffrey organised his own fake references. In view of this and the large bridging loans he's taken out; the repayments of which he certainly couldn't afford just on his salary alone; we decided to carry out an audit investigation on him. That's when the missing department funds came to light.'

Ruth Torrington's face lit up. 'Surely that's something we can remove him on if he's been embezzling funds. We can have him in the office and tell him straight. He can resign through personal reasons or we'll blow the lid and prosecute.'

The commander sighed. 'If only it was that easy, Home Secretary.' He told her. 'Sir Geoffrey is no fool. Let's be honest. He worked the vote of confidence trick quite well, knowing you were going to get rid of him, plus that signature from Lord Manning, your husband's boss.

'The problem we have now is, he has on record your continued backing. If you outed him, he wouldn't leave without a fight. He knows it could be very damaging for you. Your own position and judgement would be compromised. No doubt he would have told close colleagues with relish, how he had won you over, knowing how much you disliked him. If we were to disclose his embezzling, if it all came out in the press, the finger would also point at yours truly. The fact this had happened under your term as Home Secretary. You being his boss. Let's be honest, Home Secretary, knowing his career was finished and he could go to prison, Sir Geoffrey would drag you down as well. He'd tell the police and press that he'd come clean with you prior to being unfrocked. Admitted to you what he'd done. However, you decided to keep him on hoping to resolve and put right the missing funds to save face. Hence your quick change in backing down and keeping him on. That could spark all manners of rumours. Then the embarrassment to the PM, to the government, and only just a year into their new term.'

The colour had drained from her face. She looked at him stunned.

The Commander added, 'Believe me, Home Secretary, it wouldn't only be political ruin for Sir Geoffrey.'

Ruth Torrington looked at the Commander with pleading eyes. She said to him, 'So what can I do?'

The Commander paused, he wrung his hands in desperation. Then he stood up and moved to the door. He opened it just to check, closed it again and returned. He wanted to know if there was a camera or microphone in her office.

She shook her head.

He asked her to unplug her telephone just to be sure. Then he drew his chair up close and explained. 'We have a file on Sir Geoffrey's gay son, Francis, who's linked to a druggy pop star. The reason being, if staff have next of kin or relations that could be a risk factor to the department, then we should know about it.

'His son is currently shacked up with a famous black singer called Isaac Constantine. A rather colourful character to say the least, according to the newspapers. My contact at Briar Lodge, that's our old SAS training centre in Lymbridge, informed me Sir Geoffrey's son has enrolled there for a body guard course. Although part of the lodge is now leased for public use, we've had quite a few of our agents trained there in the military section for close protection exercises.'

The Commander hesitated and then said, 'I shouldn't be telling you this, but we still have a hush-hush brainwashing programme there. It's held in the building behind that's closed off and top secret. We use it to train sleepers. We could train his son?'

She inquired, 'What's a sleeper?'

'You know, a Manchurian Candidate. Someone we can programme to kill, then kill themselves when they're surplus to requirements. Their brainwashing is done under hypnosis, they don't know a thing.'

Ruth Torrington looked at him flabbergasted and said, 'You're joking me. Why wasn't I informed of this Briar Lodge?'

'You would have been informed, Home Secretary, after your full year term. It's a precautionary probation period the Prime Minister has set in place for all new senior ministers who come on board and have access to sensitive material. Because of what we know about Sir Geoffrey Hodder, even he his unaware of our sleeper programme.' He joked with her. 'It's the PMs way of making sure you're not a spy or working undercover for a foreign government.'

He expected her to smile but it wasn't forthcoming.

The Commander cleared his throat. 'Seriously though, it's to confirm your discretion and how you maintain staff and the controls put in place to prevent leaks occurring from your office. In other words the PM has to be assured you're the right person for the job.'

'Dear God, I only thought the Russians did brainwashing,' she said astounded. 'So you're saying you could train this Francis to be a sleeper, to be a killer?'

The Commander nodded.

Ruth Torrington asked hesitantly, 'So who would this Francis kill?'

'His father of course,' he replied. 'Then the waste of space could turn the gun or knife on himself.'

She looked horrified and said, 'You must be joking, I couldn't sanction that. I couldn't live with it. To be responsible for two deaths - murders in fact.'

'Creating sleepers, Manchurian Candidates is nothing new, Home secretary. In fact as far back as the early fifties the CIA have set up brainwashing programmes called Bluebird and Artichoke. The sleepers they created could pass from a fully awake state to a deep hypnotic controlled state. This would be via some very subtle signal that couldn't be detected by other people in the room and without other individuals being able to note the change.' The Commander lowered his voice and leaned in a little to be more intimate. 'It's been clearly shown, Home Secretary, that individuals can be induced into hypnosis by telephone, by receiving written matter or by the use of a code, some signal or words. And remember, control of those hypnotized can be passed from one individual to another without great difficulty.'

The Commander paused as if to get something off his chest. 'Again, I shouldn't be telling you this, Home Secretary, but we have just recently processed two active sleepers at Lymbridge. One of them is a Bristow flight instructor named Guy Ericson at Redhill Aerodrome. We have a spy in Iran who fed us information concerning a possible Black September terrorist attack on London this summer. We're not sure how the terrorists will infiltrate. So as to secure Middle East contracts, we know Alan Bristow Helicopters at Redhill have been training foreign pilots for some time. We believe this attack may originate from a local airfield or flying club. However, when this Guy Ericson signed up for the Korean martial arts course we saw an opportunity as a precautionary measure to programme him. This would be to eliminate any possible suspects at Redhill that we think would be a threat to our security without any repercussions to MI5. On our orders he would then kill himself.'

Ruth Torrington shook her head in disbelieve. 'You said two. Who's the other one?'

The Commander hesitated. He knew he was telling her classified information. 'She's Victoria Buxton. Her father Kenny Buxton has a front as a reputable businessman for an events' company. You know the sort of thing, a day out at Brands Hatch driving a sports car or a hot air balloon ride with a champagne lunch. Made a lot of money and donates to charities. However he's a major drug dealer. His daughter is also dating one of our agents who runs a nightclub. Kenny Buxton we're sure is financing the agent's nightclub with drug money. Whether they're in it together who knows? However, it could prove an embarrassment to the department.'

'Who's the agent with the nightclub?' She enquired.

'We keep that under wraps. Only on a need to know basis. Even the P.M. is unaware. It's kept like that as the department uses it to entertain. You know. Do our deals with the underground. Pay off the odd grass.

Because this Victoria travels with her father on business she enrolled for the bodyguard course to be on hand to protect him. Unbeknown to her, she was conditioned subconsciously as a sleeper to kill when the time is right. That would be her father Kenny Buxton. We'll make it look like an accident. Then kill herself. That way there would be no gang wars.

Ruth Torrington, still shocked by this revelation from the Commander slowly replied, 'Yes but this Guy Ericson and Victoria Buxton were conditioned without my knowledge. On the other hand, Francis Hodder I would know about? So I still couldn't—'

The Commander suddenly grabbed her elbow to show how urgent the situation was. She flinched a little as he said with a deadly serious face, 'Home Secretary, we would be getting rid of an embarrassing problem very quickly. An embarrassing problem, if left to fester, could be the ruination of this government and many political careers including yours.'

Outside her office he took a deep breath. The Commander knew he'd over stepped security. She hadn't had full clearance yet. He'd been too ingratiating. Telling her about Briar Lodge could come back and haunt him one day. He couldn't afford that. At the moment he had her confidence. However, now she knew too much. He couldn't afford that. She could pass it on to her latest fuck buddy agent Martin Lavender. He made a mental note she would have to expire when the time was right.

*

The fifth bench along from the Hanover entrance past the Boathouse Café in Regents Park was where they always met. The *WET VARNISH* sign placed on the seat this early sunny May morning kept off the elderly, young lovers and people on their tea-break. At 10:45 a.m. Commander Gregory Potting, dressed in a conservative pin striped suit, sat with the briefcase on his knees. The gold chain attached to it was locked firmly around his wrist.

It was a quiet spot over hung with copper beach and common ash trees. Another fifty yards and the park opened up into a sprawling mass of green grass punctuated by flower beds.

The Commander himself being a green fingered man appreciated the satisfying smells of rosebushes from the adjacent Queen Mary's Gardens. As he glanced at his watch, Dr Weiss appeared in the distance, his thin tall frame boldly strolling towards him on the footpath thrusting out his shooting stick with every stride as if on a military route march.

Stopping abruptly at the bench, Dr Weiss took a seat far apart without any acknowledgement. Dressed for the country with a Burberry flat cap, green hunting jacket and plus-four tweeds tucked in matching socks, his lined face winced with displeasure as he noticed and then casually flicked some grass off his tanned Savile Row walking brogues. He tweaked the end of his waxed moustache, which made him look even older than his fifty-eight years and then said, 'Did you see the roses this morning, Old Chap? I can smell the hybrids from here. The Tea Rose is my favourite. They've come out well this spring.'

Without turning, the Commander replied, 'I prefer the staid common breeds myself. The old English Maiden's Blush; now there's a white York rose not messed about with.'

'Ah, but change is the variety of life, Old Chap. We have to change things to know what they're capable of.' Dr Weiss took out a small box of snuff and after a couple of strong sniffs continued. 'Now for instance, you want change, Old Chap, or you wouldn't be sitting next to me with one-hundred and fifty-thousand pounds in your briefcase, would you?'

The Commander said abruptly, 'We require a sleeper and fast.'

Dr Weiss looked surprised. 'How fast, Old Chap? We gave you that Guy Ericson and Victoria Buxton only a few weeks ago.'

The Commander replied, 'This is a male. He has to be fully operational within twenty-one days.'

'Twenty-one days?' Dr Weiss said worried. 'We could only raise an assassin in that time; a spy would take five weeks or more due to the additional conditioning he would need.'

'An assassin is what we want, Dr Weiss. His programming is to be carried out at Briar Lodge. Your subject is called Francis Hodder. He's the son of the Director General of MI5, Sir Geoffrey Hodder.'

Dr Weiss said alarmed, 'Dear God, Old Chap, that's a bit close to home. Who's the target?'

The Commander said impatiently, 'You're not privileged to such information as you well know, Dr Weiss. Do you want the contract, yes or no?'

'Err, yes of course, Old Chap,' he replied with a nervous smile. 'I'll tell Branston and Shutler to drop everything and get onto it.'

'This comes under group two classification, as always, Doctor,' the Commander said in a barbed tone. 'Any leaks from your direction and I couldn't answer for your safety; do I make myself clear?'

The doctor shifted nervously. 'Yes of course, Old Chap. Mum's the word. However, one doesn't get the chance to process a sleeper very often. An assassin at that. The teaching opportunities would be endless to our Korean School of Blue Mountain agents. Remember you've planted two of my Koreans over in Pyongyang already this year.'

'Okay-Okay, you can have an audience but just remember you're responsible for their secrecy.' Unlocking the chain, the Commander pushed the briefcase to him.

Dr Weiss tenderly cupped the sides of it, and after looking both ways, flicked the two locks open with his thumbs. Holding the lid, he stared down at the money with a look of love a father would give being presented with his first born.

'You don't have to count it, I can assure you it's all there.' The Commander slid closer. Satisfied they had a contract he relaxed. He took out a silver hip flask and unscrewed the two small cups. He poured a measure into each and offered one. As they both downed the twelve-year old malt he said, 'Now let me fill you in, Dr Weiss, on some of the details that you'll require.'

CHAPTER FOUR

'Welcome, Gentlemen, to the Close Protection Operations Course held here at Briar Lodge Manor in Lymbridge Green.' Former retired SAS Staff Sergeant Gordon Chipley, Chip to his friends and colleagues, addressed the seven trainees with a stiff formal military salute just before breakfast in the canteen.

Wearing the regulation black tracksuit with the Blue Mountain motif printed front and back on his top, he epitomised all that was fitness and strength at forty-two years old with a six foot four-inch bodyguard frame and a full head of silver hair. His tanned features resembling a Kirk Douglas look alike stood out as he read from a clipboard of notes. 'The Blue Mountain SIA-approved Close Protection Course provides a comprehensive package of skills, delivered in a diverse range of environments and in a number of fast moving, challenging and realistic scenarios. You will learn, gentleman, a wide range of skills including threat assessments, surveillance, team work, self-defence, vehicle techniques,

IED awareness, communications and kidnap for ransom situation training.' He paused and gave them a broad smile. 'Any questions yet?' Without any forthcoming, he told them, 'Don't worry, Gentlemen, we've got three weeks to knock you into shape. However, first help yourselves to breakfast. You have three-quarters of an hour, and then we'll all meet in the seminar room.'

The seven trainees including Francis were stocky lads and without hesitation they began to get stuck in to the help yourself buffet breakfast. The course organisers had prided themselves on hearty meals and word had got around this venue provided the best, in the knowledge, an audience with full bellies was a receptive one.

By midmorning the trainees were sitting at separate desks in the classroom styled seminar theatre with its large blackboard positioned at the front. There followed a brief biography of their career and hobbies as each person stood up and introduced themselves.

Using the blackboard, former Staff Sergeant Chipley then touched on the subjects they would be initially covering over the next five days of training including: Surveillance Awareness, Responding to Emergency Medical Incidents and Trauma, Conflict Resolution Training, Assault Avoidance & Disengagement Skills, Escorting and Holding Skills, Counter and Anti-Surveillance Training with interrogation and interview skills.

Next he led a question and answer period for ten minutes for their immediate course concerns and then informed them,

'Gentlemen, thank you for your patience. We're nearly done this morning. There follows a simple I.Q. test and after that we can break for lunch.'

Walking around their separate desks he handed out the Wechsler Adult Intelligence papers and informed them they had fifty minutes for the sixty questions.

*

By late afternoon, Dr Weiss and his two colleagues had finished marking and assessing the I.Q. test papers. He summoned Chipley into his make shift office at the rear of the building.

The former Staff Sergeant stood stiffly to attention and saluted. Ingrained from years of training, old habits die hard for Chipley. Dr Weiss returned a casual salute.

He'd worked with Chipley before and knew he was reliable and discreet and followed orders on a need to know basis without asking questions. He informed him the trainees would be split into two groups as usual according to their scores. 'Chip, Old Chap, group-one with the four lowest scores you should continue with.' He showed him the names. 'I'll take care of the other three. They've displayed an unusual high percentage rate, especially one of those called Francis. Intelligence may be interested. I know they're recruiting at the moment. I want to do some further tests with these trainees. Specifically, advanced interpersonal skills, that sort of thing. You square it with them tomorrow morning, Old Chap. Tell them they're being separated for training as it makes it easier for the instructors and they'll get more one to one being in a smaller group.' Dr Weiss tweaked the end of his waxed moustache. 'Oh, and Chip, can you ensure my three are assembled in the lecture theatre at ten in the morning, there's an Old Chap?'

The former Staff Sergeant stiffly saluted and replied, 'Will do, Dr Weiss. Will there be anything else, Dr Weiss?'

'No, Chip, that will be all for the moment, thank you.'

*

'Good morning, Gentlemen. I hope your first night stay here was a comfortable one?' Dr Weiss, standing on the small stage of the lecture theatre wearing a white coat, looked up and addressed the three trainees. Also in white coats sitting by the podium were his two colleagues.

Francis, Colin and Keith nodded their approval. Sitting in the steep tiered seating they had a good view looking down onto the doctors.

'My name is Dr Weiss and this is Dr Branston and Dr Shutler.' The doctors nodded politely. 'I gather you've had it explained why we split you into two groups. Also the three of you showed exceptional high scoring in yesterday's I.Q. test.' Dr Weiss glanced down at their test papers and then continued, 'As part of this SIA-approved course we will be testing your interpersonal skills for surveillance awareness. This provides an aspect of the course which is important and goes towards achieving your certificate.' Dr Weiss nodded to the doctors and they began going from window to window pulling down the blinds.

'Gentlemen, our first test is based on spontaneous interpretation, similar to the Rorschach inkblot test, but modified to incorporate moving shapes on a screen. It will tell us how quick your brain reacts to certain shapes that in turn can govern how fast you interpret a dangerous situation. Using the pen and paper in front of you, please put down the first thing that comes into your head at the instant the screen freezes. It can be anything, a word or a shape. We shall have some Beatles music in the background for added effect.'

Using the cord, Dr Weiss pulled down the large white screen and motioned to the other doctors to dim the lights. Then he nodded to the projectionist high up. The background music consisting of Sgt. Pepper's Lonely Hearts Club Band started as the trainees concentrated on the flashing lights in front of them.

They scribbled away every time the screen froze. They hadn't noticed the doctors put on protective glasses and ear plugs. Gradually the sound became louder as the moving shapes began to throb in time with the music.

Dr Weiss watched them carefully. After a while, each one of them stopped writing and drifted into a trance. Satisfied they were in a hypnotic state, he turned off the projector and the music. With the lights switched on, he asked them, 'Gentleman, would you please come down here.'

Carefully making their way down the stairs they were seated in three chairs positioned on the stage. Dr Weiss asked them to roll up the sleeve of their left arm. They willingly cooperated while another doctor appeared with a hypodermic needle and injected each man with a measured amount of Sodium Pentothal and Scopolomine – a truth serum cocktail that had been tried and tested many times. After the injection they rolled down their sleeves and relaxed. At this point Dr Weiss knew the level-one session was a success.

He immediately pressed a hidden button on the podium and a buzzer sounded. This unlocked two doors to the tiered public gallery. Slowly people began to file in. The audience consisting of MI5 trainees studying psychiatry, psychology, hypnosis and truth serum chemistry, all wore the regulation black tracksuit with the Blue Mountain motif displayed. One by one they filled up most of the front facing seats. Most noticeable was a large delegation of Korean students in their mid-twenties wearing thick glasses.

'Good afternoon, Ladies and Gentlemen.' The doctor nodded and the delegation reciprocated with a courteous bow. 'Over the next three weeks you will see and understand the process of processing these three males into active sleepers, or better known by the book reading, film going public as Manchurian Candidates.' The audience briefly tittered and then Dr Weiss continued, 'Our trainees have been conditioned using the revised Rorschach picture test and then given measured amounts of Sodium Pentothal and Scopolomine which is a truth serum as you know. In due course I will be handing out daily notes on their exact medication requirements and dosage along with the intervals of dispensary.'

Dr Weiss smirked as he said, 'Before we go any further can I remind you, it is an old wives' tale that no hypnotised subject can be forced to do something which is repellent to his moral nature. Remember, the conception of people acting against their own interests is nothing new. We see it every day in excessiveness; eating, drinking, smoking, driving over the speed limit, ignoring diets or health checks etc.'

The audience answered with smiles and knowing nods.

Our first priority of conditioning is to take them back to their early days. To ask them various questions concerning their childhood; if they were happy or were they abused. Any other childhood memories that were notable or meaningful. Their likes and dislikes and anything else that would give us a childhood psychological profile. Eventually, our ideal candidate would be one possessing, not only good outside physical strengths as well as reacting to and handling potential situations, but also someone who would possess internal subconscious weaknesses of guilt and insecurity that could be worked by his masters to produce a sleeper assassin with incredible strengths.'

At this point the audience were already scribbling away making notes.

The doctor continued, 'Our conditioning is based upon associative reflexes that use words or symbols as triggers of installed automatic reactions. Conditioning, called brainwashing by the media, is the production of reactions in the brain through the use of associative reflexes.'

Dr Weiss gave the audience time to catch up with their notes and then carried on, 'Our aim is to implant in the trainees' minds the predominant motive, which is that of submitting to the operator's commands; to construct behaviour which would at all times strive to put the operator's exact intensions into execution as if the subject were playing a game or acting a part; and to cause redirection of his movements by remote control through second parties or third or fifth parties, perhaps even up to say, twelve thousand miles removed from the original commands if necessary. Remember, the first thing a human being is loyal to, is his own conditioned nervous system.'

Some of the audience nodded in agreement.

The doctor also informed them, 'Over the next twenty days in conjunction with their Close Protection Operations Course, our three trainees will undergo a rigorous programme of deep mental massage. This will be of various commands and errands using trigger words. Together with doses of Sodium Pentothal and Scopolomine, our trainees' will receive repetitive hypnotic intensified conditioning until they are brought to the edge, where upon their mental reflexes will be so finely tuned, they will respond and obey to any word or a sound, smell, touch, or a view and so on.'

Dr Weiss continued with the trainees' for another two hours with various tests and instructions while the lecture theatre had gradually filled to capacity. Before he finished he reminded the audience as members of MI5 Blue Mountain, the lectures were classified under the Official Secrets Act, and had a code red, For Your Eyes Only, status.

*

After seventeen days the trainees had successfully passed levels 4 and 5 conditioning. Dr Weiss knew the time was right to stage a demonstration of his work in the lecture theatre.

Ever the showman and for added effect being a James Bond fan and as a compliment to his Korean school section, he had the three trainees, Francis, Colin and Keith, dressed like Dr No in white high collar Mandarin suits with matching white medical shoes. They sat on stage and looked relaxed. Already under the control of a trigger word they were totally oblivious to the audience in front of them.

Dr Weiss addressed the audience. 'Only one trainee, which is Francis, has attained level five status. One of the main reasons for this is his childhood psychological profile. It showed under conditioning how he'd gathered mental injuries from his father during childhood; locked in a cupboard for bed wetting, being one of them as well as his father threatening to cut off his manhood.' The doctor explained, 'During his conditioning it was found that Francis is a homosexual and suffers from schizophrenia. Francis's other character is called Roxanne. It was the name of his seven year old sister who drowned in a tragic family pond accident. Although he was a year younger, his father blamed him as he was supposed to be looking after her. Roxanne was their parent's favourite. They had two previous sons who were Mongols. Then Roxanne was born. They tried again for a child hoping to have a girl. When Francis was born his mother left, thinking she had given birth to another disabled son. The father also blamed

Francis for his mother's departure.' Dr Weiss paused to sip a glass of water and then continued. 'Francis always wanted to be Roxanne. That's how Roxanne became a Transvestite. Francis wants to be a woman. He's already applied to the John Hopkins University Medical Centre in the USA for sex reassignment surgery. He was going to borrow the money for the operation. However, his male side wouldn't allow him to go through with the surgery.

'Whenever a man sexually arouses Francis there is an internal struggle between Roxanne and Francis. The male side usually wins if Francis is at ease with his partner. However, Roxanne has her needs and will slip into that character if a sudden urge arises. These sudden urges can occur if Francis thinks of his father or he's reminded of him. Subconsciously he wants to kill his father. He feels threatened by his father and yet is afraid of him. Therefore, the character Roxanne will hunt out male company and superimpose them as his father to do them harm or rob them. Under hypnosis, Francis has revealed he's done this many times over the years. The reason Francis has never been prosecuted for the ones he's harmed is that he's clever and obviously has never been caught. Secondly, due to the embarrassing situation of the victims that he'd robbed, the victims didn't want to reveal the compromising incident to the police.

'We could have used one of the other trainees with similar fractures of resentment in their psychological makeup. However, Francis's deep resentment of his father is the key to the core of his subconscious defects. Let me demonstrate.'

Dr Weiss approached him. 'Francis, when you were a child, what happened when you wet the bed?'

Francis instantly dropped to his knees and pleaded, *'Please, Dada, don't cut it off…I won't tell. I'll be good girl like Roxanne…'*

The audience shuffled uneasily. Dr Weiss faced them and smiled. 'To bring Francis back to the present we have installed in his memory a trigger word.' Dr Weiss bent down to Francis who was sobbing in tears and gulping like a small child. Making sure he had his attention, the doctor spoke firmly. 'Roxanne.'

Francis immediately raised himself and returned to the chair and stared out to the audience.

After the short applause, the doctor acknowledged their appreciation and continued. 'Francis's social and sexual dependency to lean on someone else, which in his case is his partner Isaacs Constantine, is there for us to use to our advantage during his conditioning.'

He paused to let them catch up with their scribbling and took a sip of water from the glass provided. Then Dr Weiss said, 'At this level, Francis's brain has been mentally massaged and overwritten with a new personality and a code of ethics. Consequently he has had a voice imprint etched onto his brain. This is known as the trigger. Once the trigger is activated he can no longer differentiate between right and wrong. Francis has been turned into what we call a "Clear Eyes". A fully programmed sleeper assassin. Francis has been told he is super human and all laws are written for other people. His moral code, respect for the law and fear of dying have been replaced with a personality that can commit crimes such as murder, kill on cue and have no guilt or remorse afterwards. All fear and revulsion of bloody body parts have been removed. He has a strong feeling of immortality and invincibility.

'In the event of being caught at the scene of the crime he has been given an alibi to self-destruct. Under capture he will become angry and agitated. He will present to law enforcements an image of a violent troubled past, perhaps with personality disorders. Simply a tragic nutcase who went on a senseless rampage. In this situation, as the trigger cannot be deactivated, the trainee would not remember his crime and have no memory of his masters or conditioning sessions.'

The doctor took another sip of water. 'Even under brutal torture he will not be able to remember these, because all programming is buried deep within long forgotten childhood memories which were recalled under level 3 hypnosis and erased. They were then replaced by a primary link into Francis's subconscious which is a critical application of deep suggestion implanted using a trigger word or signal. This primary link is the main connection to Francis's control as a sleeper. If Francis were to be used repeatedly we may even hook future or sub links which could represent further crimes or assignments for him to carry out. Again he would not remember his crimes, however, after the completion of these assignments a voice or signal command would smash those sub-links of conditioning and hypnosis and all knowledge of his masters without affecting the permanent primary link.'

Dr Weiss walked to the edge of the stage to convey the importance of his next experiment. He informed the audience, 'To demonstrate the effectiveness of our programming, a role play scene has been set up to show how responsive the trainees are to carry out tasks and commands. A fantasy food tasting competition has been organised whereby they have to judge meals cooked by a chef. The plates labelled A and B are in fact both empty. However, the trainees, have been informed, the food consists of Southern fried chicken with fries. They are led to believe meal A has been cooked to perfection, while meal B has been overcooked, too dry and with burnt fries.'

Checking his watch, Dr Weiss returned to the podium. He leant across and pressed the hidden buzzer. Suddenly one of the doctors appeared in a white coat pushing someone in a wheelchair. The incapacitated patient wearing a white apron with a chef's hat was strapped down and gagged.

'Good morning, Dr Schutler, I see you have brought our guest.'

Dr Schutler nodded a response.

'For the demonstration, this man,' Dr Weiss indicated to him in the wheelchair, 'will represent our chef. He in fact was released from prison two weeks ago and was staying at a halfway rehabilitation house just before we kidnapped him. Being a child molester he is currently on police records as a sex offender.'

The doctor approached the trainees and spoke to them. They immediately looked attentive. Dr Weiss sat down and said, 'Colin, please sample our chef's food and give us your views.'

Colin walked over to the table and tasted meal A. His face lit up as he bit into the invisible chicken leg and then sampled the invisible fries. With an invisible napkin he wiped his mouth and beamed with delight. Colin turned to the man in the wheelchair. 'That was fantastic, Chef, really tasty.' Then Colin attempted meal B. His face screwed up instantly as he stopped chewing. He politely held the invisible serviette to his mouth to spit out the remains. Then he had problems crunching on the burnt fries. Using his serviette he did the same with them. With a look of displeasure he said, 'That was awful, Chef, not one of your good meals.'

Keith, the second trainee, did exactly the same followed by Francis.

With all of them choosing meal A as the superior dish, Francis was asked to give his compliments to the chef. He walked over to the man in the wheelchair and pretended to shake his hand. 'That was great food, Chef,' he nodded to meal A, 'well done.' Francis then returned to his chair.

The doctor addressed the audience. 'As I told you before, Frances's level five conditioning has brought him to the point where he can murder, kill on cue and have no guilt or remorse afterwards. And to prove this, we will ask him to take out his revenge on the same chef who cooked the disappointing meal B.' Dr Weiss walked over to Francis and handed him a large butcher's knife.

The doctor faced the audience. 'Using a conditioning trigger, Francis will show you his displeasure with meal B and execute the Chef. I must remind everyone again, as members of MI5 Blue Mountain, this lecture is classified under the Official Secrets Act and has a code red status which is For Your Eyes Only. In saying that, may I point out, for some of you who have a fragile or nervous disposition or even a delicate constitution, you would be advised to turn away for the next few minutes.'

The doctor turned to Francis and said, 'Francis, don't forget to tell the Chef, Kimberly will be coming for supper.'

Francis rose from his chair. Holding the knife by his side he walked over to the man in the wheelchair. The ex-con had heard everything and shrunk back. As Francis moved in closer, the man began to struggle with his bindings. Francis stood in front of him and for a split second motioned with the knife, deciding the best position to carry out his task. The ex-con began to keen and whine with staring eyes, struggling violently with his bonds. Francis walked around to the rear of his chair deciding this was the most suitable position. As Francis's left hand grasped his head, the man kicked and struggled screeching through his gag. Francis had to use all his force to restrain him. Then pausing for a moment, like a surgeon about to make his first incision, he slashed the unshaven throat.

The audience gasped. Some of them buried their heads. One man vomited into his handkerchief.

Blood immediately spurted in a torrent onto the white sleeves of Francis's Mandarin jacket and spattered his shoes.

The prisoner's apron could have belonged to an abattoir worker. Then with a few final twitches the gurgling sounds ceased. The silence for just a moment was numbing.

Dr Weiss quickly responded. 'Thank you, Francis. Please wash your hands.' He nodded over to a young male aid who appeared with a bowl of warm water and a towel.

Francis methodically placed the knife on the table and then rinsed his hands. The water turned red as he swished his fingers. Then he returned to his chair. The other two ignored him while they stared out to the audience.

CHAPTER FIVE

The success of Isaac Constantine's autobiography, Sex, *Drugs and Rock and Soul*, had been well covered in the review section of magazines and newspapers. It was only a matter of time before he got round to book signings. Next Saturday, the famous singer would be appearing at Brooklands Book Store in Weybridge High Street according to the large poster in the window.

Martin Lavender needed a disguise. A flat cap would hide most of his dark brown hair while a thick moustache would hopefully make his film star good looks appear older. The slight stoop would finish it off and bring his six-foot-one-inch stance down to five-foot-ten. He had to remember to practise in the mirror.

As he made his way inside the Brooklands store, he immediately looked up at the ceiling. In his research he'd read the silver foil wrapped wires and ducting pipes overhead were a leftover from its former days as a shop that specialised in aircraft books and RAF memorabilia. The ceiling was supposed to represent the busy mechanics of an engine while the dull grey curved metal book racking was made to look like the sparse struts and webs of a basic aircraft cabin and finished off by oval shaped shop windows.

There was a time when the shop was going to close for refurbishment, to get with the modern times of smoked glass and chrome fittings, however, the aviation patrons of Brooklands Museum had banded together and raised a petition against this. They'd collected over five-thousand signatures. Martin Lavender had never realised there could be so many geeks involved in a cause.

As he moved further inside he noticed the framed photos displayed on two serving counters. They showed previous celebrity book signings. What was interesting, they showed exactly where they took place, and what was directly above hanging from the ceiling. The table they used was covered in books at the moment while the big fan overhead slowly turned giving some circulation on this warm early May lunchtime.

Martin's research also revealed the fan was in fact a huge steel propeller from a war time Wellington HX384 bomber. Moving closer he spotted the controls on the wall between the shop counters. The location of the variable fan speed switch made it access to staff only. Nevertheless, Martin Lavender strained his eyes to read the company name on the white plastic - Hardy and Fisher Controls Limited, Dorking, Surrey.

With a thick telephone directory he checked out their address. With his department unregistered Cortina it took less than an hour to find the company situated on a factory estate just outside Dorking Town Centre.

At a discrete distance, using a Polaroid SX-70 Land Camera, Martin took pictures of the logo design on the side of one of the company vans. The MI5 department film laboratory would take care of the rest with a correct sized print that could be pasted and lacquered onto the sides of a hired commercial vehicle. It needed to look Kosher. Brooklands Store had their own staff and tradesmen car park.

Martin called Brooklands Book Store and asked for the manager. He told them their interim free fan service was due and would it be possible to come Friday afternoon, which so happened to be the day before the book signing. The assistant manager was most cooperative. His superior being on holiday for a week had left him in charge. It was fine to come Friday at closing time. Just ring the bell by the car park gates.

*

The vehicle looked like any other Hardy and Fisher small white commercial van with its logo on the side. With the Logo stuck on with wallpaper paste, he just hoped it didn't rain. That could prove embarrassing.

With the gates letting him through, Martin parked in a bay and was then shown through a side entrance into the store. Two evening contract cleaners were busy. One vacuum cleaning while the other one polished anything that wasn't covered by a book. Looking up he noted the fan was stationary.

Martin in disguise wearing blue overalls with Hardy and Fisher printed on the back, looked the part. Wearing a roof tiler's apron and carrying a ladder over his shoulder, he positioned the steps. Then he climbed up and surveyed the scene. From up here he never realised how massive the propeller fan was or how sharp the edges were. At a top speed of 160 RPM, this baby could do a hell of a lot of damage if it came loose from the ceiling.

Security he was told would be on their rounds, but at the moment there was just himself and the cleaners.

Keeping the cleaners in view, he removed from his apron pocket a roll of insulation tape and wrapped it around the shaft of the fan. As each layer built up, he checked the thickness with his thumb nail. Digging into it until the surface felt spongy and he was sure enough he had the required amount of tape to deaden some of the sawing noise.

Just as he pulled out the hacksaw, he jumped nearly dropping it.

'Do you know how long yer gonna be, Mate?' The portly middle-aged security man had approached from behind and was looking up waiting for an answer.

'Oh, not long, Chief. Say half-hour at the most. Just got to check it out and give it a clean,' Martin Lavender replied with a reassuring smile.

The security man relaxed. 'That's okay then. The cleaners will still be here so you can let yourself out.'

Martin Lavender gave him the thumbs up. Waiting until he was out of sight, he positioned the hacksaw. The cleaners had moved away somewhere so he was safe from prying eyes.

The wires to the fan motor came down through the centre of the hollow shaft. He had to be careful he didn't nick them as the hacksaw blade cut through. A thought had also crossed his mind; they could prevent the propeller from falling. He'd have to loosen the wire terminal screws just enough, so when the shaft sheared under its own weight, the wires would pull through the terminals when the propeller dropped.

With a slow but firm action he proceeded to saw through the shaft. The tape was doing its job keeping noise to a minimum. With just over half the shaft cut through he stopped. It was a fine line, he had to be careful. Just a tad too deep and the steel propeller fan would sheer straight away and fall to the floor with a loud bang. Very embarrassing to say the least.

That was it. Job done. The rest would do its work on the day when he would be there to turn the fan speed up. Martin had calculated the vibration would sever the remaining portion of the cut, hopefully with Isaac Constantine underneath doing his book signing.

Martin cleared up methodically, not leaving any fingerprints or traces of filings. Then he extracted the fuse from the switch on the wall. He would replace that the next day and test the fan on full speed while Isaac Constantine was doing his stuff. He left a postie sticker nearby stating the fan was out of use and he would be back with a new switch tomorrow.

Satisfied everything was in order he made his way out of the building.

*

Isaac Constantine fans were out in force on this second Saturday lunchtime in May. The police had allowed some of the faithful to stay overnight in their sleeping bags as long as they kept within the steel barriers that had been erected for the anticipated crowds. By now the queue stretched down Weybridge high street and around the corner of Waitrose supermarket. Fortunately for them the warm spell had continued so short sleeve shirts and summer blouses were the order of the day.

It had just turned eleven-forty-five. According to the posters put-up, he was already fifteen minutes late. Then there was a buzz in the queue. Someone had seen a pink Bentley coming down the high street. As the car slowed to a halt outside the bookstore, the Paparazzi prepared themselves ready.

At that moment as Isaac Constantine stepped out of the car, the crowd surged. Amongst screams and shrieks, outstretched arms waved for an autograph. Some held open his new autobiography, others pleaded for a signature on a photo. Two burley minders jostled him to the swing doors of the bookshop.

Inside, Martin Lavender could hear the commotion. The white van bearing the Hardy and Fisher logo was in the staff carpark. He'd arrived with it earlier. Now wearing the regulation blue overalls showing the company name, Martin fiddled with the switch on the wall.

Because of the singer's impending arrival, Martin had gone unnoticed while staff and security organised themselves at the tills and around the book signing area before the rush started.

The table where Isaac Constantine would be sitting was still in the right place. Already a long queue led up to it, abruptly finishing where two burly security men stood. Martin had worried they may have moved the book signing area for some reason. Just a few feet either way could have rendered his plans useless.

Suddenly an announcement came over the speakers, 'Ladies and Gentlemen, please welcome our celebrity book signing of the day, Mr Isaac Constantine.'

A cheer rose up with an applause as cameras flashed and heads craned to catch a glimpse of the famous singer. Within a few minutes the queue had settled down as fans edged their way forwards wanting him to sign their purchased autobiography. Shaking their hands and smiling, he posed with them for endless photographs while press flashbulbs captured the moment.

Martin judged the time was right. He had his escape route worked out. The café upstairs on the next level, for arts, crafts and military books had a washroom. He'd placed an OUT OF ORDER sign on the door just three minutes ago.

Looking around with his hand ready, he waited until the singer was seated and book signing for a new customer. Then he flipped the fan switch to maximum speed. Using a tube of Instant Permabond he quickly glued the switch and then made his way to the staircase. Moving up the stairs, but not too fast with his prominent stoop, he made his way to the first floor.

People below glanced up from the immediate rush of wind building up. Those that continued looking would have noticed in those few seconds, not just the propeller fan speeding up but the irregular arc it was making as the whole assembly began to vibrate out of control.

Looking both ways, Martin let himself into the washroom and slid the lock. Now he had to be quick. He tore off his overalls along with the cap and moustache and stuffed them into the toilet pedal bin. Checking himself in the mirror he straightened his back up with a couple of practise exercises. It was good he could stretch at last. With a Brooklands store plastic bag filled with recently purchase stationary and wearing nice jeans and a matching blue summer shirt, he looked an ordinary shopper. Now he had to get away.

Just as he let himself out he heard a massive crash. There followed a few seconds of deathly quiet. Then all hell broke loose. Terrible screams and cries met him as he casually made his way down the staircase. People were running in all directions. Someone had pressed the alarm. Security began to assemble around an area of mayhem. As Martin Lavender descended further he could see bodies on the floor and lots of blood. One official bent over something then vomited.

Martin had to know if the job was done. He stumbled over two people with head injuries and then froze. The man bent over and vomited again. Martin could see why. The decapitation lying on the wood block flooring hadn't been clean. The black man's head had been sliced through just below the top jaw. The other half sat on Isaac Constantine's neck as he lay slumped across the table in a thick pool of blood. Women shrieked uncontrollably as officials herded them to an exit. Walking wounded and those in shock had arms around each other. They turned their heads from the grizzly scene.

Martin could see the propeller. It had landed the other end of the shop with the force. An elderly woman lay underneath it moaning with one stocking leg badly cut.

Now he had to move fast. There was no comeback with the van so he could leave it where it was.

To the sound of a distant wailing ambulance he casually passed through the swing door and headed for the station. Up ahead, traffic hesitated and pulled to one side while a police car with flashing lights and a siren raced past him.

CHAPTER SIX

Sir Geoffrey relaxed in the brown leather Chesterfield chair. It hadn't been seven minutes since he entered his Mayfair club and Jennings and his silver tray were already by Sir Geoffrey's side bearing a twelve year old malt and a copy of the Times. He took a sip and read again the headline on page two: SOUL SINGER ISAAC CONSTANTINE DIES IN TRAGIC ACCIDENT. He smiled and breathed a small sigh of relief. Above him on the walls, portraits of famous past members looked down, as if on judgement for what he'd done. Their stern faces blended with the room's dark panelling while old fashioned chandeliers highlighted deep piled Wilton rugs. The smell of brandy and cigars wafted from the billiards room. The intermittent crack of colliding balls indicated a game was in progress.

As he turned another page, Jennings had returned with a portable telephone on his trolley. 'Excuse me, Sir Geoffrey, there's a call for you.' Jennings discretely left.

He picked up the receiver. 'Sir Geoffrey, here.'

'It's me.'

'Oh…Francis it's you! So…err, so sorry to hear about your partner.' Sir Geoffrey did his best to sound sympathetic.

Francis mocked with a hollow laugh. 'If they were dishing out Oscars you'd be at the front of the queue.'

'What do you mean? I was only trying to be—'

Francis interrupted, 'I know you was responsible. The police think the fan was tampered with. I sat with them while they trolled through BBC newsreel footage. Then I recognised him coming down the stairs. No doubt, one of your agents although I didn't tell them.'

'*Agents!* What are you implying?' he said shocked.

'I enrolled for a bodyguard course recently at Briar Lodge Manor. One of your departments old training centres, remember? I was in the advanced class, perhaps even good enough for intelligence I was told. This allowed me into some off limits areas. That's where I saw the group photo. You beaming proudly with Martin Lavender third from left. All wearing the regulation tracksuit. It was the 1971 school with the names kindly printed. However, your secret is safe, for now that is.'

Sir Geoffrey bit his lip. *Shit, the picture at the training centre.* He'd forgotten about that. 'I don't know what you mean. Have you been at the weed again?'

'Not enough to know I've got you by the balls,' Francis quipped.

Sir Geoffrey sneered. 'So if you haven't told to the police, what is it you want, money? Now your pop star meal ticket has gone.'

'Twenty-five thousand, that should see me into a flat and a nice holiday.'

'Ahh, didn't lover boy leave you anything, provide something in his will?' Sir Geoffrey chided.

Francis shrugged off the remark and said, 'It just so happens Isaac left everything to his mother.'

'His mother?' Sir Geoffrey smirked, 'What would she want with money living in a mud hut in Zulu land?'

'Listen, I'm not interested in your twisted racist views,' Francis shouted. 'Are you going to come across with the money or shall I have a sudden recall of memory about the newsreel footage and your department photo while I'm at the police station?'

'Okay-okay, but I don't just have that sort of money at hand.' He slackened off his club tie in frustration. 'You'll have to give me time.'

'You've got four days, Father. Then we can meet at your club or your office to hand it over.'

'No-no, that's too risky. I know a quiet place called Giovanni's. It's an Italian restaurant just off the Bayswater road.' Sir Geoffrey used Giovanni's as a MI5 front. All the staff were on his payroll. However, it was still renowned for its spaghetti Vongole and an extensive wine list. Sir Geoffrey suggested. 'Let's meet this Monday coming. Say late, ten-thirty. It'll be quiet then.'

Francis confirmed, 'Okay and no tricks. Anything happens to me, and my new boyfriend will send a letter to the police.'

Sir Geoffrey replaced the receiver. He looked cautiously around the club lounge but nobody was paying attention. One or two members were snoozing while some others read a newspaper or doodled a crossword. He began to think. What had seemed fool proof, the perfect contract killing, had now been picked apart. And in such a short time. Then there was the prospect of a trap. Perhaps his son was working with the police. They could come rushing into the restaurant as he was handing the money over. There was no love between them, especially now Francis knew his involvement. He had to cover himself. No doubt his son would be back for more money and threats later on. The only thing was to nip it in the bud. Doctor the file of that dead nigger. Make it look like he was a high security risk with terrorist links. He had to be removed. With a good enough case, the department might get diplomatic immunity for his killing if it was kept under wraps. Sir Geoffrey's face brightened. The restaurant might be a good chance to end it. Tell the staff to make themselves scarce in case of injury; stay in the kitchen on his orders. He carried the rank. Barricade the doors in case of a police rush. Then kill his son. Plant a gun on him but fire it first. A revenge killing on his father that went horribly wrong the newspapers would say. He liked the idea and, he didn't like the idea. However, he had a bit of time to make his mind up.

*

It was a May light drizzle and the evening smelt fresh and damp as tyres licked their way along the busy Bayswater road. The taxi headlights sparkled in the wet as it slid to a stop. The fare hurriedly paid the driver and then ducked under the restaurant canopy. Francis checked the time. It was ten-twenty-eight.

Looking through the small old fashioned windows of Giovanni's, he could see the place was empty. As he entered, a burly black man confronted him. Behind in a far booth sat Sir Geoffrey and Martin Lavender dressed smartly in city suits.

Frisking him thoroughly, the big man nodded an OK to his boss and then allowed Francis to make his way to the table. He immediately switched the door sign to CLOSED and fixed a large block of wood through the brass handles to form a barricade.

Smells of garlic and prosciutto still lingered from earlier suppers as Francis slid himself into the booth facing Sir Geoffrey and Martin Lavender. The restaurant staff had been ordered to stay in the kitchen and wait until they were called upon.

After polite nods had been exchanged, Francis asked, 'Have you got the money?'

Sir Geoffrey pulled the case from under the table. 'Remember, this is a one off and final payment. Let's say for the loss of your nigger lover. You mention what you know or come sniffing again and our friend here,' Sir Geoffrey motioned his head to Martin Lavender, 'will make sure you're laid to rest by his side. Do I make myself clear?' He pushed the aluminium case across the table. 'You don't have to count it, it's all there.'

He'd had second thoughts of setting up his son and killing him. The media circus that would follow wouldn't do his image or situation any good. He needed to keep out of the public eye. There was also the threat of his son's friend sending a letter in the event of Francis's death.'

Francis slid the case down by his side. 'Listen, Father, I can promise you I have no desire to call on you again. As far as I'm concerned, you can go to hell.'

Just then the phone on the wall started ringing. The Burley aid looked over to Sir Geoffrey. Using the nod, he picked it up. He listened for a few seconds, then leaving the receiver dangling, he came over to the table. 'It's for Francis. He says it's his friend with the letter. He wants to know if Francis is okay.'

Francis smiled. 'My little piece of insurance, Father. Let me tell him I'm alright. He does worry so.'

Sir Geoffrey agreed. 'You go with him, Floyd, and check there's no funny stuff.'

'Okay, Boss.' Floyd escorted him to the phone and stood within earshot.

Francis picked up the receiver. 'Hi, Darling. Don't worry everything's fine...I love you too, honey. You've been a great shoulder since Isaac's death...Don't know what I'd have done without you.' Francis blew a kiss down the phone and then said softly, 'I love you too.'

Floyd backed off. He felt a bit embarrassed and turned away slightly.

Commander Potting, posing as his friend, told Francis, 'Don't forget to tell your father, Kimberly will be coming for supper.'

Francis replied, 'Thanks for reminding me, Darling. See you tonight.' He finished off with another kiss down the telephone.

Feeling slightly uncomfortable with it all, Floyd escorted him back to the table. Then he went back to his position by the door.

Francis sat down with a faraway look in his eyes. Fortunately no one noticed. Then he immediately winced. He asked them, 'Do you mind if I visit the washroom. Drunk too much water in the gym this afternoon.' He smiled at the pair.

Sir Geoffrey clicked his fingers and Floyd came over. 'Go with him to the gents and stand outside. Then bring him back.'

'Will do, Boss.' Floyd escorted him into a lobby and then hovered as Francis pushed open the GENTS swing door. Out of sight, Floyd relaxed against the wall and pulled his cigarettes for a quick smoke.

The smell of pine disinfectant accosted his nostrils. Francis hovered for a second and surveyed the three urinals and the one cubicle. Now he had to be quick. With Floyd outside, this was his chance. He went into the cubicle and looked up. It was an old toilet cistern with the overhead water tank. He strained and felt around the lid of the tank until his fingers touched the Glock 17 pistol. He carefully pulled it down and placed it inside his jacket. Then he went to the sink and washed his hands.

Floyd heard the hand towel being pulled and immediately stubbed out his smoke.

Francis emerged with a smile. 'That's better, I was bursting.'

Floyd ignored the remark and escorted him back.

Sir Geoffrey and Martin had relaxed. In his absence they'd ordered bruschetta and were already helping themselves from the large fancy plate provided. 'Have some.' Sir Geoffrey offered and then took another wedge and greedily began scoffing.

Martin nibbled at his while Floyd stood over by the door idly looking out of the restaurant window.

Francis took a bite of bruschetta and then went to his top pocket for a handkerchief. He politely dabbed his mouth and returned it to his inside pocket as he took another bite. In that instant the Glock appeared.

Francis fired twice. One bullet had gone clean between his father's eyes while the other one had taken off half his finger from the hand clutching the slice of bruschetta.

Martin Lavender was already up with his Walther P99 and fired twice into Francis's chest.

Sir Geoffrey had crashed backwards and was on the floor.

Francis clutched his blood soaked chest, coughed and then fell forward onto the table. His body quivered for some seconds and then remained still.

Martin Lavender reached for Francis's gun and then spun round to face Floyd who'd taken a kneeling position and was pointing his Walther at him.

Martin relaxed. 'Jesus, that was close. I thought he was going to kill us all.'

Floyd lowered his gun and breathed a sigh of relief.

In that moment, Martin raised the Glock pistol and shot two into Floyd's head. His skull exploded, blood was everywhere. Martin looked down at the staring eyes and kicked his gun away. Then he walked to the bar telephone. He dialled the clean-up number. 'Need to take away, right now, three baskets of dirty linen and a spring clean required at Giovanni's restaurant at Albion Gate W2, just off the Bayswater Road.'

Commander Gregory Potting acknowledged, 'Will do.'

Martin Lavender made his way to the washroom. In the dim light of a single bulb he washed his blood soaked hands and drank some cold water. He breathed in deeply. The adrenalin was slowing down. He stared into the mirror for a while not thinking. Then it slowly leeched into his mind. Francis? With two gunshot blasts into the chest should have fallen backwards instead of forwards. And there was far too much instant blood.

With the realisation, Martin dashed back inside the restaurant. *'Shit! – Shit! – Shit!'* Francis was gone. All that remained was a puddle of blood on the table. Martin dipped his finger and smelt it. And sure enough. 'Pigs blood,' he mumbled. *'Pigs blood and a bullet proof vest,'* he cursed. He assured himself. Commander Potting would still be pleased even if that gay bastard did escape. He wasn't going to pose a threat now his father was dead. The queer shit could go on as many gay pride marches as he liked or shack up with who he liked. It didn't matter.

CHAPTER SEVEN

They'd found another hotel just off the Bayswater Road. It was called the Grand. However, it was far from that, with the downstairs frayed reception carpet and the first floor poky room with its nicotine stained ceiling which they were looking at now.

 'My God, you could've got yourself killed. Who would have thought, his own son killed Sir Geoffrey?'

Martin kissed her tenderly on the forehead. 'I know, My Love. These days, youngsters just don't respect their parents anymore.'

They both laughed and she rolled over and straddled him. 'So, Mr James Bond, that holiday break we were talking about. Where are you going to take your Miss Moneypenny? The Caribbean, the Seychelles or perhaps the Hamptons?' She flicked back her long dark wavy hair in a haughty pose. 'I can see myself riding in an open top Bentley, off to watch polo with the other country club mistresses. All decked out in Ralph Lauren and Gucci.' Then her face dropped. 'Anything has to be better than these grotty hotels we have to find.'

'I know, My Love. Let's make it in two weeks' time.' Martin pulled her down and kissed her excitedly. 'We can really celebrate. Push the boat out. I'm meeting a contact tonight. He's got this beach side villa and a yacht in Marbella. I'll ask him if we can use it.' He grinned at her. 'I'll even teach you how to water ski.'

Suddenly Martin mounted her and grabbed her buttocks. 'Now listen, Miss Moneypenny. I'm going to show you what James Bond does with his MI5 truncheon.'

She squealed with delight and wrapped her legs around his waist. 'Come on, Mister Bond, give me your truncheon one more time.'

Suddenly, the bedside telephone rang. Martin glanced in the direction and thought to leave it. Then he glanced again.

'Leave it, Mister Bond. You've got other things on your mind,' she panted out.

Martin stopped what he was doing and lifted the black receiver. He indicated to her to keep quiet. 'Yes.'

Commander Potting told him, 'End of the bed under the sheets. Don't forget to tell Ruth, Kimberly will be coming for supper.'

'Thank you for reminding me.' Martin put the receiver down with a thoughtful expression.

Her eyes looked inquisitive. 'Who was that?'

'Oh...err just reception. Letting us know we have to vacate the room by mid-day.'

'These crappy hotels are always doing that. As if to Christ we'd want to stay any longer in this shithole!'

His concentration was back and he leant down and kissed her tenderly. 'Now,' he joked, 'what was James Bond doing before he was so rudely interrupted.'

She squealed again as he rolled her over onto her stomach. Martin said eagerly, 'Let's do it doggie style.' Behind her back his hand quickly darted under the sheets and groped around until he felt the rope and the letter. As she giggled he parted her legs and climbed on top.

Ruth Torrington always liked it this way and shouted, 'Come on, ride me, Cowboy.'

During the humping and pumping, his hand felt for the rope. He brought it up above her and made a noose and then he slipped it over her head. In those few seconds she tried to tell him it was hurting but Martin ignored her and pulled so tight his face twisted up into a shaking frothy grin. After nearly a minute, he collapsed on top of her exhausted breathing out sharp snatches of air.

Now he had to be quick. He rolled the body and went about dressing her as best as he could. Fortunately she liked it kinky, while still wearing her bra, garter belt and stockings, this saved him a bit of time. Martin searched the cheap dressing table for her earrings, wrist watch and necklace. Then he placed the forged suicide note in full view on the tatty dressing table. It stated how she couldn't live anymore with the guilt of being involved with the deaths of Isaac Constantine and Sir Geoffrey Hodder.

Martin looked at the ceiling. He just hoped the fan would take her weight. Standing on a chair he looped the rope over the blades and pulled hard. It looked like it was going to hold.

With one end around her neck he hauled the body up. It had to look as though she'd kicked the chair away. So the drop had to be just right. Satisfied, he tied off the end of the rope. Now he had to get past reception. Let them know his wife was staying on, and leave a generous tip.

*

Commander Gregory Potting stood by the window of his large office. From here he could look down on Whitehall. Across the road was Banqueting House while further down he still had a good view of the Cabinet Office. The traffic was moving well today. It was a sunny morning and he was in a good mood.

Catching his eye, he remembered his morning tea with a digestive. His private secretary, Margaret, always there on the dot with his elevenses. Commander Potting walked over to his desk and sat down. He sipped his Darjeeling and broke the biscuit in half. Then he withdrew a clutch of files. He sifted through them and reached for his ink pad and stamp. On the folders of Isaac Constantine and Sir Geoffrey Hodder he thumped down in red letters EXPIRED on the buff cover. He withdrew one more folder. It was marked Home Secretary – Ruth Torrington. With a lopsided smile he rolled the stamp once more on the pad.

CHAPTER EIGHT

It was around two in the morning when the Mercedes E220 estate pulled up outside the workshop just off Jamaica Road, Bermondsey. The sign outside stating **SAMMY'S AUTOS AND REPAIRS**, wasn't lit up. However, four of them inside were waiting.

All ears had pricked up at the sound of an engine. Someone turned the lights out. The headlights flashed twice; the signal to open the garage doors. Then the sleek silver body purred its way over the concrete dug out pit and stopped short of two mechanics with torches. A brief last look to check it hadn't been followed and then the steel doors closed around it.

As the lights went on, they got to work. Sammy Abdullah, a slim tall Egyptian with a pointed nose and dark greasy hair, took out a bundle of notes and paid the driver. He immediately made off through a side door. Then Sammy, being Mr Buxton's right hand man, barked a list of instructions and the other three started to work.

First, the upholstery and outside skins were carefully unclipped and peeled away from the door panels and seals. Then the spot welds were cut through. Finally, the yellow protection wrap was visible.

Sammy stepped forward and tugged at the packing material. As he pulled some away he revealed the first white bags of cocaine.

While the others stood back, Sammy lifted out three bags and poked his knife into the fourth. He stuck his little finger through the small slit and tasted the powder. Sammy rubbed it around his gums. The three mechanics watched him nervously. Then he nodded to them with a smile. They relaxed. From somewhere, out came a hipflask of brandy and they toasted each other. Sammy wiped the top and took a swig himself.

Within twenty minutes, they'd stashed away fifty-five kilograms of cocaine into two holdalls. Sammy barked more orders and the mechanics immediately started replacing the car trim.

*

Room service had just left. A good Bourbon with lots of ice and some canapés sat on the waiter's fancy brass trolley. Kenny Buxton liked everybody to be comfortable when a deal was going down at his Park Lane penthouse.

Kenny was smoking a large Cuban cigar. As a short fat balding fifty-eight year old South London businessman and being the owner of a few properties in the capital, he felt this was one of his good days. His other income, besides the bags of cocaine stacked high on the coffee table, was from the car repair shop and his events' company *ONE DAY WONDERS LTD*.

Kenny Buxton's wrinkled flabby face looked worried while Sammy checked out the quality of the latest shipment. Kenny made it clear to him, 'I want you to double check that shit. Even use the old method. For all we know these new-fangled kits could be faulty. Dodgy batch or somethin'. It happens.' He sucked on his cigar and scrutinised the bags of cocaine. 'I don't like being accused a cheat.'

He looked at the German, Günther Roth. Mr Luciano's representative from the North Midlands shifted uncomfortably. 'If I'm gonna cut the shit down with all that mannitol crap, I'd let them know. This is the third time we've been accused. Once it leaves here, no one touches that shit until Luciano gets it his end in Manchester.' He looked menacingly at Günther again and then turned to the two young French couriers. 'Isn't that correct?'

They sat up and quickly nodded. 'Yes, Sir. That is correct, Monsieur Buxton.'

They all watched Sammy carefully. He picked a second bag of cocaine from the bottom of the pile. Using the tip of his penknife, he carefully weighed out 20 milligrams. Sammy shook the small ampoule and then snapped off the head. With a steady hand he added the sample of drug. He held the phial to the light and began to smile as the yellow orange colour slowly changed to a dark reddish brown. Sammy checked with the kit colour chart. 'Nearly pure junk, Mr Buxton.'

'Okay - Okay, Sammy, but one last check, the old method please. Just to be sure.'

'Will do, Mr Buxton.' He lit the small camping colour gas stove that was on the smoked glass coffee table. Using the tip of his knife again, he added a small sample of cocaine to the hot plate. A laboratory clamp held the end of a thermometer against the heated surface. As the mercury level began to rise, Sammy informed the room. 'One-hundred and thirty, good housekeeping seal of approval. One-hundred and fifty, blast off. One-hundred and seventy, British government certified.' Sammy leaned closer with excitement. 'One-hundred and eighty, lunar trajectory, junk of the month club sirloin steak. One-hundred and ninety; man this is something.' The cocaine was beginning to melt. 'Two-hundred, blast off. We've got grade A poison here.'

Kenny Buxton sucked on his cigar and patted Sammy on the back. 'Music to my ears, Sammy.'

'This is over ninety-five per cent pure junk, Mr Buxton.' Sammy did some figures in his head. He leant closer to his boss so the others didn't hear him. 'Fifty-six kilograms for two mill' is a good deal we've made, Mr Buxton. It's a pity we can't cut and sell it ourselves. Think of what Luciano is going to make? He'll be dealing on this load for the next eighteen months. By the time it's got to pound and fifty pence bags he'll have made around six-million.'

Kenny patted Sammy's back again. He murmured softly, 'We don't have the set up and contacts like he has, Sammy. Luciano can get rid of this shit a lot better than we can. We mustn't be greedy. Our operation is just to move it on to the highest bidder, remember that.' Kenny lightened. 'And for arranging this, Sammy,' he whispered. 'There's a nice little bonus coming your way.'

Sammy beamed at his boss.

Kenny turned to the German. 'You tell Luciano he's getting a good deal.'

The German held out his hand. 'I vill tell my boss to expect good stuff this time. I have seen with my own eyes, yes?'

Kenny shook it and mocked, 'Now you go and tell Mr Luciano you have seen with your own eyes, yes?'

After the German left, Kenny retorted, 'Fucking Krout!'

Sammy with the two young French couriers placed the bags of cocaine into vapour sealed x-ray proof bags, then concealed them inside two rucksacks and the linings of their rolled up sleeping bags.

When all was finished, the young couple, dressed as backpackers touring Europe with their hairy sheepskin waistcoats and urban camouflage trousers, hoisted up their loads.

With maps in hand and tin mugs swinging from their rucksacks adorned with foreign stickers, the couriers made their way to Victoria Station left luggage desk. Kenny Buxton had been using this drop off since 1971.

Although the old fashioned left luggage lockers with their key would have seemed safe. They'd had a spate of station break-ins late at night. Nothing had been stolen. However, a damaged lock showed evidence that an attempt had been made. To reassure the public, most London stations had a manned left luggage desk. This was very convenient, since over a period of time they'd lost merchandise through vigilant police raids of houses and garage lock-up searches. Now, two years later using this method, they'd managed to keep one-step ahead of the narcotics squad. With the stuff buried in left luggage, it was out of the way and off their hands temporarily.

The French couriers asked how much for the rental and then signed for their rucksacks and pocketed the ticket.

With their arms around each other like young lovers on holiday, the couriers walked off to Victoria tube station, while on the way, kissing now and again and very content with their agreed £4,000 pay-off and the small complementary dope bags. The agreement being, half the pay-off money when they'd returned the left luggage ticket to Kenny as proof of delivery. This would give Kenny time to arrange his handover deal. To get the other half of their payoff, the couriers would take the ticket and collect their rucksacks and bedrolls as planned, and then deliver to the car boot of a Mercedes on the third floor of a car park in Ealing.

CHAPTER NINE

Martin Lavender was pleased with his successful contract on Isaac Constantine and Ruth Torrington and his bonus of five-hundred pounds. Things at the moment couldn't be better for Martin.

On a MI5 high flyer salary and the successful owner of Studio 21, an upmarket nightclub that was making good money, he felt a celebration was in order.

His nightclub STUDIO 21, a venue for diners and clubbers just off Streatham high street was previously a corner supermarket. He'd purchased the business two years ago and struggled at first to make ends meet. It had been a bit of a gamble, however, business had picked up considerably over the last six months, so much so, he'd completely refurbished the interior.

Fortunately, he never had to borrow any money. STUDIO 21 had become well known and the in place for upmarket, fashionable and professional people who required their presence to be discreet and away from prying eyes and the press photographer's flash bulb. His nightclub membership was in high demand, in fact there was a waiting list.

Never in his wildest dreams could he of imagined his little side-line would become so profitable. Now they were flocking in droves to his club. He'd like to think, it was the food and music that was swelling the numbers in the diner and on the dance floor. However, in reality, they'd come for the sundries on offer. So much so, that demand outstripped supply.

It never surprised Martin who queued up with their coat ticket when transactions were taking place in the back office. They could be labourers, doctors, judges, solicitors, famous footballers, chefs, meat packers, dentists, welfare workers, you name it. They all wanted a piece of cocaine, or nose candy or Charlie for those that used the American terminology.

Indirectly, it was his brother Dave who got him into this profitable scam. Dave worked as an assistant manager for a left luggage chain at Victoria Station. It was Maria, Dave's dozy assistant, who'd managed to get the left luggage tickets mixed up one time. So Dave, while swearing under his breath, had to sort it out. Going through bags trying to find some identification or an address, he found the cocaine by chance hidden in rucksacks. It was always the same two French couriers dressed as students that dropped off the coke and then collected it at a later date.

While his brother Dave had the coke, he quickly removed a third of the original pure stuff. Then making up the weight and quantity with a mix of mannitol, he carefully resealed the bags and replaced them back in the courier's rucksacks. Martin then sold what they'd stolen at his nightclub.

*

This Friday evening rush-hour, Martin Lavender was traveling back from his MI5 department on a crowded Tube train reading the Times Newspaper. However, his concentration was elsewhere. Tonight he was going to celebrate. Push the boat out. It was all planned. He'd go down on one knee and propose to Vicky his girlfriend.

They'd first met at Briar Lodge Manor when he was her instructor for a bodyguard course she had enrolled for. Since then he'd been dating her for six months. Victoria Buxton, a twenty-eight year old petite five-foot four South London girl with gorgeous long blonde hair and a face and figure that could grace the cover of any fashion magazine. She worked as marketing director for her millionaire father Kenny Buxton.

Vicky, as she liked to be called, would be coming round tonight for their usual Friday evening takeaway, or so she thought.

The underground, packed as usual was warm and sticky. Martin had managed to find a seat and was thinking of the surprise evening ahead. Slowly he began to feel something digging into him. He shifted uncomfortably and then lifted himself slightly and felt behind. His fingers clutched at a wallet. Sitting down again, he stared at it.

Martin looked warily either side. Nobody had seen him pick it up.

Using his newspaper as a shield, he discretely opened the wallet and found around £150 in ten and twenty pound notes. He also found a Youth Hostel card with a name and telephone number scribbled in Biro. He nonchalantly checked both ways again and dug his fingers into the other little pockets of the wallet and suddenly clawed at a ticket. He slowly unfolded it.

It was for left luggage. Martin frowned. He recognised the company name on the ticket heading.

Once he reached his stop, he made his way to one of the telephone booths inside West Brompton Station and dialled his brother.

'Dave, it's me.'

'What is it?'

'Listen, Dave, I found a luggage ticket. Looks like one of yours. Someone dropped a wallet on my train.'

'So?'

'In the wallet was a Youth Hostel card and a scribbled French name.'

Silence, then, 'Could be anybody, doesn't mean just because they're French–'

'Dave,' Martin interrupted. 'Better check this out. We don't want any fuck ups. This is our biggest cut yet from them.'

'Okay, okay. Read me the ticket number and I'll go and have a look.'

Martin scrutinised the ticket. 'Zero, zero, three, nine, five, four, one.'

Dave replied, 'Hang on, I'll check.'

Martin flicked through his newspaper. His eyes didn't focus. He turned a couple of pages and then his brother was back.

'Shit, would you believe it?' Dave said, in desperation. 'It's the actual ticket.'

'You're kidding me,' Martin said. 'What are the bloody chances of that? Look, when do they collect?'

'In a couple of days for fuck sake,' Dave said panicking. 'How the fuck could they lose a ticket?'

'Listen, calm down,' Martin tried to relax him. 'We've got to get it back to them. If they can't collect, then it becomes complicated. They don't know me. I'm just an honest Joe returning a lost wallet.'

'Mart', don't draw their attention to us, for Christ's sake.' Dave was really panicking. 'Remember we're cutting their shit by a third with mannitol, then selling on the pure stuff. They just have to assume everything's Kosher when they come and pick up. If they suss what we're doing, we'll be hanging from meat hooks.'

'Okay I said calm down, Dave. I'll phone the number on the Youth Hostel card. Get them to collect the wallet. It'll only be those usual couriers. They won't recognise me. I'll do it now.'

'Let me know how you get on,' Dave said anxiously.

Martin ended the call. He made sure the ticket went back exactly how it had been folded and in the correct wallet compartment. If they asked him about it, he'd tell them he did see a ticket of some kind and act blasé about it. Martin prepared himself. He cleared his throat and took a deep breath. Then looking at the Youth Hostel card, he dialled the scribbled number.

'Reception, Bayswater Youth Hostel.'

'Oh, err, Good afternoon. Thought I'd better phone. I've found a wallet to day with a Youth Hostel card inside with the name Arnaud on it. I wondered if you'd had one reported missing?'

'We have actually. A French couple staying here reported it late this afternoon. If you hold on I'll check there room.'

Martin could hear himself breathing rapidly while he waited. After thirty seconds he heard muffled talking and then.

'Ah, merci beaucoup!' The voice was ecstatic. 'Many thank you. I fear I lost my wallet this afternoon on a train. I 'ad a lot of money inside it. Around one-'undred and forty pounds I think.'

Martin corrected him. 'One-hundred and fifty to be precise. I live in Chelsea, number thirty-seven Cheyne Walk. If you want to pop round and collect, I'll be in from seven p.m. onwards tonight.'

'Je vous remercie de tout cœur. Err, 'ow do you say, I thank you from the bottom of my 'eart.'

Martin laughed. 'No problem.' After repeating his address slowly, he ended the call. Then he phoned his brother again. 'I think they swallowed it.'

'Are you sure, Mart?' Dave sounded very scared. 'They didn't sound funny or anything? Perhaps it's a trap. Perhaps they're on to us. They followed you on purpose. Seen you collect the good shit. Sussed we're shafting them. Dropped the wallet so you'd find it. To find out where you live…Jesus Christ, Mart', we're fucked.' Dave started to blabber. 'They're gonna kill us. *I don't wanna die, Mart' –I don't wanna die—'*

'*Can you shut the fuck up?*' Martin shouted and then checked sheepishly if anybody was looking. 'Calm down for Christ sake. It's gonna be okay. Listen, stay low. Have someone else handle the baggage, like that dumb cow Maria you've got there. Go sick for a few days. I'll call you.'

*

By eight-thirty that evening, everything was ready. The table laid, the chef doing his thing in the kitchen. Martin had showered and was taking advantage of another warm May evening as he chilled out on the balcony of his apartment overlooking the street. Lights were appearing with activity on other balconies as people sat around on fashionable leather sofas with their first of the evening cocktails.

The restaurants below were gradually filling up. Casual Armani and Dior dressed couples promenaded hand in hand and gazed through windows at enticing menus.

Martin was on his first slurp of the day, a chilled Sancerre. He looked back through the balcony curtains. He was a materialist and couldn't help it. His trappings of success bore witness to that. The white walls with their limited edition Hockney prints. The Bugatti furniture. The massively expensive white and black Persian carpet you could lose yourself in, and frequently did with Vicky astride him. The tinted Louis Poulsen ceiling lights that could relax your mood after a hard day. As for the Amode dining table and chairs, that cost more than his father ever earned in a year.

He thought of Vicky. He was definitely feeling horny tonight. Then the front door buzzer sounded.

She stood there looking stunning, wearing a little black Fendi number and matching high heels. He kissed her in the hallway. She responded and pushed herself against him. He was hard and she felt it. Martin wanted to take her now. His hand cupped her bum. He felt the suspender strap. Jesus! She was wearing those, his favourite. He wanted her up against the wall now. Hoisted up, legs around his waist like they'd done so many times. But it had to wait - the chef in the kitchen - the surprise candlelit dinner. Martin eased off and whispered, 'Later, after my surprise.'

Victoria joked, 'I thought *that* was the surprise.'

He kissed her and led her by the hand into the dining room.

'Jesus! What's this,' she gasped.

Martin had spent a lot of money and it had paid off. The table and the mood looked stunning. There were candles everywhere. The gold plated cutlery and candelabra glinted amongst the tiny flames. A bottle of Dom Perignon sat in the ice bucket. As if on cue, the Bang and Olufsen came alive and sent Mantovani wafting through the curtains.

Victoria kissed him. She started to say, 'What's this–'

Suddenly the Italian chef emerged in his whites, sporting a huge floppy hat. He bowed to them both and said, 'I am pleased to meet you, Miss Victoria. I hope you enjoy my cooking, yes?' He offered his hand and she sheepishly shook it. 'Now, if you are ready I will serve.'

They both nodded and took their places.

Alonzo reappeared wheeling his trolley with an assortment of highly polished copper pans. He smiled to them as he removed a lid and served slow poached Moulard duck foie gras. It was her favourite. Martin had remembered.

There was silence for a couple of minutes as they sampled the hors d'oeuvre. Martin looked up and raised his glass of Sancerre. Victoria followed and they toasted each other. Then she cheekily licked her lips at him.

'You've earned your brownie points tonight,' she said.

He responded licking his lips and replied, 'I know.' Then they collapsed into laughter.

Next came the buttered poached lobster with Chanterelle mushrooms and black mission figs in Pimentòn oil. As Alonzo uncorked the Dom Perignon, Martin moved his chair aside and went down on one knee. He took out the £4,000 diamond cluster engagement ring.

Victoria breathed in sharply. She'd never seen anything like it. She slowly took it out of the small satin box and muttered to him. 'Dear God, Martin..It...it must have cost you a fortune?'

'I know, it was worth it though,' he said. 'But more important. Will you marry me?'

Victoria slipped it on to her finger. It fitted perfectly. Then she looked up. 'Yes of course I will.' Pretending to be serious she added, 'Provided you can keep me in a manner I'm accustomed too.'

'I'll do my best,' he joked. Then they kissed.

Alonzo applauded and took a photo of them both showing off the ring with Martin's camera. Afterwards came another toast followed by an assortment of desserts including ice cream, chocolate and candies.

By ten o'clock, after seeing out Alonzo who was more than happy with his large tip, they were warming up together on the sofa. Martin, with his shirt open, had his hand inside Victoria's panties while she had her hand inside his flies. Suddenly the front door buzzer sounded.

Martin remembered. 'Shit.' He pulled himself away. 'Sorry, Love, I forgot all about them.'

Victoria sat up. 'Who's that at this time of night?' She straightened her dress and arranged her hair.

'Oh, err, I found somebody's wallet today on the train. Had an address inside. Told them to call round and collect it.'

Tucking his shirt in and doing up some buttons, he made his way into the hall. Martin looked through the security peephole. A young couple wearing bobble hats and sheepskin jackets hovered outside. 'Yes, who is it?' he said over the intercom.

'Are, merci, we 'ave come to collect the wallet, thank you.'

Martin hesitated, they were alone. There looked to be no problem. He opened the door on a chain. They both smiled at him through the small gap. He said to them, 'One moment, I'll go and get it.'

A few seconds later he returned and handed them the wallet. They thanked him with big smiles. The scruffy young man checked its contents and then peeled off a £20 note and offered it to Martin.

'No please, that's okay. Really you don't have too.' Martin held up his hand to kindly refuse the offer.

'Please take it.' The young man said again.

Suddenly the young woman crossed her legs with a moan. 'May I use your washroom, Sir? We've been drinking with some friends and I'm afraid, my bladder is bursting. 'Ow do you say, I've been caught short.' She giggled.

Martin hesitated. He didn't want to draw attention. Make them suspicious. He smiled and told her, 'Of course you can.' He unhooked the chain and let her in. The boyfriend hovered. Martin turned and pointed to the cloakroom toilet. 'It's in—'

Within a second, the cattle prod came out from the rucksack and discharged 30,000 volts into Martin's neck. He jerked into a fit and hit the floor. Victoria raised herself when she heard the commotion. 'Martin, are you okay?' She hurried to the hall and saw the scruffy young man standing over her fiancé.

CHAPTER TEN

The smelling sorts brought him round. His head felt like it was being squeezed inside a cider press.

'ARGH,' Martin flinched. The sharp slap across the face was the final jolt into reality. His blurred vision began to focus on his surroundings. There was a bare light bulb above. It reflected off some grimy broken windows and a puddled floor. The discarded steel drums with the strong smell of cellulose and various coloured stains on the concrete chipped walls indicated a derelict spray shop or paint warehouse.

'Shit.' Another sharp slap made him focus intensely now at his tormentor. Sammy Abdullah, disguised wearing a balaclava with a slit for the mouth, leaned into him. Three other men dressed the same stood around.

Fear was creeping over Martin fast. What had happened? Where was he? Where was Vicky? And above all else, what was going to happen to him?

Stripped of his clothes apart from his pants, he was tied to a chair with rope. Someone behind grabbed his head and turned it. They wanted him to see. He was made to look at them.

The French couriers were hanging upside down from hooks. Blood dripped off them and spattered the floor. The bodies swayed and twisted gently. From the mutilated hands it was clearly visible they were tortured before having their throats cut. Martin tried to look away but his head was held firm.

Sammy told him, 'These are the couriers that called round on you. They told us they lost the wallet and you'd found it. We had to be sure you hadn't been inquisitive with the left luggage ticket while you had the wallet in your possession. This is their punishment for being careless with the ticket and trying to do a runner with half of their courier fee. They were stupid.'

Sammy smiled. He gripped the arms of Martin's chair and leaned into his face. 'Which now leaves you. What we have to ask ourselves is; did you out of curiosity go and check out the luggage once you found the ticket? Might be something worth pinching? Admittedly, there was money in the wallet. But then there could be more valuables and money in the left luggage.'

Martin shook his head vigorously. 'No - no, honestly I never did. I just phoned them when I found the wallet.'

'But what if you checked out the luggage first. Found the stuff. Then got cold feet. Realised you was into some heavy shit. Told the desk that you found the ticket; wanted to look through the luggage for an address so you could return it. Showed the desk what you'd found. They would notify the police. Set a trap for us. Perhaps they even promised you a reward?'

'No please believe me.' Martin gulped. 'What stuff? I don't know what you're talking about.'

'You see, we have to be sure it's safe when we collect.' Sammy patted his head affectionately. Martin flinched away.

'We can make you talk, you know.' He clicked his fingers.

Another man stepped forward with a cattle prodder. He jammed it against Martin's neck and delivered a reduced charge of 25,000 volts.

Martin's body shuddered in fit. *'Arghh! – Arghh!...Please God, no, I'm telling the truth...Arghh.'*

The man stood back as Martin released his bladder. Urine spilled through the wicker seat onto the floor.

Sammy menacingly gripped the arms of Martin's chair again and leant in close. 'That is nothing to what we shall do to you. I will ask you again. Is it safe for us to collect?'

'Yes—Yes, dear God, whatever your talking about it's safe. I've told you I'm telling the truth...Please no more.'

Sammy nodded to the man. He jammed the cattle prodder into Martin's neck again.

'Arghh! – Arghh! – Arghh! Fuck you mother — Arghh! Please don't, God, please–Arghh!' The shuddering stopped. Martin was sobbing in agony.

Sammy gripped his chair again. 'We have all night to do this. I'll ask you again. Is it safe to collect?'

'Yes, I've told you.' He gulped for air and cried out, *'I don't know any more. Honest please!—I'd tell you if I did.'*

He wrenched Martin's hair lifting up his head.

Martin's face was contorted in agony as blood shot eyes with tears pleaded to be believed.

He let his head drop. Sammy pondered in thought and said, 'For some reason you may be telling the truth.'

Martin was slumped over, exhausted in pain.

Sammy clicked his fingers and the aid threw a bucket of water over him.

Martin stirred with the sudden coldness.

Then Sammy dragged up a chair and sat on it back to front facing Martin. He slapped his face again to make him look up and take notice. 'Now listen carefully. I can't risk any of my own. You'll have to do the collecting for me. That's the only way we'll find out if you're telling the truth.'

'I am telling the truth,' Martin blurted out in sobs.

'Okay - Okay, but just remember. We're holding your girlfriend, Victoria.'

Martin looked up in terror. He'd just assumed she'd managed to get away or hide from them. Not seeing her tied up with him, he'd kept quiet.

Sammy smirked. 'No, she didn't get away. We've got her and she's perfectly safe, provided you do as you're told.' He leant in, 'But if it's a trap, if it isn't safe, then she will be killed.' Sammy grinned at him. 'Of course we'll have our little bit of fun with her first.'

Martin pleaded. *'Please don't harm her. She's totally innocent, I beg you.'*

'Then you will do as we say?'

He meekly nodded.

'Cut him free.' Sammy motioned to the man. 'Give him his clothes.'

Martin rubbed his wrists. He raised himself and felt groggy. Sammy informed him, 'You will have to stay here tonight. There's a couch you can use with a toilet and shower. If you try anything, your girlfriend dies. Don't forget.'

At gunpoint, he was led into a disused first aid room. The strong musty smell was overpowering but at least it was reasonably clean compared to the rest of the place. He was given a bottle of mineral water and a toilet roll and then locked in.

Martin lay back on the first aid couch and checked his watch. They'd forgot to take it. The time was 2:45 a.m. As he closed his eyes he pondered, what would they have done to him if they'd known the real truth? What a mess he thought. MI5 wouldn't be pleased either, knowing he was creaming off a mobster.

The following morning his door was unlocked and he was handed a set of used clothes. Sammy, still wearing his balaclava, shouted to him, 'You have ten minutes to get ready, put them on.' Then he locked the door again.

Dressed in moccasins, holed jeans and a Tibetan lamb waistcoat he looked the part. Martin peered at himself in the cracked mirror. With the pulled down bobble hat and sunglasses, he could pass for a backpacker traveling around Europe.

Sammy realised they might want to see some identification of Martin at the luggage desk. Sometimes the ticket on its own wasn't good enough. Sammy had worked on the passport of the courier who was hanging upside down. Scratching the photo a little with a pin and some added tea stains would stop any close scrutiny.

Martin just hoped he wouldn't be recognised at the luggage counter. Some MI5 staff used the station. He'd made himself available more than once to some of the girls in the typing pool. For one of them to spot him at the station and start asking awkward questions would be curtains. Especially for Victoria.

Martin also hoped his brother had heeded his advice and taken a couple of days off. He just wanted it to run smoothly, do exactly what they wanted for Vicky's sake.

Dave's stand-in at the luggage desk, Maria, was a bit of a dozy twat which was fortunate. Martin had only met her once. She definitely wouldn't recognise him dressed like this. It was unlikely she'd even recognise Father Christmas with her earphones plugged in to her transistor radio and chewing gum.

Dave was going to get rid of her. She'd cocked up a few times handing out the wrong luggage or getting the tickets muddled up. But she was cheap labour and would do for the meantime. However, this time it had to run smoothly. No mix-ups and without a hint of recognition. Otherwise they'd put two and two together and he'd really be in the shit. That working over he'd received would be nothing. A mob like that would have contacts everywhere. No matter where he ran, they'd find him. And there was Vicky to think of. Would they let her go after all this? Hopefully her captors hid their faces.

Martin knew he was in a catch twenty-two situation. He had to go along with it. What else could he do with Vicky's life at stake? Even if he tried to raise the alarm or do a runner, they'd probably have a gun on him.

Martin's mind was racing in overdrive when suddenly the door was unlocked and two men roughly hauled him out in front of Sammy.

Sammy gave him the luggage ticket. 'Now these are your instructions, listen carefully.' Sammy checked his watch. 'The time is now nine-fifty-five. You will go to Victoria Station and pick up the rucksacks at the left luggage desk. Then you will proceed to the station taxi rank. A cab will meet you there at approximately ten-fifty. Don't worry, he'll recognise you. You will instruct the driver by showing him this address.' He handed Martin a piece of paper with the details. 'He will take you to this warehouse. You will drop off the rucksacks at the rear of this building by the fence. You will tell the driver, you're a volunteer worker and the dossers that use the warehouse require some clean clothes, blankets and tinned food. Then you will continue to your apartment. If all goes well, your girlfriend will be released within the following hour.'

He gave Martin £30 in £10 notes. 'This is for the luggage rental and the cab. Remember, any hiccups in the plan and your girlfriend will be killed immediately.'

Sammy came closer. 'If you go to the police afterwards, no matter how much protection you are guaranteed, we will find you and kill you. Nobody escapes our clutches.' Sammy took out a photograph of Alonzo, the chef Martin had hired. He showed it to him. Sammy smiled. 'He died under torture. We had to make sure if he knew anything or was part of a trap.'

Stripped naked and hanging upside down badly beaten, the bloody mess dangling in the photo made him feel sick. Martin quickly looked away. He'd made up his mind. If he and Vicky ever got out of this he'd finish with it all and take her on a long holiday somewhere.

Then Martin was ordered into the rear of a small commercial van. He sat in a crouched position. The driver was partitioned off. Sammy leaned through and reminded him, 'Remember, two people will be watching you all the time.'

Martin nodded to confirm he understood. Then Sammy locked the rear doors.

As the van pulled away, he wondered why he wasn't blindfolded. Then thinking more clearly, he could see why. The warehouse was derelict. They'd probably use it just the once and then be gone. And they knew he wasn't going to show the address to anyone apart from the cabdriver. Vicky's situation took care of that.

Looking through the small rear windows, he began to recognise where he was. They'd passed Southwark Park on his left. That meant they were traveling down Jamaica Road following the Thames. Next, he caught a glimpse of Tower Bridge.

Martin rested his head back against the side of the van. The bumpy ride didn't help. He closed his eyes, wishing this nightmare would end.

CHAPTER ELEVEN

On the station platform, he discretely looked around. Martin couldn't see anybody suspicious eyeing him up. That was hardly surprising. The mob were probably more sophisticated than that.

As he moved towards the left luggage counter, he checked to see who was serving. Dave was out of sight, thank God. He could see Maria was on her own. Martin pulled down his bobble hat further, then approached. 'Excuse me.' He handed her the ticket.

The pretty, twenty-two year old cocked her head to one side as if she was listening to a particular track. With her earphones in and chewing nonstop, her short jet-black hair with its little white quiff stood out against the dull grey uniform she had to wear. Maria looked at the ticket then disappeared around the back.

Martin waited. He cast his eyes over all what was going on. People milling about, noises, echoes, the smell of diesel engines, doors slamming, whistles blowing, the information boards flicking over. A West Indian man on the sound system informing commuters of delays and maintenance work. The smell of coffee and burgers from a takeaway.

With two rucksacks she appeared again. With great effort, she lifted them onto the counter. Maria hesitated and then said, ''Ave yer got any ID, Sir?'

Martin took out the passport and gave it to her. She looked at it nonchalantly, turned it over, looked at him, then the tickets on the rucksacks. 'That's fine,' she said. She handed him back the passport.

Martin breathed a sigh of relief.

Maria stamped the ticket and scribbled a receipt. 'That'll be seventeen pounds, Sir.'

He took out the money and paid her. Then he hoisted a rucksack on his back and carried the other one in the crook of his elbow to the taxi rank.

By the time he got to the queue of taxis, he was sweating. The warm spell this May was continuing. He checked his watch, it was 10:45a.m. As Martin nudged forwards in the line of waiting people, a driver shouted to him, 'You're with me.'

He looked across and saw FOR HIRE light up. Martin walked over and passed the piece of paper through the window. The driver studied it for a few seconds. 'Okay, Guv', do you want a hand with those?'

'No, I can manage.' He removed the rucksack from his shoulders and lifted them both into the taxi and then climbed in. He sat back wondering if the cabby was in on the deal or had just been hired to drive him somewhere.

During the journey, Martin agonised on what to do. Should he tell the cabby the truth? Get the police. Hope there was still a chance of saving Vicky. Problem though, what if the driver was involved, part of the gang? They'll know he grassed. Better to keep quiet.

After a twenty-minute drive, they entered a potholed road to a warehouse. The taxi moved cautiously around to the rear. Martin looked for any signs of movement, but nothing. By the gates, he told the driver to stop. 'Just got to drop these off,' he said with a smile. 'I'm a volunteer worker with the Samaritans. It's tinned food and blankets for the dossers that sleep rough in the warehouse.'

He climbed out and then dragged the rucksacks off the seat. Martin pushed them together against the rusting wire fence hoping he'd been seen. Show them he'd kept his side of the bargain.

He stood for a while, but still no signs of movement. He got back into the cab and told the driver his apartment address. The taxi slowly pulled away and bumped along the potholed drive until it reached the busy main road again. As the cab swung left, it moved sharply into a layby and stopped.

Martin leaned forward. 'What's the problem?' he asked.

'Sorry, Sir, have to make an urgent call.' The cab driver pulled out a walkie-talkie and muttered a few words. Martin strained to listen but he couldn't quite hear. Just as the cabby put the receiver down, all hell broke loose.

Suddenly, three marked police cars and an Austin J4 police van with sirens blaring and flashing blue lights appeared from nowhere. They swung past the taxi into the warehouse slip road like a bat out of hell. Martin looked on speechless. The cabbie turned to him and made light of it all. 'Probably found someone without a TV license, Sir.' Then he swung the cab around and followed them into the warehouse entrance.

As they approached, a police car blocked their way and two armed officers raised their semi-automatic carbines. Martin froze. Then he heard shots fired and someone calling over a megaphone. 'Throw down your weapons, you are surrounded. Come out with your hands in the air.'

In the distance, six police officers in riot gear suddenly appeared all carrying semi-automatic carbines including teargas. Then more shots sounded and thick yellow smoke began to billow out from broken warehouse windows. Lots of shouting followed.

Martin watched transfixed through the cab window as three men came running out of the smoking building firing machine guns from the hip. They were cut down immediately by the police in a hail of bullets.

The two officers motioned with their guns for Martin to get out of the taxi. He did as he was told.

'Down on your knees with your hands behind you,' one of the officers barked.

Immediately a set of handcuffs snapped around his wrists. Then they hauled him to his feet. 'Now move.'

They marched Martin to where the bodies lay on the floor. Already a pool of blood was spreading from each one. An officer covered them over with a tarpaulin sheet.

Martin protested, *'Listen, I've got nothing to do with this. I was forced to bring the bags. They kidnapped me and my girlfriend! They're holding her hostage somewhere.'*

'You can tell it all to the Inspector, Sir,' one officer replied.

Detective Inspector Collins with two police constables feverishly searched the rucksacks and bedrolls. All they found was dirty washing, maps of London, plastic plates and a first aid kit.

'Shit!' The short balding, middle-aged Detective Inspector looked at his men. 'Either we've been tricked or Sammy Abdullah has been shafted?' He kicked the rucksacks in temper. 'This could have been a good pinch with the drugs.'

At that moment, DS Reynolds with three of his men in riot gear approached. 'Found two dead bodies inside, Sir, but no other weapons or drugs.'

'Okay, Reynolds, get this area taped off for the forensic boys and better call the Morg'.' DI Collins kicked the rucksacks again. 'Fuck it! The real catch got away. The real Mr Big himself. All we got now is five stiffs, and still nothing on Sammy Abdullah.'

Martin was shoved into a police car. He protested again, *'Listen, they've got my girlfriend. You've got to find out where she is. They said they'd kill her if they didn't get what they wanted.'*

'Yea, Okay - okay,' the officer said. 'We'll take a statement when we get to the station.'

Martin sat back, there was nothing he could do. Being handcuffed he felt even more frustrated. If anything happened to Vicky, he'd never forgive himself. It was his fault he'd got her into this miss. He decided there and then, no more wheeling and dealing. He was finished with it all. They'd just have to cut their losses.

Martin had to think clearly. He lowered his head. That stupid bitch at the desk had given him the wrong rucksacks. If the ones with drugs were still in left luggage, he'd get Dave to hand them to the police. Dave could say he'd found the packages by chance, while searching for an address or a contact number as there'd been a mix up with the tickets. That would show the mob and the police the luggage desk were totally innocent. Knowing she had no part in it, they might release Vicky. Martin clenched his fists and screwed his face up with regret and guilt. He realised now what a fool he'd been. He knew the way to go. He and Dave would wash their hands of all this shit. For once get a decent night's sleep instead of wondering all the time if they were going to be found out. Yes that was it. He'd made up his mind no matter how much Dave would moan.

At Savile Row Police Station, Martin was un-handcuffed. Then he was cautioned and searched. Still protesting his innocence and his fiancé's life threatening situation, he was escorted to one of the cells.

An hour later they came for him. Flanked by two police officers, Martin was taken up a stony flight of steps and then along a busy office walkway comprised of people at desks working typewriters and filing systems. Finally, they reached Incident Interview Room No.2.

DI Collins and DS Reynolds were already seated behind a large table with a coffee each. A pitcher of water set amongst glasses, a telephone, some statement sheets and a tape recorder were also at hand.

The tall slim young fair-haired DS Reynolds began, 'This interview is now being recorded on the twenty-fourth of May in the year nineteen-seventy-three at sixteen-hundred hours. I am Detective Sergeant Reynolds, also present is Detective Inspector Collins and the defendant Martin Lavender.'

Martin gabbled his story. He knew time was running out for Vicky, if she wasn't dead already. *'I found this wallet. This couple came to collect it. They used this sort of rod to electrocute me. They kidnapped my girlfriend and then killed two other people, including a chef I hired to make dinner. I woke up in this derelict factory. I was tied up. They electrocuted me with this rod again. Kept asking me if it was safe.'*

Martin showed them the burn marks on his neck and then continued, *'They gave me a left luggage ticket and forced me to go in disguise to Victoria Station to collect those bags. Then get a taxi to that warehouse to drop them off. I swear I had no idea what was in those bags, what they were after. You must believe me. They've got my girlfriend, said they were going to kill her. You've got to find her before it's too late.'* Martin stood up, *'Don't just sit there, fucking do something!'* He banged his fist on the table.

DI Collins told him, 'Sit down, Mr Lavender. All in good time.' He made some notes and then looked puzzled. 'So why did they torture you? For what reason?'

'Perhaps there was something in the wallet. Something that would incriminate them,' Martin replied. 'As I said, they kept asking me if it was safe.'

DI Collins stroked his chin thoughtfully and then asked him, 'So where did you exactly pick up those rucksacks?'

'From the left luggage desk on the station platform. That's why they sent me with the ticket, in case I'd been to the police and they were walking into a trap.' Martin half raised himself from his chair and protested, *'They made me go, said they'd kill my fiancé if I didn't. There was nothing I could do.'* He slumped back feeling helpless and finished by saying, 'Then I proceeded to the station taxi rank and was met by a cab.' Martin looked thoughtful. 'So how did you find the warehouse?'

DI Collins smiled. 'PC Williams was our man driving the taxi. We've been tailing that drug boss, Sammy Abdullah, for a long time. But he's not the real Mr Big. The real Mr Big has always been careful. We could never find anything on him or his side kick, Abdullah. We just didn't know how they moved the stuff. How it came in or went out.'

While the Inspector took a sip of his coffee, DS Reynolds continued, 'A German, Günther Viess had been spotted. He's a little hood who works for a narcotics mob in Manchester. We'd heard something heavy might be going down. So this morning we did our usual tail on Sammy Abullah leaving his premises. As always, he hailed a cab. We were ready for him with our own taxi driver. Then we followed him to Victoria Station. We had him covered. Then he paid our driver to wait for a man dressed as a backpacker with a couple of rucksacks. With you clambering in, we had a good idea. With the address you gave him he radioed through. After that, we lost Abdullah. He ducked down into Victoria tube amongst the commuters.'

Then the Inspector pushed some mug-shots across the table to Martin. 'Do you recognise any of your kidnappers?'

He picked up the photos, flicked through, then stopped. 'Yes - yes, these two.' He handed them back. 'That's the couple that came to collect the wallet, the ones who jumped me. They sounded French. She wanted to use my toilet, so I let her in. They were dressed like a hippies, you know, that backpacker look wearing moccasins and a bandana.'

DI Collins looked at the photos Martin had picked. 'That's Bono and Claudine. Two French pushers who work for Sammy Abdullah. Bonnie and Clyde we call them. They've both done time for handling narcotics. Haven't seen them for a while. We know Abdullah works for a drug lord who on paper is a respectable businessman. Mr Big, as we call him finances the deals. He has buyers in this country and Marseille. Probably where they've been. Some of his stuff must go by boat. Airports are too risky for him. Trouble is he's too slippery for the coast guard.'

Martin shouted at them, *'Look, enough of this waffle. You've got to help my girlfriend.'* He leaned forward. *'She's going to die, don't you understand. They're holding her somewhere. Did you search all of the warehouse?'*

DS Reynolds assured him, 'Mr Lavender, we've got men out now looking for your–'

Suddenly the telephone rang. DI Collins picked it up. His face lightened after fifteen seconds. 'That's good news.' He cupped the receiver and said to Martin, 'Your girlfriend Victoria is safe. She managed to escape from the boot of a car.' He continued with the call, 'Any luck with the drugs?– Shit. Anything we can pin on a Abdullah?– Shit.' He slammed the phone down.

Martin collapsed into sobs. 'Thank God - thank God.' He took a moment to compose himself. He wiped his face with his sleeve. He looked at the DI with pleading eyes. 'Where is she now?'

'We've sent a car to have her picked up, Mr Lavender. Don't worry, she's unharmed.'

Martin held up his hands in exasperation. 'Jesus, this is all my fault because of the wallet. I should have just left it there. Let someone else pick it up. But like a Good Samaritan...' He shook his head and slumped back in his seat. However, he was thinking, *how much longer can I manage to play the innocent?*

After further questions and a much appreciated cup of tea, Martin turned as the door opened and Victoria under escort walked into the interview room. Martin immediately stood up and rushed towards her. They embraced each other with hugs and kisses. 'Dear God, Vicky, I can't believe you're standing here. I thought they were going to kill you.'

Victoria in tears, sobbed out, 'They fired electric shocks into me with some sort of prodder. Wanted to know if it was safe. I didn't know what they meant.'

Martin sat her down. 'You poor thing.' His anger rose. 'What did those bastards do to you? Do you need to go to a hospital?'

'No - no, I wasn't molested, nothing like that.' With his arm around her she carried on. 'I woke up gagged and blindfolded. They kept me in this room. No idea where I was. But I couldn't tell them anything. Then they threw me into the boot of a car.'

DS Reynolds handed her a glass of water. Victoria gulped some of it and then continued, 'It seemed I was driven for miles. Then they stopped. I heard the boot lid open. They dragged me out. I thought they were going to kill me.' She broke down sobbing. Martin comforted her. She dabbed her eyes with a tissue.

'Take your own time, Miss Buxton,' the DI said, patiently sitting back with a sympathetic expression.

'Then they untied me, but kept my blindfold on. Told me to start walking. Not to look round. Then I heard them drive away. When I took off the blindfold, it was pitch black. I was in a country lane somewhere. I walked and walked and then saw a light. A farmhouse. The old couple let me in and called the police.'

DS Reynolds asked her, 'What did your kidnappers sound like, Miss Buxton? Did they have an accent? Sound foreign? Call out a name by mistake?'

'I think one of them may have been foreign,' she said shakily, 'but I'm not sure from where. I was so scared I wasn't taking anything in.' She sobbed again and Martin hugged her.

'You're a very lucky lady,' The DI told her sternly. 'A lot worse could have happened to you. Those men would have stopped at nothing. You were very brave, Miss Buxton. You did well to keep your cool.' He glanced at Martin. 'Are you sure you both don't need medical attention?'

'I'm fine,' Martin replied.

'And I'm fine, really,' Victoria said. 'The old lady at the farmhouse was a retired nurse, bless her. She was fussing around, checked me out for shock and concussion, but I'm okay.'

After being shown the same mug shot photos, Victoria shook her head. 'I never got to look at any of them. I was blindfolded the whole time. Sorry I'm not much help.'

'You're a credit to your fiancée, Miss Buxton. He should be very proud of you,' the DI said with a smile.

Victoria returned the smile and cuddled Martin.

Quite satisfied their stories corroborated with one another and after signing and dating statements, the Detective Inspector terminated the interview. He gave the couple his card with a contact number. This was in case they remembered something else or were worried about their safety. He knew Sammy Abdullah and no doubt his boss Mr Big, had little time for grassers, coppers narks or informers, even less for witnesses that could lay something on them.

CHAPTER TWELVE

Driven back to Martin's apartment by police car, they decided the first thing on the list was to raid the refrigerator. They heaped the leftovers from last night's fancy meal onto the kitchen table and tore into it like a couple of street urchins that hadn't eaten for a week.

With Lobster juice pouring down their chins, they feverishly sucked on the claws, crunched on mouthfuls of salad, made doorstep sandwiches filled with the remaining terrine of foie gras, in between slurping ice cold Sancerre straight from the bottle, and then falling into fits of laughter as they belched away in turn. Finally, they attacked the half segment of Black Forest gateau using their hands.

Martin and Victoria sat back, their faces covered in chocolate. They didn't care.

'Jesus, was I hungry,' she said, wiping her top lip and then sucking gateau off her fingers.

'Me too.' He looked at her and then with an exaggerated sweep of his tongue he licked off some remaining cream around his mouth.

'You going all purvey on me?' Victoria said, leaning towards him and placing her hand on his crotch.

'Now listen, the future Mrs Victoria Lavender, you won't be able to lick your fingers like that at swank dinner parties.'

'So?' Victoria started to unbutton her top. 'Are you going to lick them for me?'

They both leapt at each other. Martin had his hand up her skirt while her leg wrapped itself around his waist. She was biting his neck trying to rip his shirt off. Martin had his trousers down at his ankles. He was trying to wrench off her panties while trying to keep his balance. Then he stumbled. Resting against the edge of the kitchen table to steady himself he wasn't going to risk it to the bedroom. No point in breaking your neck for a good screw he thought.

Then it came to him. He said to her, 'You know, I've never done it on a table before.' While she clung on, he took the tablecloth with his free hand and gave an almighty wrench.

The remains of their left overs including plates, bowls, cake stands, breadboard and empty wine bottles crashed to the floor. The carpet tiles cushioned most of the impact apart from two busted plates.

Victoria looked at him nonplussed.

'Saves doing the washing up,' he joked. With another wrench, Martin tore off her panties and hoisted her up onto the kitchen table. Then he wrestled with his underpants and frantically leapt on.

As he got inside her, she bit his neck and shouted, 'Fuck me! My Hero.' And Martin did the best he could for the next seven minutes.

Finally, exhausted, he rolled over, then checked himself, suddenly aware of the table edge and the drop beneath. They lay on their backs panting hard, staring at the kitchen ceiling. Then they started laughing. The absurdity of it, how they must look.

'If my aunt Alice could see me now,' Victoria said, 'she'd have a fit. She doesn't think butter melts in my mouth, the sweet old thing.'

Martin looked at her, all serious. 'Who the fuck is Alice?'

They exploded into laughter and lay there holding hands.

Within twenty minutes they were sharing a bath. Sitting at opposite ends of a gold plated Villeroy and Boch with clawed feet and matching taps, they toasted each other with the last of the Dom Perignon. Victoria raised herself and wobbled slightly. She steadied against the black and gold mosaic wall tiles. 'Hoosh for another boshttle of bubbly?'

'Good idea, Vicky.' Martin laughed. 'There's a cold one in the fridge, and mind how you go.' He watched while she put on her robe and then disappear through the bathroom door.

Martin laid back fully contented. He'd had his fill, food wise and a good screw with the most beautiful girl you could ever wish for. Now he was sipping champagne in a luxury bath in the knowledge that he still had enough money.

After this latest cocaine cut he'd hand in his notice with MI5. As far as he was concerned, his new boss Commander Gregory Potting could go and hang himself. No doubt they had shit on him but he didn't care anymore. He would sell the club and retire with Vicky somewhere exotic. He hadn't told her yet. But she'd come round once she saw the beach house he wanted to buy in Bermuda and the beautiful yacht. And she could always fly home for weekend trips to see her friends and family. He could afford it.

Victoria returned with a new bottle. She passed it to Martin who fumbled with the silver paper and the wire cage, then he eased out the cork. As it popped, they both cheered and she held out her glass.

Martin glugged a quarter glass and said, 'Not getting back in?'

'Na, my fingers start wrinkling up if I'm in there too long.' She sat on the plush satin covered stool and proceeded to dry her hair.

Just then the gold plated telephone on the bathroom vanity unit rang.

'Get that for us, Vicky. Maybe the police again.'

She moved off the stool and picked up the receiver.

After some crackle of background interference a distinguished voice said, 'Is that Victoria Buxton?'

'Yes, who's speaking?'

Commander Potting told her, 'Don't forget to tell Martin, Kimberly will be coming for supper.'

'Thank you, Inspector, I'll let him know.' Victoria replaced the receiver. She was in deep thought for a second and then went back to the stool and continued drying her hair.

'Who was that?' he asked

'Oh, just the police following up. Wanted us to report any suspicious activity and to lock all doors of a night.'

Martin rested back. He held his champagne glass against his chest and closed his eyes. The drone from the hairdryer was making him sleepy. His mind wandered back to the interview room. There was something, some detail he'd thought of and then forgot. Not surprising with all the other stuff that had gone on. It had been nagging at him, like knowing a face but not remembering the name.

He opened his eyes and watched her. The way her hair rippled and danced with each swoosh of the dryer. Her bathrobe untied showing her gorgeous breasts, nipples still firm even after lovemaking. The swan neck, twisting and turning in motion with her long white slender arms. Not a blemish in sight, he thought. Skin like virgin snow. Her engagement ring sparkled and faded as it caught the tiny beams of the ceiling spotlights. Instant and gone he thought, like a shooting star. Martin closed his eyes again. Then he remembered.

He sat up and looked at her. 'Vicky.'

'Yes, Dear.' She turned to him with a smile.

'There was something I wanted to ask you.'

'What's that?' She turned off the hairdryer and wrapped a towel around her head.

'At the interview with the police, you told them you'd been tortured with a cow prodder and tied up. Arms and wrists. Where's the marks? And the ring, they never stole your ring? And the photos they showed you. You never recognised the two that jumped us at the flat?'

Victoria sighed and then smiled at him. 'Dad and I didn't know how it was being cut. Who was shafting us? It was either the couriers, and they said nothing even when their fingers were being chopped off. Or it had to be the station luggage handling; that was the only other place. We checked out that drip brother of yours. Followed him to your club. That's where I conveniently met you again. We'd met before at Briar Lodge Manor, remember? You were my instructor for the bodyguard course. Well, it took us some months to suss it. Everyone was keeping quiet. Then we made some calls, leaned on a few people. Local dealers were saying they were getting some grade A shit for a change. And you were refurbishing your nightclub like a man that had won first dividend on Littlewoods. Didn't take long to add up.'

Martin looked like he'd seen a ghost. His mouth opened and shut and opened and shut again like a goldfish peering out from its bowl.

'Fortunately for dad, the girl on the counter fucked up. Gave you the wrong bags. I expect they've got rucksacks coming out their ears holiday time. Anyway, all the police got was dirty washing and a handful of bums who were excess to requirements.'

Martin spluttered. 'Your far'… your father deals in drugs? But that's impossible.'

Victoria turned as the bathroom door pushed open. 'Ask Mr Buxton yourself.'

The short fat balding fifty-eight year old South London businessman stood there smoking a large Cuban cigar. 'Hi, Vicky.'

'Hi, Dad.' She rose and kissed his cheek.

Kenny Buxton said, 'So this is the little shit you told me about.'

'It sure is, Dad, and this little shit is no more.' Victoria picked up the hairdryer and fumbled with the switch. 'You know, Martin, we could have been a great team together. However, as they say, never mix business with pleasure.' With that, she threw the hairdryer into the bath.

They both ducked at the white flash. Martin continued to shake and jerk for a full ten-seconds. Smoke curled out from his singed scalp with the strong smell of burning.

'That'll teach you to fuck with me.' Kenny Buxton leaned over him as if he were still alive. 'And never dry your hair in the bath. It can be dangerous.'

Victoria asked, 'Dad, what about his dick-head brother?'

'Oh, I've got something a little special for him.' Kenny with a smile, lost himself in thought for a few seconds and then said, 'A spot of fun with a welding torch.'

CHAPTER THIRTEEN

Film director Dimitri Irwin, known throughout Hollywood as - The Master of Disaster - stood on the centre court at The Wimbledon All England Club looking up making a frame with his fingers. The smell of damp grass hung in the air while he discussed with his film crew the scene where the IRA attack the crowd. 'I reckon if we shoot in the afternoon and have the choppers coming over the court from the east, then we won't have to worry about direct sunlight.'

Dimitri Irwin was telling the crew, 'We've got to get a move on, try and finish this scene within a couple of weeks. We're already in early June and I haven't got fifteen minutes of film yet. This picture has to be finished, in the can and distributed by the end of the year, otherwise the studio's in deep shit and my neck is on the line.' The director took a puff on his large Cuban cigar and then said, 'That's come straight from the vice president of the studio. He informed me they already have 1974 mapped out starting with a new picture schedule in January, hopefully using the initial profits from my film for financing.'

While the director spoke, Norma his secretary scribbled notes down fast.

Dimitri Irwin, holding a copy of the script, pointed. 'The IRA will attack using choppers flying over the centre-court crowd and jettisoning aviation fuel from hanging buckets. Then they'll drop flares to start a massive fire to kill as many people as possible.' He grinned and said with sarcasm, 'As this attack is for the IRA cause because of the British intervention in Northern Ireland, let's hope a peace treaty isn't signed between governments before the film is released. Otherwise, it could be a sensitive issue and they might postpone distribution. Then we *would* have egg on our faces.'

A few of the film crew laughed nervously.

The film director looked at his notes and then continued, 'Because of casting problems, we're going to have to shoot a lot of the outside action scenes first to make up time. They still haven't come up with a leading man yet. It's either going to be Sean Connery, Charlton Heston or Steve McQueen. Either way, they'll have to have a good plausible Irish accent.' Chewing his cigar, he turned to his secretary, 'And make a note, Norma, they're not going to be being paid a million bucks to be on my set sounding like John Wayne.'

She hastily jotted down what he'd said and then looked up. 'Mr Irwin, Sir. I was informed to tell you, we do have a leading lady for the film.'

'We do, who the Christ is that?'

'It's Faye Dunaway, Mr Irwin.'

'Faye Dunaway?' He said with another sarcastic swipe. 'Well at least *her* fans might come to see the picture.' The director glanced at the seating. 'Are the extras signed on for the crowd scenes?'

'Yes, Mr Irwin.' Dave, his young assistant director confirmed. 'We have four-thousand of them on a two day notice to turn up when required.' Dave checked the script. 'They'll be sitting beyond the protection of the roof in seats along the west side of the stand in the first front rows.'

'OK, that's good.' The director relaxed a little and puffed his cigar. Then he remembered. He turned to Norma and Dave again. 'Have we got the helicopters organised?'

'Yes, Mr Irwin.' Dave flicked a couple of pages of notes and then looked up. 'We've managed to hire two S-61N Sikorsky helicopters with pilots from Alan Bristow Ltd at Redhill Aerodrome. They've been briefed about carrying fire-fighting water buckets.'

The director stroked his chin thoughtfully. 'We'll have to check with the stunt coordinator the allowable amount of water that can be dropped on the extras. Too much of it will be like a ton of lead on their heads. We'll check with health and safety. We can always back it up to look more, using hoses. Make a note to arrange with Wimbledon fire brigade.'

The director chewed his cigar and then added, 'As planned, we'll drop the real fuel and ignite on a mock up shot using mannequins; somewhere safe. Perhaps that

Redhill Aerodrome has a practise area for firefighting? Make a note.'

Dave, scribbled away and said, 'I'll get on to it, Mr Irwin.' Then he remembered. 'Oh, Mr Irwin, just a reminder. We'll have to tell the London Emergency Services Liaison Panel when we're filming the helicopter scenes. They have a no fly zone policy over the club during tournament fortnight because of any real terrorist attacks.' Dave gave him a nervous smile. 'So ideally, Mr Irwin, filming the helicopter scenes would have to be completed before the tournament starts.'

The director threw his arms in the air in shear desperation. 'But that's only four weeks away, as if I've got nothing else to worry about.'

*

Guy Ericson stood up and wobbled a bit. He liked a drink and he was enjoying himself. He raised his glass and slurred out to everyone around the table. 'Here's to our Iranian trainees and may...' He took a slurp, 'And may their choppers stay up and never let them down.'

The other British flight instructors cheered and raised their glasses. However, the rest of the middle-eastern pilots didn't understand the joke. They hadn't quite mastered the crudities of English.

Amir Halabi, had. He had a joke book tucked under his pillow back at Redhill Aerodrome. He was the only pilot drinking, much to the disgust of Fadil Baba his direct supervisor.

Fadil had brought the five trainee pilots over from Iran so they could qualify for their commercial licence. This would enable them to fly the twin turbine 28-seater S-61N Sikorsky helicopters. It was all part of a flight exchange training programme run by Bristow Helicopters Limited at Redhill Aerodrome. For Bristow to win contracts for their operations, a certain number of pilots had to be of Iranian origin. When trained, these pilots were to be employed for a new oil rig support shuttle service that Bristow were enlarging in Iran. This was to ferry workers back and forth in Ahvaz for the National Iranian Oil Company. However, Fadil and his pilots also had their orders from Beirut. As a Black September group, they were committed to carry out a large scale act of terrorism on mainland Britain.

At the moment, Fadil and his pilots were staying at the training accommodation of Nissan huts set up at Redhill Aerodrome.

Fadil, already qualified, had worked the Iranian oil wells for two years. He'd joined Bristow's overseas development in 1971 and within three months had obtained his commercial license and been made a supervisor. Being the supervisor in Iran had allowed him some access on planning their training schedules in the UK. Now with the other five pilots he was celebrating their success.

Guy Ericson could relax. As head of flight training for Bristow, he'd done his job. Well, almost. Just the filming exercise to be carried out at the Wimbledon All England Club and then they'd all be gone. Off his hands after three months and back to Iran, thank God. The responsibility and demands of the training programme sometimes got him down.

As a side-line, Guy Ericson also ran a skydiving business. He rented a small hangar with an office at Redhill Aerodrome where he kept his own light aircraft.

With a co-pilot he payed by the hour, he used a four seater single engine Cessna 182 Skylane to carry out tandem sky diving trips for anyone that wanted to pay the £28.

Thirty-four year old Guy however, at six-foot-two-inches with his dark wavy hair and Rock Hudson good looks, liked the women and it cost him an expensive divorce. This coupled with the 1973 recession, high unemployment and a downturn in the economy, meant that people weren't spending on luxuries and so his business wasn't doing well at the moment. He knew he would have to make decisions soon on whether to continue paying rent and costs on a declining side line one man operation.

His wages as Bristow's flight chief just kept his head above water, and he was making sure to take advantage of tonight's celebration with its free meal and booze. Bristow helicopters had paid for the slap-up dinner as a reward for the Iranian pilots obtaining their commercial license. It was all a bit political. There were still a couple of contracts up for grabs back in Iran.

The six pilots, according to their Muslim religion, could only eat halal food and drink tea apart from Amir Halabi. He had relaxed since being in England and was on his fourth brandy and coke. However, the rest of them seemed to be enjoying the evening out and looked reasonably happy. As happy as one would expect living thousands of miles from home in a Redhill Aerodrome Nissan hut, smelling of stale sweat most of the time.

Gatwick Manor was busy this Friday night. The smells of sizzling steaks, cigars and coffee wafted through a packed dining room. The pianist in his white jacket was softly clinking out an old Frank Sinatra number.

Guy Ericson was in the Gents toilet standing at the urinal when Amir Halabi walked in. 'I never been in such posh toilet,' Amir slurred out.

Ericson, sucking on a fat celebratory cigar raised his head back and chortled.

Amir looked across and said, 'I would to thank you, Mr Ericson, for kind and generous hospitality. Although I think music be better if they played good jazz...eh...yes?' He laughed at his own remark.

'No problem, Amir.' Ericson had finished and was zipping up. 'How's yer friends out there? That Fadil looks like he could do with a good woman.'

'Ah, Fadil is serious man. I think misses home. You know, he our boss back in Iran. Oil Company made him responsible we all get our license.'

'Do you have anybody back home, Amir?' They were standing in front of the large mirror drying their hands and double-checking the zipper. Ericson preened himself although he was seeing double. With his slim build and good looking features he knew he could turn a few ladies heads. And frequently did while he enjoyed playing the field.

Twenty-five year old Amir Halabi on the other hand looked the complete opposite, being short and on the portly side with heavy features and bushy eyebrows. Sporting a typical Palestinian full beard and cropped black hair he looked middle-eastern.

Amir glanced behind, it was all clear. He took out a cigarette and lit up. Then inhaled deeply. 'Eh, I like girls, especially naughty girls like back home. Type you pay for, prostitutes, yes?' He nudged Ericson and they both rocked with alcohol-fuelled laughter. 'But here, I have not found. For the others those women strictly off limits you understand.'

Ericson asked amongst a cloud of cigar smoke. 'So what do you lot do in yer spare time?'

'Oh, just cinema usually, that and Salat at our mosque.'

'Salat, what's that?' Ericson swayed trying to concentrate.

'Prayers, five times a day,' Amir said with a sigh.

'My God, Amir, that's a lot of praying, Son.' Ericson put an arm around Amir's shoulder. He took a long drag on his cigar and looked at the end thoughtfully. 'Listen, Amir, I always say a man's gotta have a good screw at least once a week.' They both laughed.

Then Ericson became serious. He looked over his shoulder just to check and then spoke softly. 'Like you, I like naughty girls, yes? I find myself a nice woman.' Ericson took his arm off Amir's shoulder and tapped his nose.

Amir didn't quite get it. He gestured, *what*, with his hands.

Ericson wobbled more and put his arm around Amir's shoulder again. He looked left and right and then said softly, 'I find one that goes like a fucking rattlesnake.' With that, he creased over laughing hanging on to Amir.

Amir looked a bit shocked. 'What, you have own whore - Prostitute?'

He put a finger to his lips and shooshed Amir.

'You lucky son of bitch,' Amir slowly breathed out. Then his face lit up. 'I suppose she not have friend?'

Ericson was feeling in a good mood. He tapped his nose again and took his arm off Amir's shoulder. He wobbled reaching inside his jacket. He fumbled a bit and then pulled out his wallet. Ericson tried to focus as he gingerly picked a card from a compartment with lots of other cards. He handed it to him.

Amir scrutinised the name. 'Roxanne, you know her? Pretty, yes?'

Ericson returned his arm around Amir's shoulder and said, 'She's a friend of the one I use. I've never had to call on her but she's always handy as a backup, just in case.' He gave him a lopsided grin. 'Believe me I've seen her, she has a face and an arse to die for.'

Amir read the card. 'I telephone this number between 10:00 p.m. and 10:30 p.m. Yes?'

Ericson nodded.

Amir asked excitedly, 'I ring number for good shag, yes?'

Ericson threw his head back with a laugh and said, 'You do that and say, a friend of Tina recommended you.'

Amir asked, 'Who is Tina?'

He tapped his nose again. 'Some things are best not spoken about, Amir.'

'How much Roxanne? Is expensive?'

Ericson pondered and then said, 'Twenty quid should cover it.'

'Thank you, Mr Ericson.' Amir shook his hand. 'I will keep secret. Just between two of us.'

CHAPTER FOURTEEN

'Because we have no other pilots at hand, this will be a good exercise for your firefighting capabilities.' Guy Ericson as head of training was explaining to Fadil and his pilot group in the briefing room at Redhill Aerodrome. 'The film studio is paying Bristow Helicopters a lot of money for the hire of our services. The director wants everything to run smoothly so we have to give them value for money. Over in our fire training area, the film people will be building a mock-up of the Wimbledon centre court seating while using mannequin's for the crowd scene. You will be required to fly over them and release aviation fuel from hanging buckets, then set fire to the mannequin's by dropping flares. Also they want the same stunt carried out with live people over the real Wimbledon Centre Court. This will be using water instead of aviation fuel. They will mix the film to simulate the real attack.'

Ericson paused to look down at his notes and then said, 'No doubt, some of you in your careers will be called upon in emergencies to water bomb installations on fire using hanging buckets. Especially over oil wells and rigs. Rigs in particular can be volatile bitches. A bit like a woman who's been cheated on.'

Some of the pilots smiled and then Ericson joked, 'The Met boys reckon 1973 has been the hottest this April and May so far since records began. If that's the case, you could all be deployed helping Surrey fire brigade for the summer.'

They smiled again.

'Anyway, I'll be pinning up a notice on the board for the film schedule within the next few days so keep your eyes peeled.' As he gathered up his things he asked them, 'Any questions?'

Fadil raised his hand. 'Will there be extra pay for performing film stunts?' Fadil Baba at thirty-four years old with his thick mop of curly jet-black hair and a small fine beard that circumnavigated his tanned face, spoke for the rest of the group. He looked more Palestinian than the others with his wiry frame at five-foot ten-inches and a proud middle-eastern nose set between heavy dark eyebrows.

'There will be no extra pay, but you will be covered by the Actors Equity Union card. This includes accident and life insurance.'

Fadil mumbled under his breath, 'Well that is comfort to know.'

Ericson remembered. 'Oh, and before I forget, I was given some free ground entry passes to hand out for the Wimbledon Tennis Championships. I'll pin them on the notice board in the canteen so you can help yourselves.' Ericson hovered.

'Is there anything else?' After a silent pause he said, 'OK, dismissed all of you.'

*

At their secret rented two-bed flat above a tobacconist shop near Southfields Station, Fadil had the attention of his five pilots. 'We must speak English all times outside of aerodrome. More we speak their crap English and dress like British infidels, better chance we not draw attention and keep our cover. Also, we think we being followed; then keep away from here and never anything on us that could be incriminating in case we caught or killed.'

They had just finished supper. A large metal cooking pot with soiled paper plates bore witness to the remains of lamb Mansaf cooked in yogurt on rice. The rich spicy smell still hung thick as the pilots passed around a hookah. In turn, it bubbled away as they inhaled the sweet shisha tobacco.

While they sat, Fadil stood by an ordinance survey map of Wimbledon Common pinned to the wall. He was telling them his revised plans for their attack. 'This to be Black September's retaliation for Israel's Operation Spring of Youth, when previous April you remember, British and American supported Israeli commandos killed three of senior Fata members including beloved leader Abu Youssef.'

On cue, the rest of them stood up and raised their right arms in a clenched fist salute and shouted, 'Death to infidels and all Allah's enemies. 'Alla Akbar, Alla Akbar.'

Fadil waited for them to quieten down and then continued, 'Comrades, Fata have kept us in dark on strictly need to know basis. This in case our cover blown as well possibilities being captured. MI5 have ways making you talk that newspapers not disclose. As you been trained as commercial helicopter pilots to work oilrig shuttle service back in Iran, we now have real purpose for training. I now tell you we have choice of two targets. The Epsom Derby in June or All England Wimbledon Tennis Championships, also June.'

Fadil, including his five pilots, <u>Hirad</u> Alizadeh, Jamal Abboud, Amir Halabi, Arif Nahas and Hashim Mustafa were originally from Palestine. They had all fled to Syria and then to Iran after the September conflict when King Hussein of Jordan declared military rule. This resulted in the death and expulsion of thousands of Palestinians from Jordan. All the pilots had lost family during the uprising. Now they lived and breathed revenge against the Jews including the British and the Americans for supporting Hussein. This was also for the land they had lost in the West Bank during the Six-Day-War.

'However,' Fadil gave them a wry smile, 'it seems as British say, we got lucky. The Wimbledon film stunt exercise to carry out would be perfect cover for attack.'

'Our honourable leader, Sala Khalif, considers kamikaze. To crash into crowd. The problem of this, to ensure massive casualties using helicopters, would depend on angle of attack, speed of descent being accurate to hit dense public areas. We could end up killed with minor dead and nothing to show.

It has to be something spectacular, something remembered to further cause of PLO and EL FATA.'

Again they stood up and raised their right arms in a clenched fist salute and shouted, 'Death to Allah's enemies. Alla Akbar, Alla Akbar.'

Fadil smiled at their fanaticism and then continued, 'Flight Chief Ericson, requires that we water-bomb Wimbledon Centre Court crowd for film to pretend IRA attack using gasolina; all for making of Hollywood blockbuster.' He paused and then his face filled with enlightenment. 'What if we *really* bombed crowd with gasolina? Switched water for aviation fuel, last thing. Could be done, but requires planning.'

Fadil began to pace the room and then stopped. 'Switch have to be quick though. No time for security on ground, get suspicious. If we hide fuel truck on Wimbledon Common, say here, or here.' He pointed to the map. 'We could ditch water, fill buckets with fuel, then fly over and douse crowd. At same time drop flares. Then make escape as infidel's burn.'

Fadil punched the air and shouted, 'Death to infidels and Allah's enemies. Alla Akbar, Alla Akbar.'

On cue again, the rest of them stood up and raised their right arms in a clenched fist salute and shouted, 'Death to infidels and Allah's enemies. 'Alla Akbar, Alla Akbar.'

Fadil shouted, 'We here to burn them. We here to burn infidels in name of Allah.' He raised his hands submissively and the others followed. 'Believers, take neither Jews or Christians for friends while we here in country of idolatry worship. We seek out Zionist enemies relentlessly. Slay them wherever we find them. Make war on Zionist unbelievers and allies. Make war on them until Allah's religion reign supreme. Make war on them so Allah chastise them and humble them and grant us victory.'

Then all in frenzied unison, 'Death to infidels. Alla Akbar, Alla Akbar.'

When they had quietened, Fadil became solemn. 'Salah Khalaf, our Black September leader be pleased of our attack. If successful and we manage get back to Beirut, we be protected by Fatah, with new life, new identity. Salah Khalaf has promised.'

For communication with Salah Khalaf and the Fatah network in Beirut, either by telephone or wire, they used an encoded script. The script codebook was held at the flat in an overhead toilet cistern protected by a waterproof plastic bag. Along with this were three handguns. Two Walther PPKs and a Browning Mark 1.

Fadil looked down as if to compose himself and then said, 'An escape network for us being set up, but in reality our chances slim. We probably become martyrs for cause.'

Again, they cried out, 'To die for Allah is greatest wish.'

At that moment, Amir Halabi reached for his wallet and took out his Black September badge. He kissed the small fabric shield that showed crossed machine guns and muttered a small prayer. Sewn on uniforms back in Beirut as part of their allegiance, it was now a good luck charm for Amir.

However, Fadil spotted him. 'Amir, I know it is FATA holy ensign, but must not carry with you. You must keep here for safety.'

'I sorry, Fadil. Of course, I forgot. I will do as you say.' Amir was secretly having none of it. As long as he carried it with him, he was sure it would bring him luck to survive or a quick painless death. Either way, during the fighting, he'd carried it through the Six-Day-War and he was still alive and in one piece.

CHAPTER FIFTEEN

Amir Halabi combed his dark frizzy hair over a small bald spot that he'd noticed and finally smoothed it down with Vaseline. He always carried a tube when he was paying for it; sometimes they even thanked him. Then he bared his tobacco stained teeth into the cracked mirror. He grinned again and pushed his long nose up to reduce the slight bump and to make it look less prominent. Amir liked to think they thought of him as handsome, even though deep down he knew they probably didn't give a flying fuck, as long as they got their twenty-quid at the end of the shag.

Standing in the Wimbledon Station phone booth, Amir read the card again he'd been discretely given. **For lessons in French, contact Roxanne on 01-946 0147 between 10:0 p.m. to 10:30 p.m.** He was feeling excited. His hand shook slightly with anticipation. He wondered if he should haggle over the shag rate of twenty-pounds. Then again best not to, he thought.

Don't want to start off on the wrong foot. Amir picked up the receiver and dialled the number.

*

At evenings and weekends, whenever possible, the pilots used the Southfields flat. The Fazi Mosque nearby was a legitimate excuse to get away from the aerodrome. The flat was where they could quietly plan their operations. With the existing two beds and sleeping bags, they would sometimes stay overnight. Then in the morning, catch the early train back to Redhill and sneak into the aerodrome perimeter through a hole they'd cut in the fence. Thankfully, the security wasn't tight. In the adjacent washrooms the pilots would change into pyjamas and a dressing gown, to make out they were on a toilet visit in case they were spotted.

That Sunday afternoon at the Wimbledon flat, Amir was combing his hair in the mirror while the others chilled out watching the television and reading newspapers. Wearing a green Ben Sherman shirt with matching flares and chisel boots, he was excited. Amir preferred to dress Western style instead of the traditional thobe thawb jubba cloak and sandals with a keffiyeh tied around his head looking like Yasser Arafat. His date with Roxanne was for 3:00 pm. He had his excuse. 'So none of you keen to come and watch rugby at Twickenham?' He knew they wouldn't be interested.

Fadil spoke for all of them, 'Na, that infidel boring game, we'd rather watch a donkey pee in road.' The others raised their heads and sniggered then went back to what they were doing.

Amir breathed a sigh of relief. Now he had the afternoon to himself and his date. Thinking about it, he was already getting a hard-on. He made sure the others didn't notice.

*

One of Commander Potting's MI5 agents had managed to find a Roxanne card by pure luck. In line with the London Emergency Services Liaison Panel, agents were on standby alert combing Wimbledon and Southfields areas for suspicious IRA terrorist activity for explosive devices left in public places including telephone boxes. With the All England Wimbledon Tennis Championships coming up at the end of June, security was paramount. Nevertheless, Francis Hodder, Roxanne to the punters, had served his purpose and was now a liability.

Rather than put a contract out for him and have to negotiate awkward questions from the press if a leak occurred about his death, it was best if he was caught in the act as a sleeper killing someone. Knowing all trace of his conditioning would be wiped from his memory, his captors would be left with a transvestite who just harboured a grudge against his father and any man that reminded him of his father.

Using Roxanne's card, Commander Potting put a tap on the telephone box at Southfields. When they heard the conversation between Amir and Roxanne and their ensuing date, the Commander telephoned as a prospective customer and told Francis Hodder, 'Roxanne, don't forget to tell Amir, Kimberly will be coming for supper.'

The final part of the Commander's trap would be to catch Francis when he killed Amir. Have the police waiting for him.

*

Now they were lying back on the tartan blanket that Francis had brought along, most thoughtful. Smoking a cigarette each, both of them were looking up at the overhanging branches of the sycamores and horse chestnuts. How romantic. The west side of Wimbledon Common this sunny afternoon was quiet for early June. Just the raspy sounds of a magpie and a distant cuckoo filtered the peacefulness.

Amir sniffed the woodland smells. It made him feel good being out here. Far better than the smell of the stuffy Nissan hut. He lifted himself on one elbow and stroked his date's slim stomach while Francis inhaled deeply on a menthol cigarette.

'You see, reason I do this because girlfriend not understand me. We not had it for ages.' Amir took a drag of his cigarette. 'I feel can talk to you, Roxanne. I suppose lots your clients tell you woes? You are first person I confided in, you know that?' He reached for his jacket and took out his fancy snakeskin wallet. He thumbed through a thick wad of notes and then withdrew twenty-pounds. He placed the notes seductively, just above Francis's shiny leather crotch pouch. 'There's bit extra, in case, I can have bit extra?'

Francis's gaze never left the wallet, as though a hypnotist was dangling it on a piece of string.

Amir continued. 'Mother understood me but father never did.'

Francis's eyes rolled mentally as he patted Amir's thigh in an affectionate gesture, as though his situation was understood. As if he really cared.

Amir asked, 'Was it same with your father, Roxanne?'

'My father?' Francis turned and looked at him sharply. 'Don't you mention my father?' With a look of hate he pounced on Amir, sitting on his chest pinning him down. 'Do you hear me?'

'Yes – yes, I sorry to mention father.' Amir stared up at him wide eyed. He was scared.

Then Francis's expression became empty as if he'd drifted somewhere. Suddenly the face cringed with fear. He whimpered, 'Please, Dada, don't cut it off...I won't tell. I'll be good girl like Roxanne...'

'What?' Amir said shocked. 'What you talk like that for?' He tried to wriggle but Francis had his full weight astride him.

Francis immediately regained his composure. His face softened. 'I joke with you. Pretend I'm your little girl.'

'Ah, English joke. I see.' Amir relaxed back on the tartan blanket, however, his eyes said it all. He knew there was something wrong.

Francis leant over him and said with a mocking smile, 'So Mr, My Girlfriend Doesn't Understand Me, wants seconds does he?' He dropped a hand and started massaging Amir.

Amir laid back. 'Mohamed, that feels good.' The sensation had numbed his awareness. He closed his eyes in ecstasy.

With the other hand, Francis felt for the handbag and flipped the gold clasp. The grip of the bone handle knife felt good like a hard dick, while six-inches of Sheffield steel glinted in the sunlight. Then with a sudden cry of exertion, the blade disappeared into the throat of Amir Halabi pinning him to the ground.

Francis looked at him and smiled as he coughed and spluttered. The butcher's knife holding rigid as his body twitched around it with staring eyes that said, *I can't believe you did that.* And all the while, the pool of red spreading as movement and sounds began to cease.

With a *schluck,* the knife came out. Francis wiped the blade with a handkerchief and placed it into his handbag along with Amir's wallet. Then he set about clearing up.

Commander Potting had followed and watched them through his binoculars from a secluded position in the park. He'd taken it upon himself to finish the job. The less people knew about something then all the better, he'd always maintained. And he should know. Secrecy was his business. Now all he had to do was get to his car phone and report a murder.

The Commander, wearing his Burberry flat cap and wax hunting jacket with tweeds tucked into an expensive pair of leather boots, quickly made his way out of the woods along the gravel track to the Windmill carpark. Pleased there were only a few cars where he'd parked, he strode over to his black

Rover PB Saloon and climbed into the plush leather driver's seat. Turning the ignition, he lifted the receiver of his Motorola car phone and dialled 999.

The line was dead. He feverishly tried again cursing this time. The line was still dead. 'Bugger! Bugger! Bugger!' He slammed the receiver back into its holder.

On a number of occasions he'd experienced a system breakdown. Now wasn't the time to have one. Knowing Francis Hodder would be making his getaway, he pulled out of the carpark and headed for his MI5 office. He might get another chance to set Francis Hodder up, but that would have to wait. There were other things more important now. Like a possible London terrorist attack. Information trickling through highlighted it could be IRA or Black September.

CHAPTER SIXTEEN

The alarm woke Fadil the next day. He was the first to rise at five o'clock. Every Monday morning was a rush to get washed and ready for the journey back to Redhill Aerodrome. As they all slowly clambered to their feet and used the bathroom in turn, it wasn't until they were having tea and toast that the realisation suddenly dawned.

Amir was missing.

After a brief search of the flat, Fadil addressed the situation. 'Maybe he met woman or perhaps got drunk. Maybe slept it off somewhere?'

Jamal Abboud, a twenty-nine year old Palestinian and Amir's pilot friend, looked worried. 'What we say to Ericson?' Jamal at six-foot-two with a short back and side's dark brown haircut was unofficially second in command of the terrorist group. With his muscular figure and sharp features that included a close shaven face of light olive skin, he looked the most European looking of the group, and as far as most women would judge, the best looking.

The others looked at Fadil for an answer.

Fadil told them, 'We tell truth, he went to watch rugby match and never returned.'

*

The following lunchtime while they were seated in the aerodrome canteen, flight Chief Guy Ericson approached them with a solemn expression.

Minutes later, Fadil and the pilots were in the flight chief's office accompanied by Detective Chief Inspector Graham Regis - a middle-aged heavy built man with receding grey hair wearing a conservative tweed suit. By his side was Plain Clothes Detective Sergeant John Dicks - the slimmer and younger of the two with a dark haired crewcut and sporting a light grey mohair suit with hand-stitched lapels.

As Guy Ericson nodded the OK, the Chief Inspector addressed them. 'I'm afraid I have some bad news for you all. It concerns your pilot colleague, Amir Halabi. He was found murdered yesterday afternoon on Wimbledon Common.'

There was a gasp from the pilots. Two or three put a hand to their mouths in shock.

The DCI continued, 'A woman walking her dog discovered the body. He'd been stabbed through the neck. Police immediately searched the area. His flight license was found in the pocket of his jacket. His assailant must have missed it. That's how we traced Amir Halabi to Redhill Aerodrome.'

The DCI checked with his notebook and said, 'It looks like robbery. The body was stripped of all identification including, what appears to have been two rings and a wristwatch. No money or wallet were found amongst his clothes or around the scene of the crime.

'For the moment, we are working on the theory that the deceased knew his killer. Perhaps while engaged in a sexual liaison. There was a flattened area of grass that looked like a blanket had been laid out. His clothes show no signs of a struggle or blood stains from the attack.'

The DCI checked with his notes again. 'We believe his murder is the work of a prostitute the press have dubbed, The Beauty Spot Butcher. Only this time the robbery turned to murder. A number of other young men have discretely reported being attacked and having their money and wallet stolen.'

The DCI glanced at the Flight Chief for confirmation and then said, 'So you can be eliminated from our enquires we have set up an interview room. This is to give us your detailed whereabouts from yesterday lunchtime to seven o'clock in the evening.'

Starting with Fadil Baba, they filed into the Flight Chief's office and spent fifteen minutes each, giving similar alibis. This confirmed a visit to Southfields Mosque early afternoon and then on to the cinema in the evening. The DCI had obtained a slightly false account of how they all had seen Amir go off to his rugby match at Twickenham from their sleeping quarters at Redhill. Then they'd taken the train from Redhill Station to Southfields Fazi Mosque. This was for Takbir at Salat al-'asr. The imam at the door of the mosque could verify their alibi. After prayers, it was on to *The Sound of Music* at Southfields Plaza. Fortunately, this had been true and they'd all kept their ticket stubs.

After the interviews, the police asked to see Amir's locker. A search provided no obvious clues or incriminating evidence. Nevertheless, they took away with them a hairbrush and two pairs of his shoes.

Fadil relaxed. It seemed to have gone smoothly. However, he had a nagging feeling.

After work, on the pretence of going to the Southfields Mosque, they decided to hold an emergency meeting at the flat. While they were seated, Fadil paced the floor and offered his concerns. 'It looks though we are in clear for moment that is, with cover still intact. However, how we *really* know?'

Jamal Abboud spoke up. 'Being his close friend, I know he liked women. But around us, where did he get chance to meet someone?'

Fadil stopped pacing and then said, 'What if he met prostitute, arranged to meet by telephone? Every telephone box has cards advertising sex.' The others nodded. 'We will search his things, let us get going.'

For the next twenty-minutes, they checked under Amir's mattress, his small wardrobe, inside the sleeves of his jazz records, his rolled up prayer matt until finally, as someone was flicking through the pages of his Salat – Amir's Muslim prayer book, a card fell out.

Fadil read the card aloud. 'For lessons in French contact Roxanne on 01-946 0147 between 10:00 p.m. to 10:30 p.m.'

Jamal Abboud shouted, 'Stupid fool must have been seeing prostitute. But I swear, he never told me.' The others looked at him with serious concern, half-believing.

Fadil looked hard at them. 'None you others knew of this?'

They all shook their heads.

Fadil sighed. 'We have big problem. It unlikely he was killed by this woman.' Fadil looked at the card. 'Most likely him killed afterwards by her pimp or maniac.'

Jamal Abboud interrupted. 'What if Roxanne did have pimp or somebody? Perhaps Amir set up to be robbed and murdered. What if he seeing this Roxanne for some time? Fool may have told her things to show off. Let it slip what we planning.' Jamal had a frenzied look in his eyes.

Fadil acknowledged him, 'You have point, Jamal. However, what happened to his Fata badge and Wimbledon ticket? I know he kept them in wallet.' Fadil pondered, he stroked his beard. 'If he set up by this Roxanne after he told her things, maybe she and pimp have put two and two together. They could go to police; pretend found his wallet, suggest an attack, even collect fat reward.' Fadil thought for a moment and then said, 'Because recent IRA bombings, police offering up to thousand pounds for information resulting in arrest of terrorists. Meanwhile we could be walking into ambush. They be waiting for us.' Fadil thought for a moment and then added, 'Worse still, perhaps police are lying. They have wallet. Established Amir was terrorist in wrong place at wrong time. His murder pure coincidence. However, with pilot license, his Fata badge and Wimbledon ticket, they worked out, attack by us could be imminent.'

Jamal added wide eyed, 'Police be watching us right now.'

The others mumbled in agreement.

Fadil relaxed. 'On other hand, perhaps we getting too paranoid. Police on high alert for any suspicious activity. If they thought in any way we be threat to people in this country, we would be behind bars at moment. They not allow us to operate if there was risk.'

'So what we do?' Jamal asked. 'Is it still on?'

Fadil answered him. 'First things, first. We have to find whore Roxanne. Find out what she knows. Then kill her. After that, I will contact Salah Khalaf. See where we stand. No doubt, if he not know, he will know soon enough of Amir's death through his contacts. Just hope he has not washed his hands of us being sloppy with security.'

CHAPTER SEVENTEEN

That evening at the flat, while they expectantly huddled around Fadil and the telephone, he made the call. It was five-minutes past ten when an elderly woman answered, informing him she was not Roxanne and he had the telephone box on Southfields High Street. Fadil apologised, left it for five minutes and then tried again.

After four more attempts listening to the engaged bleeps he tried again. This time he heard the normal ringing tone. But after hanging on for a while and no-one picking up, he decided to leave it for the night and try again the next day with a stake out on the telephone box.

By ten-fifteen the following evening, they were on their third black coffee. The Wimpy Bar on Southfields High Street sat directly opposite the telephone box. Sitting at the window, Fadil and Jamal had a good view. It was a warm early June evening again and the telephone box had seen some activity, mostly elderly people and a teenage couple who'd squeezed themselves in. However, there'd been nobody hanging around resembling a hooker on the game.

Fadil was fed up. He put his head in his hands and mumbled, 'There is only so much infidel crap coffee you can drink in evening.'

Jamal wasn't paying much attention, he mumbled something back and then leaned forward nearer the window. 'Dear Mohammad, look at that!'

Fadil sat up and looked in the direction of where Jamal was pointing. He strained his eyes.

He seemed to appear out of nowhere. Walking leisurely towards the telephone box swinging his handbag, wearing a red PVC miniskirt with matching top and high heels, he certainly fitted the part. With his black fishnet stockings and Cleopatra wig, he hovered as he got to within listening distance and stepped inside the telephone box.

They were sure this was it. As planned, Fadil made his way to the Wimpy pay phone booth in the lobby by the toilets. He could see Jamal as he dialled the number. He listened to the dialing tone and gave him an excited thumbs-up. All of a sudden, there came an answer.

'Hello.'

'Oh, err, could I speak to Roxanne, please?'

'Speaking.'

'Err, I found card for French lessons and wondered if we meet?' There was a pause. 'Hello, hello, are you still—?'

'I'm still here. How did you find my card?'

'Well…err, it tucked away in phone box I was using.' Fadil noted the voice sounded deep. Slightly masculine or it could be a heavy smoker.

'What's yer name?'

'Danny…Danny Ferrero.'

'You're not the filth are you trying to talk foreign? I don't hold lessons with coppers who want to entrap me.'

'No - no, I from Zardinia. Came over here as small boy with parents many years ago.'

'Your foreign accent sounds shit. I think you're putting it on. You're lying for some reason.' With that, Francis hung up.

Fadil heard a click and then the disengaged tone. Jamal was already outside when Fadil made a quick exit.

From across the road they watched Francis leave the telephone box.

Francis proceeded to make his way at a leisurely pace along Replingham Road. Jamal as instructed, crossed over and followed parallel with Fadil at about forty-feet behind.

After a short while, Francis turned left into Pirbright Road and made his way towards the entrance of a block of flats. There was a lift but he didn't use it.

Fadil waited until Francis had turned the first corner at the top of the stairs and then whispered to Jamal, 'You know I think this is man in drag as they say.'

Jamal said puzzled, 'Drag, what you mean?'

Fadil explained, 'Man dressed up as woman. He too big for woman. He even walk like man, has legs of man. You know, like man you can rent back home in Tehran in whore houses of Citadel.'

Jamal grinned. 'Ah Citadel. I have not visited but heard many stories.'

Fadil looked up the stairs and motioned for Jamal to stay behind. He went up cautiously and as he tiptoed nearer the top, he got the smell of stale urine and takeaway curry. He beckoned Jamal and then continued up the second flight of stairs.

Francis's high heels clacked on the concrete steps until the third floor. He moved off the landing and then slowed along the hallway as he approached his front door. Francis stopped to get his key.

Looking up near the top of the stairs, Fadil could clearly see Francis. No point in any rough stuff on the landing, he thought; wait until there inside.

Jamal had arrived just behind him. He stopped instantly when Fadil raised his hand. Then they watched Francis go in and shut the green council flat door.

Fadil took out a purse and stuffed it with twenty-pound notes until it bulged with temptation. They both smiled at each other. Jamal waited as instructed until called, while Fadil, checking all was clear, knocked on the front door.

He could hear the television and had to knock again. Suddenly, there was a rattle of a chain and then just a gap. 'Yes,' he said.

Fadil politely held the bulging purse. 'I'm sorry to disturb, I think you dropped this on stairs. I live above on next landing and followed you up. It is yours, yes?'

It looked very attractive sitting there in Fadil's hand with pound notes bulging out of the top. In those few seconds, Fadil could see the cogs turn over.

Francis's eyes never left it. With some quick thinking, he ruffled the hair of his Cleopatra wig in astonishment. 'Oh thank you-thank you, I've been searching frantically for it, I wondered where I lost it.' Francis took off the chain and poked his head out with a smile. With a nonchalant glance either way, he took the purse and extracted ten pounds. Francis handed him the tip.

Fadil doffed his cap. 'Thank you err misses...'

'I'm Roxanne and thank you for finding it.'

Fadil offered his hand. Francis timidly shook it. This was Fadil's chance.

Like a striking rattlesnake, he struck Francis's carotid artery with a Karate-chop. Francis collapsed like a sack of potatoes. Jamal sprinted along the landing and helped Fadil drag him inside. They closed the front door and immediately taped his hands and legs, and then across his mouth. A strong smell of fish and chips came from the kitchen. Probably the remains of tonight's early supper.

While Francis lay in the hallway, they frantically searched him; ripping buttons off as they checked out linings and pockets, even inside his bra and panties. 'Well we know we've got Roxanne.' Jamal nodded to the tattoo on Francis's arm. Then he pulled back with alarm. *'Dear Mohammad! You was right.'*

Fadil stopped and looked at him. 'What?'

Jamal arranged his clothing so he could see.

Fadil put a hand to his mouth in shock. Then burst out laughing. Jamal joined him, their shoulders hitching for some time until, wiping the tears from their eyes, Fadil said, 'No wonder Amir wanted to… wanted to keep quiet about *her*. I mean *him*.' They collapsed again laughing, this time holding on to each other bent over until, the sound of Francis coming round stopped them in their tracks.

They quickly got serious. Fadil instructed, 'Leave him for moment, Jamal, while we search place. We have to find wallet or anything else he has on Amir. You start in bedroom and I'll look in sitting room.'

Fadil rummaged through Francis's large shoulder bag and found a garter-belt with fishnet stockings, handcuffs, a dildo and a small-coiled whip with leather thongs attached. Then in a hidden zip pocket, he discovered a rent book and a diary. Tucked in the diary were half a dozen business cards. The business cards were for French lessons advertising an experienced sophisticated international lady going by the name of Roxanne.

Fadil breathed a low sigh. On the back of one of the cards, the name Amir was scribbled. Flicking through the diary he suddenly froze. In the address section he also saw the name Amir. Underneath was written, flat 127B, Wimbledon Park Rd, Southfields. (near the station).

Fadil couldn't believe it. 'The stupid, dumb shit,' he whispered. 'He told her where he lived.' He flicked some more pages and then suddenly stopped. His hand shook slightly. The name Guy Ericson and in brackets (pilot) stared at him with a Redhill phone number. Fadil gave a low whistle. Pocketing the card and carefully tearing out the incriminating pages from the diary, he carried on searching until a red leather album in the bookrack caught his eye.

Full of old photos, mostly of a man and a young girl; it appeared to be a scrapbook.

Fadil thumbed through the pages and noticed the edge of a folded newspaper clipping stuffed in the lining on the inside of the back cover. Slightly discoloured with age and delicate looking, he carefully unravelled the piece of paper. The headline gripped his attention:

Young Local Girl Drowns in Family Fish Pond

Kent News Roudup

A seven year old local girl, Roxanne Hodder from Maidstone in Kent, was found drowned last Tuesday in her family fishpond. A neighbour in the adjacent garden spotted her face down in the water and alerted her father. Although family friends were quick to carry out artificial respiration, she was pronounced dead at the scene of the accident shortly after the ambulance arrived.

It is still not clear how the tragedy occurred while she was playing with her six year-old brother, Francis.

Their single father, Mr Hodder, who cares for the children was too distraught to comment and was being comforted by friends and neighbours.

Francis was quietly moaning on the floor, struggling with his restraints. Fadil shouted to him, 'Shut up, you Miserable Whore.'

Just then, Jamal called from the bedroom. 'Fadil, quickly, look what I have here.' He held up the small polythene bags he'd found under the mattress.

Fadil carefully slit one and dipped his finger, then licked it. 'Cocaine,' he exclaimed. 'The whore must be earning good to afford this stuff.'

While Francis was still moaning, they dragged him into the lounge. Fadil reached for the television and turned up the volume. Jamal had filled a glass with cold water and tossed it at him. Francis flinched as it hit his face. Then they hauled him onto the sofa. Fadil sat next to Francis with the point of an Italian stiletto pressed on his cheek. He was wide-awake with his eyes open in terror. Fadil told him, 'I am going to remove gag. If you make sound, I will dig eye out. Is that clear?'

Francis nodded.

Jamal sat the other side of him. He'd found a large breadknife and held it to his ribs. A shriek of pain followed as Fadil pressed in the stiletto just below his eye and drew a small spot of blood.

Fadil asked him. 'Why did you kill Amir? And not lie otherwise I will blind you.'

Francis gulped with fear, 'I swear I didn't. When I left him he was alive.'

Fadil pressed the knife and drew more blood.

'Please - please believe me, it must have been some maniac who killed him. How could I? I'm just a prostitute – a woman,' he pleaded.

Fadil sneered. 'A woman? I think not, you Disgusting Whore, or whatever you are. Was it your pimp?'

'No - no, I don't have a pimp. I work alone, honestly. You can ask the other girls on my patch.'

Fadil relaxed. He moved the knife away. 'What did you do with wallet, his badge, his ticket?'

'I never had them, he just paid me twenty-pounds and I left him lying on the grass.' Francis said in panic, 'You must believe me, please. Somebody must have watched us. Killed him after I'd gone.'

Fadil hit him with the back of his hand. 'You lying whore.'

Francis cried out and flinched at the sting, the mark growing vivid on his cheek.

He shoved the diary into his face and pointed to the entry. 'How you know Guy Ericson?' He instantly put the stiletto to his eye again. 'I know if you lying.'

Francis moved his head carefully. He looked at the name. 'Oh him. Tina gave me his number as a favour. I've never met him.'

'Who is Tina, and why did she give Ericson's number?'

'Tina's a friend on my patch. She does massages and stuff. She told me she's seeing this Ericson. We swop clients to help each other out. You know... if one of the punters wants something a bit special. But I've never used him, never had to.'

'Did Amir talk about himself? What he did? Did he talk about Ericson?' He pressed the knife.

Francis panicked. 'No - no, I'm telling the truth. All we talked about was music. We had a mutual liking for Oscar Peterson and Count Basie.'

Fadil thought, knowing Amir liked jazz there was a ring of truth in what he said. 'Did Amir ever use Tina?' He pressed the stiletto hard this time and blood trickled down his cheek.

He yelled, *'No, he never did, I swear. She would have told me.'*

Fadil shouted at him, *'Give us Tina's number, her address.'*

'I don't have her number or address. She's not in my diary, honest. Look for yourself.' Francis collapsed sobbing.

He didn't bother to look. He was probably telling the truth.

Fadil and Jamal moved away from him and spoke quietly to each other.

Jamal whispered anxiously. 'What about wallet? This whore lying. Maybe gave to Ericson or police for reward?'

'Maybe, maybe not,' Fadil replied. 'Could be some other dumb shit stole it? Took money then threw wallet away. We have to take chance. Attack still on until we told otherwise.'

After a couple of minutes, they approached Francis and smiled. 'We going to let you go. If tell anyone or police about this, we come back and kill you. Understand?'

He nodded to Fadil.

Fadil came and sat by his side. He wanted to relax the mood. 'Now listen,' he said with a smile. 'We lock you out on balcony, yes? So have time to get away. Is that clear?'

'Yes - yes, of course, I understand.' Francis was doing his best to be agreeable.

'Would you like powder to calm nerves?' He took out the bags of cocaine. 'We found under your mattress.'

Francis's eyes lit up. 'Yes, Jesus, I could do with a snort.' He eased a little, knowing they wouldn't be offering stash if they were going to kill him. They'd keep it for themselves or sell it.

Fadil grabbed a saucer from the coffee table and made two lines. 'Ah, need something,' he said. In the kitchen, he found some drinking straws. With scissors from the cutlery drawer he snipped one in half and then returned to the lounge. He held the straw while Francis sniffed.

With hands tied behind his back, it was difficult. However, within seconds he'd managed to clear both lines. He sniffed hard again but some white powder remained around his nose.

Fadil tucked the other bags of cocaine inside Francis's bra. Then he stuffed a handkerchief into his mouth.

Francis shook his head with a muffled protest.

Helping him up to his feet, Fadil joked to Jamal, 'I think young lady needs some air.'

With Francis trying to pull back, they hauled him out onto the balcony, swiping their way through washing hung up on a line. The sound of distant televisions competed with one another while a neighbour's record player blasted out a Tom Jones hit. That was good; hopefully they wouldn't be heard.

Francis had an uneasy feeling about this. He started to plead and whine through his gag.

'That better, some fresh air.' With exaggeration, Fadil breathed in and then exhaled. He looked across from the balcony. 'What great view. I do so love evenings over here. Much cooler than where I from.'

Then with lightning speed, they grabbed his waist and legs and hoisted him up until he rested half way over the safety railings.

Francis kicked and moaned through his gag, his eyes bulged in terror as he looked down.

While Jamal held him securely, Fadil cut the tape to his arms. At the last minute, while Francis dangled over the edge, his hands swiped wildly to grab hold of something. Then Fadil wrenched the handkerchief from his mouth and Jamal cut the tape to his legs.

With one last ear-piercing scream from Francis, they upended him and he disappeared into the car park below followed by a muffled thud.

Fadil and Jamal concealed themselves against the balcony wall, waiting for a light, a commotion, someone appearing; but nothing.

They eased and smiled to each other.

Before they left the flat, Jamal forged his hand writing in the diary. He scribbled a suicide message indicating his involvement as 'The Beauty Spot Butcher' and that he simply couldn't live with himself anymore after what he'd done.

CHAPTER EIGHTEEN

After the police had photographed Francis's body, clothed and unclothed, along with height and weight details; all garments were collected and itemised for trace evidence.

After his big toe had been tagged, his body was slid into the police morgue refrigerator while a pretty crime lab technician named Sally, who'd just come on shift, pencilled in the work schedule for the autopsy.

Having been pronounced dead at the scene of the suicide by the ambulance team, Francis's body had shut down from the injuries of the fall with no heart rhythm on any of the monitors after failed cardiopulmonary. Then later unbeknown to medical staff, he experienced an autoresuscitation. A spontaneous return of circulation to the heart through a build-up of released chest pressure. Although rare, Francis experienced Lazarus syndrome. And now he wanted to be free of his stainless steel temporary coffin.

At this moment, Francis was cold as well as angry. However, there was nothing that could be done. They'd all come and gone. Poked and prodded. Made a few tasteless remarks. Shone a torch into his eyes and made out the death certificate.

Francis wanted to scream at them. *I'm not dead you fucking idiots. Look closer, can't you see. My eyes are still watering, you pricks.* However, he knew they couldn't be bothered with some drugged up hooker in drag, who as far as they were concerned had committed suicide by jumping off a balcony with a stash of cocaine stuffed inside his bra.

Committed suicide, like fuck. I'd like to get my hands on that Moslem crap who did this to me. That's a bit remote now, lying stark naked in a mortuary fridge wrapped in a sheet with the prospect of having vital organs examined or removed. Francis had heard the police pathologist requiring an autopsy to establish a firm forensic link between the Beauty Spot Butcher and the victim found stabbed on Wimbledon Common.

They'd said, no family or even friends had come forward to identify my body. Not surprising being stitched up by that suicide note as The Beauty Spot Butcher, even though it was the truth. What do they know? I've still got a mother in Newcastle. Admittedly, haven't seen her for years since she cleared off when I was a kid. To them though, I'm just another statistic. Another dead whore that nobody will miss.

All of a sudden Francis blinked. *Jesus, I can move my eyelids.* Then some feeling was coming back into the toes and fingers. *I can move them, dear God.* Francis tapped the side of the steel drawer. *Tap hard enough and they'll hear me before they freeze my nuts off as well as take out my giblets. Shit, what's that smell?* He was beginning to get a whiff of formaldehyde and surgical spirit. The strong pungent smell started gagging the back of his throat.

The pain was coming back. The same pain Francis felt when he bounced off the soft top of an 88 Series Land Rover and then hit the concrete road. The right knee and left wrist burned, like someone was driving a hot poker through them. *Still, better to have feeling than no feeling and the soft top did break the fall.*

Suddenly distant footsteps sounded louder. Then the steel drawer was being pulled. As Francis breathed in, he closed his eyes.

*

'Who's next?' Dr Blanchard had just come back from lunch and peered over Greg's shoulder at his workload.

'I can never make out Sal's writing.' Greg said. 'She booked this one in early this morning. Looks like a young male named Francis Hodder with a question mark against it.' He screwed up his eyes again and then dropped the pad down. 'This one apparently had been using a false name according to last night's police report. Goes by the professional name of Roxanne when giving French lessons. But they're sending over dental records so Phil can give them the once over.'

'Sounds a colourful character. Okay, Greg, let's have a look.'

Greg stopped pulling on the drawer, he'd just remembered. 'Oh! By the way, Sally went home sick. She'd gone before I arrived. Left *you* a scribbled note in *my* IN tray for some reason.'

'Just the two of us then?' Dr Blanchard said as Greg pulled out the body. With that, a rush of cold air hit their faces. 'So what have we got here?' The doctor looked at the notes. 'Murder suspect on drugs fell from a balcony with possible internal trauma to the rib cage and spine.'

Greg pulled down the sheet. 'Jesus Christ!'

Both of them winced. There was no face. Dr Blanchard looked at his chart then looked at his colleague. 'There's nothing here to say there'd been a sex change operation.'

Greg looked at the toe tag. 'On here it says Francis Hodder. But as I say, it could be a false name.'

'This is very confusing. You sure we got the right one. It could be in another drawer, Greg.'

'As I said, Sally booked the body in early this morning,' Greg flicked through the autopsy schedules. 'All we got is two other males in here; that's a hit and run and a shooting.'

'Check out the other drawers,' Dr Blanchard said pulling open another one. Lifting the sheet, he inspected the tag on the big toe and then both leaned over the 32-year-old Caucasian with a .38 bullet hole between his eyes. 'This one's all present and correct.'

Greg did the same with the hit and run, checking the big toe label against his pad.

They looked at the three remaining drawers. 'Let's just double check.' Greg quickly pulled the handles, however, at a quarter of the way he instantly knew they were empty.

'How the Christ was all this missed?' Dr Blanchard had returned to the female and was looking at what remained of a face. He leant over her. 'And where's all the chest injuries from the balcony fall?'

Greg looked at Sally's sheet again. 'On here she's got male marked up. She's crossed out something else in the distinguishing marks box. It looks like Rox…tato… something. I can't make it out. But I don't understand…she wouldn't…' Greg didn't want to say too much if Sally had fucked up. He got on with Sal' but could sense a gigantic bollocking coming her way.

Dr Blanchard pulled the sheet down further and then threw down his pad in a temper. 'Bloody hell, the bodies not even cleaned. She's still wearing a ring?'

Greg moved closer and lifted the hand. His rubber glove inspected the cheap silver ring on her engagement finger. He looked puzzled.

'Don't just look at it.' Dr Blanchard's sarcasm had surfaced. 'Take the bloody thing off and log it.'

Greg did as he was told and then stopped. He was looking at something else.

'We'll have to get in touch with *Miss* Simmons,' the doctor hissed. 'See what this mix-ups about.' First names were always dropped when trouble was brewing, Sally's included. The doctor was in a mood now, noisily searching his work area for the address book. 'Have we got her home number, for Christ sake?'

'I think it's there…somewhere in…the.' Greg stood back and put a hand to his mouth. He started whining and making a strange keening noise.

The doctor looked up with a start. 'Christ sake, what's up, Greg?'

Greg pointed, but backed away from the body. He dropped to his knees and started rocking backwards and forwards drooling with tears streaming down his face. 'No…Please… no…please God no…'

Dr Blanchard froze in shock. He stared at Greg mortified. 'What is it…Greg…what's happened?'

Greg pointed with a shaking hand, and all Dr Blanchard could hear was gibberish. He looked at Greg on his knees and then walked slowly over to the body. 'What the hell are you going on about?' He looked at the corpse and then looked back at Greg. 'What?'

Greg was sobbing, 'Not her…not her…' A thin drool of spit was swinging from his chin as he lifted his arm and pointed again.

Dr Blanchard peered over her. The face was a mess with frenzied incisions. It looked like somebody had slashed it to ribbons with a razor. Then he checked the legs and thighs, but still nothing unusual. He cast a glance back to Greg who was buckled over sobbing deeply.

The abdomen, the breasts, the shoulders revealed nothing. He looked around the bloodied neck. The doctor lifted the hand. He examined the ring closely with a slight look of indifference, as a jeweller might when being asked to buy it and knowing its cheap value.

That's when he spotted it. Just under the left armpit. Dr Blanchard leaned closer and saw the little red heart with the arrow. He read the tattoo. Then he read it again. *Sally loves Greg xx…*

CHAPTER NINETEEN

The following evening they called an emergency meeting at the flat. Fadil, including his other four pilots, Hirad Alizadeh, Jamal Abboud, Arif Nahas and Hashim Mustafa sat on mats with grim expressions while Fadil addressed them. 'The whore Roxanne is dead. However, we have problem. He had Guy Ericson's phone number in diary. He swore he never met him, but could been lying to save himself. Maybe Ericson bisexual as well. Maybe Roxanne passed on Amir's pillow talk to Ericson. Who knows what Amir said under influence of alcohol, drugs or sex? Perhaps Ericson knows attack by us is imminent. Maybe he wants to collect fat reward of thousand pounds put up by police for capture of IRA or anyone committing terrorist acts. He is keeping to himself otherwise we be locked up now.'

Arif Nahas raised his hand to say, 'Boss, I think Ericson waiting for chance, biding time for more information, then when is right, shop us and collect fat reward.'

Fadil agreed. 'You could be right, Arif. None the less, being close to mission we not afford to take chances. We have to kill Ericson and soon the better. Our leader Salah Khalaf would demand it.' Fadil looked worried; he paused and then said, 'I will contact leader tomorrow. He not be pleased. As they say, "We fucked up." A man down, my carelessness, my stupidity. I should been more strict with Amir knowing his history with call girls. It was on file.'

Jamal sympathised, 'You could not done more with him, Boss. He beyond control. Not committed enough.' The others nodded in agreement.

*

Fadil was owed some leave although it was a busy week. Alan Bristow's shuttle service were using Fadil's group as part of their final training, to ferry people back and forth to the Royal Tattoo and The Horse Show at Windsor Castle. Flying twin turbine 28 seater S-61N Sikorsky helicopters, the group would cover for Fadil while he'd squared it with Guy Ericson to have the following two days off.

Using the code sheet he kept in a polythene bag hidden in the toilet cistern; he constructed a message to Khalaf.

The next morning, Fadil took the train from Southfields to Redhill. On the way he was thinking - *That stupid dumb shit, Amir. He'd broken orders. What had he got mixed up in? Some whore named Roxanne and God knows what else.* Fadil knew he had to be careful when he explained the problem.

Salah Khalaf took no prisoners. All the group including himself were expendable. Khalaf could easily arrange a hired assassin from Europe to pick them off quickly. His influence had no boundaries.

Fadil knew, even though he considered himself a true Palestinian and fought with Fatah in three wars, with his mother and sister getting killed during the September uprising when their house had suffered a direct hit by the Israeli's, that wouldn't count for anything now.

Only two nights ago at their Redhill sleeping quarters, he'd been blindfolded and roughly pushed against a wall. Someone had shouted, ready, aim - fire! That's when he'd started pleading and Jamal had shaken him out of his nightmare.

Should he mention the wallet? That could be a death sentence. Khalaf would be saying or worse still, thinking; if you knew he kept details in a wallet that could be lost or stolen, why didn't you rectify this at the time?

Then there was the killing of Roxanne and Guy Ericson's name being in his diary? Again, best to keep quiet. No point in complicating matters further. He had enough on his plate explaining the death of Amir.

As a Fatah operations leader, he'd been given Salah Khalaf's contact number. Only to be used for dire emergencies, otherwise strictly out of bounds.

Fadil would not dare to compromise or presume on Khalaf's Beirut connections, or to jeopardize any more the fragile trust they must have in him now. However, this was an emergency.

The other evening at the Southfields flat, the group had argued with him not to phone. Just kill Ericson, find the wallet if possible and carry out the attack, then contact Khalaf. However, Fadil needed clarification if the attack was still on; or if they'd been abandoned with a contract on their heads. He needed to sniff the air. Gauge the atmosphere. Were they doomed or had they been given another chance?

*

At Southfields Station, he made his way to one of the two phone booths just inside the entrance. Fadil checked the line by feeding four-pence into the coin box and telephoning Redhill Aerodrome reception. When they answered, he apologised with a wrong number excuse and hung-up. Fadil copied the pay phone number and quickly encoded it.

Then he took the train to King's Cross-Station. A cacophony of diesel smells mixed with whistles and doors slamming met him on the platform while a West Indian man gave out train times and delays over the speaker system. From there, Fadil flagged down a cab to take him to the Hilton Hotel, Park Lane. The tall Hilton loomed large above as he stepped from the taxi while the doorman acknowledged him and asked if he had luggage and required a porter? Fadil declined and on giving him a generous tip, paid the driver and then made his way through the heavy smoked glass swing doors.

Holding his expensive leather suitcase, he eyed reception with its flurry of cosmopolitan guests. Fadil waited for the right moment and then stepped forward. 'I would like to send a cable.'

'Thank-you, Sir.' Donald, the man at the counter with his name badge pinned to his smart reception suit, fussed with some papers and then passed him a blank form.

Using his notepad, he copied down the encoded message on the wire form that cryptically asked his wife to telephone him tomorrow at 10:30 a.m. at their Southfields hotel address.

Within minutes on the long line beneath the sea, the brief personal note flashed its way towards the lair of Salah Khalaf in Beirut.

The following day, Fadil was back on Southfields Station at 10:00 a.m. He placed an out of order sticker on the side of the phone booth and sat within hearing distance on the platform bench with a newspaper. At 10:32 a.m., a telephone ring jerked his head. Fadil quickly ensconced himself inside the booth and picked up on the third ring.

Despite the scratchy connection, he recognised the voice of the senior Beirut officer and personal secretary to Khalaf. After Fadil had given a brief greeting of, 'As-salaam alaykum,' there was silence and then the voice of Salah Khalaf came on.

'What went wrong?' Salah Khalaf asked

Fadil said nervously, 'May peace, mercy, and blessings of Allah be upon you. Oh, Honourable-One.'

'Yes-yes-yes,' Kkalaf said impatiently. 'Tell me, what went wrong?'

Fadil cleared his throat and explained, 'Amir was just in wrong place at wrong time, Oh Honourable-One. He liked to go walks in park on his own. He must been attacked by unknown infidel robbing scum.'

There was silence the other end. Fadil could hear breathing. With his free hand, he took out a handkerchief and dabbed his sweating forehead. It seemed an eternity before Khalaf spoke.

'As long as Amir had nothing on him that could be incriminating,' he said, 'your mission is still on. Have you decided the target?'

Fadil quietly breathed a sigh of relief and said, 'Wimbledon Tennis Championships, Oh Honourable-One. It would be great Black September showpiece if we kill enough people. The infidels are making big budget film here and have hired expertise of company. As pilots, we been contracted to help in attack scenes. We been given chance to fly over crowd and jettison water from hanging buckets. But at last moment we swap water for aviation fuel and drop flares to start massive fire, to kill all infidels.'

There was silence and then Khalaf said, 'You have done well, Fadil. You have redeemed yourself. Now listen carefully, within three days you will receive a coded letter addressed to your Southfields flat. The letter will contain a key for a left luggage locker on Wimbledon Station. In the locker, you will find a package left by our contact from the Embassy. It will contain new passports for you all. Make sure to memorise your new names. There is also a set of vehicle number plates, to swap over in case you have to steal a car. If you do not use them, make sure they are destroyed. So we know the goods are with you and no one else and the attack is still affirmative; leave the message September Sun in capitals in the personal column of The Times newspaper. Ensure it is carried in the Wednesday 23rd of June edition. If it is not there, I will assume the attack is off and you are on your own. Do I make myself clear?'

'Yes, Oh Honourable-One.'

Salah Khalaf continued, 'After the attack, the authorities will be watching all the airports. So I have included rail and ferry tickets with money for your journeys from Dover to Calais then through France and Italy to the port of Genoa. From there a steamer will take you all to Beirut. Details are inside. Allah be with you.'

Fadil was overcome with the news and said again, 'May peace, mercy, and blessings of Allah be upon you, Oh Honourable-One.' Before he'd finished his thank-you, the phone was dead.

As he replaced the receiver, it rattled for a second in the cradle. His body shook with nerves. He looked around and tried to compose himself. For a second he wished he'd come clean about the wallet. Then he remembered how he'd witnessed failure. Seen men's hands cut-off with the axe for lies and deceit. Fadil assured himself the wallet didn't matter. The others would be glad with the news he had.

Fadil glanced around. No heads look down quickly. It was dangerous to communicate with the Middle East, but their dilemma demanded taking the risk. Grateful Khalaf had given them another chance he could now concentrate on the attack plans, but first, Ericson had to be eliminated. It had to look good, an accident in front of everyone. No mess-ups this time. Khalaf had only so much patience.

He remembered, Ericson had informed him they were scheduled to film action scenes at the aerodrome fire training area to simulate an attack. It demanded tipping aviation fuel onto thousands of seated mannequins and setting light to them. This could be the opportunity they were looking for.

At a brisk pace, he made his way out of Southfields Station and then suddenly stopped. The writing on the billboard outside the newsagents glared at him. **The Beauty Spot Butcher Escapes From Hospital.**

Khalaf was true to his word. Three days later, Fadil received the letter with the key and made his way to the station left luggage locker. He checked the package contents. Everything was there as promised with more than enough money. No doubt, the extra was to bribe the captain of the steamer at Genoa.

CHAPTER TWENTY

With a bit of free time on his hands this weekend, Guy Ericson was sifting through some unpaid bills and red reminders from his private business while sitting in his office that he rented at Redhill Aerodrome. Grateful for the wage he collected from Bristow Helicopters every month as their flight chief, he had to face facts. Without a steady flow of customers who wanted to pay the £28 for his parachuting and skydiving trips at *Ericson's Para Jump and Skydiving School Ltd*, he would have to close down soon. This year, the money coming in from his small enterprise wasn't covering his receptionist wages or the rent on his office as well as the aircraft hangar that housed the four seater single engine Cessna 182.

His expensive divorce and financial settlement two years ago, which included a re-mortgage on the house he was living in, hadn't helped either.

This Saturday lunchtime it was sunny again with blazing June weather and Guy was taking advantage of it with his office door and windows open. He could see the aerodrome field and its control tower from here. It brought back memories as a boy when his father, a war time pilot in the RAF, used to take him to Biggin Hill and the Farnborough air displays. It was there his fascination of aeroplanes and is ambition to be a pilot first began.

Guy, sitting in for Pauline his receptionist while she was on her lunch break, looked up at the knock on the door.

Guy breathed in. She was gorgeous. He thought he recognised the very attractive twenty-eight year old blonde from somewhere but he couldn't put his finger on it.

'Hi, I'm Victoria but everybody calls me Vicky.' She held out her hand and Guy responded with a courteous shake.

'I'm Guy, how can I help?'

'I'm the marketing director of my father's company, *One Day Wonders Ltd.*' Victoria explained to Guy, 'We're looking at the possibility of incorporating skydiving and parachuting into our events catalogue. I wanted to see what it was like first hand to free-fall from an aeroplane. So here I am to book one.' She finished off with a beautiful smile.

For a second, Guy was rooted to the spot, speechless. Victoria was wearing an expensive black Fendi trouser-suit with matching shoes and handbag. He hadn't been close up to anything so desirable for a long time.

She raised her eyes in anticipation, waiting for him to respond.

He realised he was staring. 'Oh, yes, I'm sorry. Please forgive my manners. It's just...' Guy suddenly remembered.

'Now I know where I've seen you. It was at Briar Lodge Manor, some months ago. I was doing a martial arts course. You were in a different group but we used the same instructor if I remember.' Guy thought for a second. 'Now what was his name? Martin…somebody?'

'Lavender. Martin Lavender,' she confirmed with a smile.

'That's right. I remember he owned a nightclub somewhere. He was always handing out free entry passes for it. Did you ever go?'

Victoria's smile dropped a notch. 'Err no. I'm not into nightclubs.'

Guy now remembered her father was head of an events company. He'd read a business profile about One Day Wonders Ltd and its chairman Kenny Buxton the wealthy entrepreneur and self-made millionaire. It was the second biggest event specialists in the country. The article had gone on to mention Kenny Buxton opening a children's hospital wing at Reigate General and donating for a new playground area in Redhill Park.

Victoria had also read the same business article about her father. However, she knew it wasn't One Day Wonders Ltd that had made him a self-made millionaire. It was his drug running.

Guy felt a bit of flattery was in order. 'That outfit you're wearing. It's simply stunning.'

'Why thank you,' Victoria said with another big smile.

Guy pulled up a chair for her and cast a quick glance. He could see no engagement or wedding ring.

'Would you like a coffee? I've just made some,' he offered.

'I'd love one.'

Guy poured two mugs from the percolator and pushed one, along with a plate of chocolate biscuits, across the table.

'You don't mind if I dunk, do you?' she said with a giggle, taking a biscuit and dipping it into her coffee.

'No - no, whatever turns you on,' he responded with a smile.

'It takes a wee bit more than that to turn me on,' she said with a cheeky grin.

Guy gave a nervous laugh. His head was spinning. Was she sending out all the right vibes or was he misreading the situation?

Guy reminded himself he was a professional, and business came first before pleasure. *Get her to part with money and book a jump, then play footsy if she's still willing* - and would he love to play footsy with this one.

Sitting on the edge of his desk, trying to keep it light-hearted and informal, Guy explained to Victoria the ins and outs of a sky diving. 'You'll be tandem jumping from ten-thousand feet out of a plane attached to a professional.' He smiled at her. 'Believe me it will be an exhilarating experience for you.'

Victoria beamed back at him while he continued. 'It begins with an hour of tuition on jumping and landing techniques before going up in the plane. After that, you'll get securely harnessed to an instructor.' Guy picked up the bookings sheet and then looked up. 'Looks like that will be me,' he said with a grin. 'Then you'll be helped with the jump by the dispatcher.'

Victoria looked at him puzzled.

Guy laughed. 'That's the man who pushes us out. Then you can enjoy about thirty-seconds of free-fall, which is completely incredible.' Guy reassured her, 'Don't worry, I'll open the parachute and control the descent.'

'Wow,' she said, 'I can't wait.'

After a further half-hour tour of his hanger and letting her sit in his Cessna aircraft, Guy could feel a mutual attraction forming between them. During their conversation, they even discovered they shared the same Taekwondo martial arts sport. Victoria was a brown belt in karate and had her own personal coach, while Guy, a black belt 2nd Dan, belonged to a martial arts club in Reigate.

As Victoria booked her tandem jump, Guy couldn't wait for next weekend to come.

*

On the following Saturday, Victoria arrived at Redhill Aerodrome. It was a perfect morning as she began her training. Watching her practise landing techniques, Guy had told Victoria she looked a natural.

After being harnessed together, Guy enjoyed the intimacy of being so close to Victoria. They were taken up to ten-thousand feet in the single engine Cessna. Attached to Guy, she made her dive, screaming with enjoyment during their thirty-seconds of free-fall until the chute opened and they floated down, taking in the scenery for the rest of the descent.

Victoria was so excited, she reckoned it was the best thing she'd ever done.

Guy sensed the mood and suggested dinner together that evening. She agreed with a big smile.

He booked a table at Botticelli's in Banstead Village. Very posh and renowned to be expensive with its indoor floodlit waterfall and live jazz quartet. Victoria of course, had been there many times. Guy wanted to impress, it had been his usual eatery in the days when he was flush. He still had an account with them that was handy when he was strapped for cash.

That evening she looked amazing with her blonde hair cascading down the back of her red velvet trouser suit and matching high heels.

Guy felt all eyes were upon them. Her for being so beautiful and him for being the lucky one to be with her as the waiter showed them to a table by the waterfall amongst the subdued romantic lighting.

Holding their menu cards, Guy made small talk but wanted to find out more about her. 'So, Victoria, do you have your own place?'

She slapped his arm playfully. 'Call me Vicky, as I said everyone does.'

'Sorry, Vicky,' he grinned, 'I must remember.'

'My own place? Not at the moment. I live with my father on the Pilgrims Way Estate in Reigate.'

'Wow, that's a bit exclusive. Let me guess how many bedrooms,' he joked. 'Now I reckon you've got seven, not counting the servants quarters.'

She laughed. 'Not quite, there's nine actually including a lodge as well as an indoor and outdoor swimming pool. Then there's the riding stables and of course the obligatory tennis court.'

'With all that, who would want to move?' Guy quipped.

'Well,' Victoria looked pensive. 'At the moment, I've never felt the need to move and find my own place and independence and all that. With an annexe all to myself, the property is more than big enough to satisfy my needs and privacy. My mother died of cancer seven-years ago. So it's just been myself and dad. It would have to be something special,' she met Guy's eyes for a second, 'to make me want to leave.'

He caught it and was inwardly excited. Even though it was early days, everything seemed to be going well. As the evening progressed, Guy became more smitten and Victoria Buxton was giving out all the vibes to show she was interested.

It was after the poached pears in Armagnac; she reached across the table and grabbed both his hands. 'Guy, I want you to know I'm really having a great time.'

For a split second, he was lost for words. Guy was dizzy with happiness. He kissed her hand tenderly. 'I'm having a great time being here with you, Vicky.'

From then onwards, they talked and laughed, sometimes just smiling at each other as if there was no one else in the room.

Within the next couple of dates, Guy Ericson was totally infatuated with Victoria. He couldn't think of anything else. He'd never felt this way about a woman. He was so in love, it hurt. The fact she had a rich father also helped. Guy's mind was swimming with possibilities: Marriage. The family money. His own company incorporated into the successful Buxton operation. Being on the board of directors. Perhaps his ship had sailed in at last.

They spent the next three weeks together. Guy couldn't get enough of Victoria, buying her presents, treating her to lunches, dinners, even a weekend away in Milan. For her it seemed the same. She'd told him she was only really happy when they were together. A happiness she only thought was possible in novels.

It was during their shopping trip to Milan, Guy proposed. He'd gone down on one knee in La Malmaison, an exclusive restaurant just off the Zona Greco Strada. Victoria thought he'd dropped something. Then, with all eyes on them, Guy pulled the little box and flipped the lid. 'Vicky, will you marry me? You'd make me the happiest man in the world if you said yes.'

Victoria with tears in her eyes said, 'Of course I will, My Darling.' She slipped on the beautiful engagement ring and then leaned forwards and kissed him.

Guy had primed the Maître d' beforehand when Victoria had visited the rest room. All the diners applauded the smiling couple, with a new bottle of champagne being delivered on the house to their table.

The engagement ring had cost Guy a fortune. Most of it was on hire purchase from a Hatton Garden Jeweller.

However, he believed in the theory, one must speculate to accumulate.

Arriving back from Milan with his bride to be, he had firmly made up his mind. He was going to finish it with Tina.

CHAPTER TWENTY-ONE

Wearing a dark blue pin stripe suit for the board meeting - his mother always said it made him look slimmer and taller - Graham Lumley, as finance manager of *One Day Wonders Ltd*, tried to persuade Kenny Buxton the chairman, that their liability insurance was being stretched taking on skydiving. Already paying high premiums for their hot air ballooning he couldn't see the reason why the company needed to expand anymore.

Graham Lumley stood and raised himself without the others seeing his feet under the table and, with a nervous posture argued, it would be better to buy into other franchises with safer sports rather than have a skydiving operation.

However, Kenny Buxton refused to listen. He'd seen his major competitor, *Great Days Out Ltd*, take over franchises on three airfields in Kent and Surrey. And he wanted to use Redhill Aerodrome as an inroad for his own company and to stop further expansion from his rival. He argued, there was a potential market for young people who wanted a buzz these days. With the increase in sponsorship for charities and the rest, skydiving and parachuting fitted the bill. He envisaged the profit margins could be very healthy.

As usual, once Kenny Buxton set his mind to something, like a dog with a bone, he didn't let go. Graham Lumley knowing he was on a lost cause, sat there sulking for the rest of the meeting; and Graham had plenty to sulk about.

He'd heard the rumours, mostly office girl talk, Victoria Buxton had found herself a new beau and was getting married.

Graham had always fancied Victoria. They'd gone out on a couple of dates but nothing had come of it. The third time he asked her out she politely refused. Told her friends he wasn't really her type; a boring four-eyes she'd said, just talked about work all the time.

Thirty-six years old and slightly overweight at five-foot-eight-inches with a rear bald spot amongst a remainder of dark thinning hair, Graham at first glance, could have been mistaken for an oriental with his thick glasses and slightly flat features.

It was Graham's career mission to end up with the governor's daughter and have Kenny Buxton as his father-in-law. Graham envisaged marrying Victoria and living in Weybridge or Virginia Water in a large detached house within its own grounds - having all the trappings of success - holidaying in St Jean-Cap-Ferrat - cruising on his own flying bridge motor launch with lazy afternoons spent on deck with select friends, nibbling at a fussy lobster salad with foie gras complemented by an ice-cold Sancerre.

Now his easy path to the top, becoming finance director, becoming part of the Buxton family seemed shot to threads. To make matters worse, he'd heard Victoria's fiancé owned a skydiving outfit at Redhill Aerodrome and Kenny Buxton already had his arm around the shoulder of his future son-in-law for a buy in.

To rub salt into the wound, Graham had been called in by the chairman to carry out an exercise to determine past skydiving and parachute jump fatalities. Kenny Buxton wanted to know how high risk his new expansion venture was going to be and the company's position on insurance costs and liability cover. In Kenny Buxton's office, Graham had mumbled, 'Will do, Sir. I'll get onto it straight away.'

With a, 'Good man, Graham, if you could let me have your report within a week or as soon as possible please,' from his boss who didn't bother to look up. Graham closed the door and sloped off with his shoulders down.

The following few days, Graham sifted through data statistics that had been kindly faxed through by the British Parachute Association including newspaper reports. It was one of those headlines that grabbed Graham's attention. It was a four-year-old news item from the Redhill Tribune that caught his eye.

Woman Dies in Parachute Jump at Redhill.

By Phil Reed: News correspondent

Caroline Scott fell to her death when her parachute failed to open properly on her first charity jump at Redhill Aerodrome. The two-month pregnant 26-year-old had

plummeted from a height of six-thousand feet after her main parachute ripped and became entangled in her reserve chute. Her fiancé, a director and instructor of the skydiving company she was using, was too upset to comment.

CAA and BPA inspectors are currently carrying out an investigation on the accident.

Graham mumbled under his breath, 'Good God.' He flicked through the phone directory until he found the Tribune number for the editor's desk and picked up his phone.

'Tribune news desk, can I help you?'

'Hi, I'm after a reporter by the name of Phil Reed about an article of his some time ago.'

'Phil Reed you say. I don't think we have...' Short pause then came some muttering to a colleague... 'Hello, sorry about that, I can give you his extension, one-four-seven or I can try and put you through?'

'Put me through please.' Graham strummed his fingers until he heard the ringing tone.

'Phil speaking.'

'Oh, hi, err...I'm Graham Lumley. I came across one of your old news articles in the Tribune concerning a parachute accident at Redhill Aerodrome and wondered if you could help me. I'm carrying out an accident survey for my company.'

'Well, I don't know. I mean...I'm not into surveys.'

'No - no, I'm not doing a survey,' Graham gave a nervous laugh. 'It's just this specific accident.'

'Well I'm a bit busy...but...go on, how far back are we talking?'

Graham scrutinised the date. 'It was the 10th of July 1970. A young woman fell to her death. Her parachute failed to open.'

'Oh, yea. Now I remember,' the reporter said. 'She was pregnant or something.'

'That's the one,' Graham said excitedly. 'Did you get to speak to her fiancé? You mentioned him in your article.'

'Her fiancé? Now come to think of it…bit of a cold fish… if I remember, he didn't exactly look devastated, considering he was the instructor and had arranged it all.'

Graham asked, 'He didn't give any reasons for the accident then?'

'He didn't want to be interviewed; I suppose he thought it would be bad for future business. Told me to clear off, said he had nothing to say.'

Graham sighed and then asked him, 'Don't suppose you remember his name?'

'No sorry, Mate, can't…now hang on…Everington or Erlicsome … something like that. He did own some sort of skydive outfit at the aerodrome. We did follow up the case. There were some rumours about tampering with the chute, incorrectly packed. At the inquest however, the accident inspector reported insufficient evidence. The Coroner overruled foul play and recorded accidental death. The young woman's parents were devastated; they started shouting out at the verdict.'

Graham didn't want to push it. He could probably find out more from Coroner's records if he wanted to pursue it further. 'Many thanks, Phil, sorry to waste your time, I owe you a drink.'

The reporter replied, 'No problem, Mate.'

Graham leaned back and stared at his office ceiling. Should he confront Victoria with what he'd found out about Guy Ericson? Or find out more? He could of course try and make contact with the dead woman's parents. Graham reasoned, *shouting out at the verdict, as the reporter had conveyed, seemed to infer they had deep rooted suspicions. Then again, who am I to question things if a Coroner rules accidental death? However, what if this bloke is Victoria's fiancé? What if he's a gold digger?* His mind was running riot. *What if he's done it more than once for some sort of profit? What if he's got some sort of plan for Victoria once they're married? Gets himself on her Will?* The thought of facing her father at a similar coroner's inquest with the knowledge, he knew her husband had a shady past. Her father shouting at him. If only he'd spoken up earlier, her death may have been prevented. Everybody looking, pointing a finger at Graham Lumley because he was too afraid to speak up.

Graham buried his head in his hands; he knew he was getting paranoid. He took some deep breaths and then composed himself. He decided, *I'll tell her father. Just tell him what I've found out. Then he knows and I've covered myself. He'll probably tell Victoria. She'll think I told her father out of jealousy because she didn't fancy me and I'm stirring it up because she's with someone else. Well, that's her problem.*

The following morning, Graham submitted all his figures on skydiving and parachute jump fatalities and a copy of the newspaper report together with a memo of his conversation with the reporter.

Kenny Buxton was busy, he never looked up. 'Thank you, Graham, just leave it on my desk.'

'There is something, Sir, I think you should–'

Graham was cut off. 'Yes, thank you, Graham, I'll read it in due course.'

With his shoulders down, Graham mumbled, 'Thank you, Sir,' and closed the door.

CHAPTER TWENTY-TWO

Tina had phoned Guy on his office phone. 'Can we meet for dinner, somewhere posh as it's my birthday? You haven't forgotten have you?'

Guy had forgotten, but there was still time to buy a present. 'No I haven't forgotten, My Love.' He wasn't seeing Victoria tonight, it was her friend's birthday and so she was out celebrating with the girls. 'I'll pick you up say around eight?'

'Okay, don't be late and like I said, let's go somewhere special, cos it's a double celebration,' she coyly informed him. 'I can't say over the phone but I'm sure you'll be pleased.'

Guy knew Tina was on the pill and they hadn't had it for a while, as far as he could remember, so hopefully he could rule out that she had a bun in the oven.

'You haven't won the lottery have you?' he joked.

'Ah, I'm not saying, wait and see.'

Guy had met Tina just after his divorce. It was from one of those girlie magazine back page adverts for massage parlours.

She was aged thirty-three years old with pointed features and mousey swept back hair fastened with an Alice band. Wearing her tanning cream, Tina always looked as though she'd been on holiday. Although she had a so-so face, it was her fantastic figure that first attracted Guy when she mailed him her photo wearing a bikini.

Tina worked from her sixth-floor council flat in Wimbledon as a masseuse and did a bit of prostitution if the massaging side was slack. Although she never told Guy. They'd been seeing each other for nearly five months and, what started out as great sex with a free massage thrown in, had slowly for Guy, cruised its way into a platonic and mundane relationship. The recession had seen her massage parlour clientele dry up. So she never had any money. She'd hinted more than once about getting engaged. As far as she was concerned, Guy was the sugar daddy with his own aeroplane business.

However, Guy felt he was suffocating. Tina was getting too clingy and quite frankly, now he'd met Victoria, dating them both was costing him a fortune.

That Tuesday the 12th June being Tina's birthday, she'd insisted on being taken to Botticelli's in Banstead Village. 'Do you remember you used to take me here quite a bit when we were first dating? Then you became a Meany and we started having takeaways,' she poked him with the reminder.

'Who'd of thought the bottom would drop out of my flying business. I'm still struggling now,' Guy nervously said as he eyed the prices on the large menu card.

The Italian restaurant was half-full as Tina selected the Lobster Thermidor and a bottle of Bollinger champagne. Guy smiled weakly and went for the Caesar salad.

'So, what's this big surprise then?' He said with a false grin.

Tina clutched his hand and looked lovingly into Guy's eyes. 'You're going to be a daddy.' She giggled, 'Isn't that fantastic.'

Guy, still trying to hold his smile, was churning inside. 'That's great, you're expecting a baby?'

'Our baby, my Darling.' Tina squeezed his hand.

Guy's smile dropped slightly as he muttered, 'I thought you were on the pill?'

'Mistakes do happen, Darling. But like it says on the box, not one-hundred-per cent safe.' Tina noticed the slight change and gripped his hand anxiously, 'You are pleased, aren't you?'

Guy forced a smile and dutifully reciprocated, 'Of course I'm pleased, Love. I couldn't be happier.'

For the rest of the meal, Guy couldn't get a word in. Tina mapped out his whole life. 'Look, I can help out,' she told him. 'I've got some small savings put by. We could have a white wedding, nothing fancy. Then for our honeymoon, we could have a two-week cruise in the Caribbean. I want to see all those places they show in the holiday programs. St Barts, St Kitts, St Lucia and of course Barbados.' Then Tina turned the conversation to more practicable things on the home front. 'Oh, and I could give up my council flat and move into your place. And we could turn that spare bedroom you've got into a nursery. You'd have to clear out all that stupid sports equipment first,' she playfully tapped his arm. Having been to his house a few times, she'd seen it being used as a gym.

Guy's mind was in a daze, his head was spinning.

Tina looked at him with excitement in her eyes. 'So when do you reckon I can move in?'

Guy tried to stall her. He told a fib. 'Err, well you see I'm having a new central heating system put in. The place is an absolute mess at the moment; it would be a couple of weeks at least.'

'Make sure they put a big radiator in the spare room for our little one,' she giggled patting her tummy and squeezing Guy's hand again.

Before desert had arrived, Guy was feeling sick to the stomach. Of course, he hadn't told Victoria about Tina. Far too late now. It looked like all his well-laid plans with Victoria could be wiped out in a flash; or in his case, a dodgy contraceptive pill.

He needed a stiff drink.

While Tina tucked into a strawberry truffle desert with a Remy Martin VSOP sauce; he'd suggested the inexpensive three scoop ice cream; she reminded him with a grin she was eating for two now; he drowned his sorrows with three large Jack Daniels.

On the way home, Tina was still excited, she didn't stop talking.

It was a hot evening around ten-fifteen and the windows were down. The steady drone of traffic helped to drown out her constant twittering about wallpapers and new curtains.

'Also we could install a hot tub. Your garden's big enough,' she said. 'My cousin in Canada has one. They're the latest thing,' she informed him.

Guy nodded and pretended to look keen, but he was building up inside. If she didn't shut it, he was going to explode.

Finally, while waiting at traffic lights, Tina dropped another bombshell. 'Guy, darling,' she hugged his arm affectionately. 'Would you mind if my elderly mother came to live with us? At the moment she's in a horrid rented flat. She'll be no trouble and you still have a spare bedroom.' Tina didn't wait for a reply and insisted, 'She could babysit the odd night and it would be cheaper for us in the long run, rather than paying out all that money to have her in an old peoples home.'

Guy could take no more. He clenched his fists in temper and punched the steering wheel. *'Can you just shut the fuck up for one second?'*

Tina pulled away and burst into tears. At that moment, a car drove up alongside. The driver heard the commotion and leaned across to enquire, 'Is everything all alright?'

Guy told him, 'Mind your own business and fuck-off.'

The driver seemed concerned about the distressed woman and tried to engage her in conversation.

Spurred on by the Jack Daniels and with Tina trying to hold him back in tears, crying and yelling, telling him not to be silly; Guy got out of his Jaguar and slammed the door. He shouted to the driver, 'Did you hear what I said?' walking menacingly towards him.

At that moment, the lights changed and with a two-fingered gesture, the Audi roared off.

Guy slid back in next to her and apologised. He put his arm around Tina. 'Sorry, Love. It's just, my flying business is making me stressed out.' He fibbed again. 'I had to get rid of another pilot today because of no work.' He lifted up her head and kissed her. 'You know I love you and I really am looking forward to the baby and your mother coming to stay.'

By the time they'd reached her place she was twittering on again making plans.

As Tina left the car, he told her, 'I'll see you on Wednesday and stay over. We'll have a nice bottle of wine and a takeaway, watch the TV.'

She beamed back a smile.

However, on the way home Guy was thinking. *What am I going to do for fuck sake? Come clean, tell Victoria about Tina. Then what? Stringing her along all this time, she would never forgive me. Then there's her father. It was Vicky who persuaded him to take on Ericson's Para Jump and Skydiving School. And remember, the contract's not signed yet. And another thing, if I was going to have kids, I'd rather have them with Victoria than that gold digging cow.*

He had to act quickly or lose everything just like his father. As he drove, his mind went back to when he was eleven-years old.

His father, after leaving the RAF at the end of the war, ran a successful TV rental company. He had five shops spread out locally. Then gradually the price of televisions came down.

People started buying their own sets instead of renting. One by one, his father had to close the shops. His income wasn't enough to pay the mortgage. The rows at home started between his parents. Then he was pulled out of private school and went to a state owned. Eventually his mother upped and left. After she divorced and took his father to the cleaners, she married a wealthy stockbroker. Her difference in life style was apparent with a seven-bedroomed house in Virginia Water including indoor and outdoor swimming pools and a new Mercedes in the sweeping manicured drive.

With visiting rights, he started seeing her once a week, but that gradually decreased as she clearly became disinterested and grew fonder of her new husband's existing children.

His mother was just another gold digging bitch, he thought, like his own wife had been. She'd upped and left when the recession began to bite, when things started getting tough. Found herself a richer beau.

As his car came to a halt, he was at breaking point again. He began punching the steering wheel, yelling, *'Fucking bitches! - Fucking bitches! - Fucking bitches!'* until his knuckles ached too much. Then he broke down sobbing.

*

That Monday evening, Commander Gregory Potting sat late in his Whitehall office and rolled the business card through his fingers. He looked at it again. ***TINA WARFIELD MASSAGE SERVICES. Book a massage from £5* per Hour. If you want a***

soothing massage from a gorgeous woman, you should know that you've come to the right place. Home visits a speciality. No hidden charges. Telephone Wimbledon 20375.

The secret tap on Guy Ericson's telephone, installed by a fake gas meter reader, had provided the card and the info about his girlfriend's services which included her little side-line working as a call girl.

The Commander knew a decision was imminent. He was thinking, Dr Weise had informed him that Francis Hodder, at the time of his sleeper conditioning, had admitted under hypnosis that he knew Tina Warfield. That was while he was working as the male prostitute Roxanne. However, Dr Weise had also admitted the conditioning of Francis Hodder hadn't been full proof. Mostly because of the deep rooted Roxanne character that already existed. That meant the Roxanne character might remember things. In particular some of the events that happened at Briar Lodge Manor. And in turn, Tina Warfield could have told Francis Hodder about her boyfriend, Guy Ericson.

There was no doubt, Francis Hodder had to expire, and the sooner the better.

There was something else that nagged. Was Ericson's sleeper conditioning now questionable? He could have told Tina about Briar Lodge. Who knows what he could have said to her while drunk or snorting cocaine while having a soothing massage?

The Commander considered his options. Guy Ericson was a MI5 Sleeper. Programmed at Briar Lodge he was their man at Redhill Aerodrome to report back any suspicious IRA or other terrorist activities and eliminate them if need be. Local airfields like Redhill were being watched by the security forces. They knew for terrorists it was only a short hop into London to cause maximum devastation for their cause.

It hadn't been the first time that the Commander had thought about the Iranian pilots under Ericson's charge. *Were they a bunch of terrorist's right under their noses? If they were, where would they attack? Then again, there had been no indication.* All he could do was rely on Ericson.

The Commander sighed. Maybe he was getting too paranoid.

Ericson was now dating their other sleeper, Victoria Buxton. Her brief under conditioning was to kill her father when the time was right. Nevertheless, the Commander knew Tina Warfield had become expendable. And it was a good opportunity to test the assassin potential of Guy Ericson.

Commander Gregory Potting checked his watch. It was coming up to 10:00 p.m. Recent phone taps had highlighted Guy Ericson spent Monday nights in with Victoria Buxton at his house. No doubt a takeaway while looking at the television and then a good screw.

He picked up the green receiver and asked to be put through.

'Is that Guy? Commander Potting here.'

'Speaking.' Guy Ericson hesitated. 'Commander—'

'Listen, Guy. Can you tell Tina Warfield, that Kimberly will be coming for supper?'

'Well yes...' Ericson took on a faraway look and then composed himself. 'I'll do that as ordered.' The telephone clicked and Guy Ericson was left holding the receiver.

*

It was another warm June evening as Guy took the smelly council block lift to Tina's sixth-floor flat. He was sweating profusely and knew he should have left his flying jacket in the car, but then again, in this sort of dodgy area of Wimbledon, would it be there when he arrived back? And flying jackets didn't come cheap.

He'd called round to Tina late on the off chance with a big bunch of flowers. Told her, 'Sorry it's such short notice but, could we do tonight instead of Wednesday? I've got to attend a health and safety pilot meeting at Redhill tomorrow night.' Guy followed up his white lie by adding with a sympathetic face, 'The meetings usually run late with people nattering on, so if you don't mind?'

Tina beamed at the expensive flowers and said, 'Okay by me, come in.' As she closed the door, she gave him an affectionate peck on the cheek and told him, 'Help yourself to a drink while I take a shower and put my face on.'

Guy followed Tina into her poky council flat lounge. He was met by the distinct smell of a curry. The remains of last night's half-eaten korma still lay on the small makeshift dining table along with the cartons it came in. She took the flowers filled a vase and arranged them.

Guy had it planned and this was the moment. As she turned to thank him again, he struck her with a karate chop to the neck on the carotid artery.

Tina collapsed like a sack of potatoes, making him stumble back. As he laid her out on the carpet, she twitched a couple of times and then remained unconscious.

He'd learnt the move in his martial arts training. Hitting her on the carotid sinus at a right angle, fools the body's natural method of monitoring blood pressure. A sharp blow kids the brain to shut down because of the instant surge in blood pressure.

Guy checked for a pulse and it was still healthy. That was good. He had work to do. Then panic overtook him. Guy stepped back and put a hand to his mouth. 'Dear, God, what am I doing?' He started shaking. *This is madness. I can't kill her, I can't go through with it. There's still time. Wait until she comes round then apologise. Tell her you saw a wasp on her neck and struck out as a nervous reaction. Better to stop now than get caught. I don't fancy slopping out every day for the next thirty-years in a stinking prison cell or even worse, getting raped or gangbanged in the showers.* Guy closed his eyes and clenched his fists. He tried to compose himself. *What's the alternative? Losing Vicky, the loveliest thing in the world. Losing the most lucrative contract I'm about to sign with her dad. Having him, a millionaire, as my father-in-law with a seat on the board and all the trimmings that go with it, or carry on working for peanut wages as a flight instructor for Bristow Helicopters.* For once, the high life was in Guy's reaching distance. His boat had finally sailed in. All he had to do was complete the final push.

He took some deep breaths. He looked at his hands. They'd stopped shaking. There was something else in the back of his mind, more important, why he had to complete this. He looked vacant into space for a second and whispered, 'Kimberly.' It was then he decided, there was no turning back.

First, he must find her diary. It had his number.

Guy began searching, and within a short time he sat down with it and flicked through to check if he was mentioned anywhere. Then he carefully tore out the page that had his phone number, as neatly as possible to make it look like it wasn't missing. Guy checked the rest of the place for wall pads, calendars, address books and anything else that could identify him. He made his way to the telephone in the hall. There was no answering machine and he'd been careful only to phone her from a call box when he was two-timing his wife. Now he was grateful. No phone records linking back to him.

Using her handwriting, he forged a suicide note in her diary - ending it all. It briefly stated, she couldn't face bringing a baby into a world like this. The shame of not knowing who the father was. Sorry to let everyone down. He left the diary open on the coffee table.

With his handkerchief, Guy retraced his steps wiping everything he could have touched. Then he gingerly opened the balcony door and peered out.

It was quiet as he parted the washing on the line and looked over the rail. He went back inside and dragged Tina to the entrance. He went out to double check. It was dark now and all the kids he'd seen earlier on their bikes or kicking footballs were hopefully indoors.

Guy scanned the other balconies. He could hear faint music and conversations, possibly televisions competing with one another. With no one around, he quickly dragged Tina to the edge of the balcony. Lifting her under the arms, he hauled her up so she was hanging over the rail.

Guy checked himself and waited. Listening out, peering into the dark.

Tina hung there like a collapsed drunk.

With the all clear, he pulled down the washing line and made a noose. Then Guy slipped it over Tina's neck. He gauged the length and tied the other end to the balcony railing. As he stooped to grab her legs she kicked out in reflex. Tina was coming round. She started moaning. He gripped her waist and tried to lift her, but she was fighting with him, trying to push him away. Tina clutched his jacket and held on. He tried to prize her fingers off but she scratched him on the wrist.

Although groggy, it was as if she knew she was in a life and death situation.

Guy cursed under his breath, 'Don't fuck with me, you Bitch.'

Tina started yelling. He had to shut her up. In panic, he punched her on the chin and her head snapped back, making her somersault over the rail.

In that instant, he saw her drop and then suddenly the head snapped back and he heard the crack as her neck broke.

Guy ducked down and waited. Then he tentatively leant over the balcony rail. The body of Tina twitched a few times and swung widely for a while and then began to settle down to a gentle sway while slowly spinning at the same time.

Guy continued looking with his heart pounding, breathing in sharp snatches of air, expecting to see lights coming on, people on balconies, a crowd forming below; but nothing.

He went back inside and pulled the curtains. Guy switched off the lights. He stood there shaking, thinking what he'd done. He took deep breaths, 'Come on, pull yourself together,' he muttered.

Guy looked through the security peephole - no movement. He put his ear to the front door - no sounds. He eased the front door open and slipped outside. As it clunked shut, Guy winced.

He made his way to the lift and pressed the arrow for down. He heard the doors instantly close below him to move up. That was good, it wasn't in use. When it arrived, he got in and feverishly pushed the button for the doors to close.

It seemed an eternity all the way down. Guy had his finger on the G button the whole time, in case anyone wanted to get in. Whether it made any difference he wasn't sure.

As the doors opened he covered his face. He needn't have bothered. No one was around as Guy made his way by foot out of the estate. He didn't use the car park. He'd read in the newspapers that some council estates were installing cameras. Guy wasn't chancing it.

He'd parked in a quiet cul-de-sac a quarter of a mile away. As he approached, he cast a quick glance. The wheels were still there. No damage or bottles jammed under the tyres.

Guy slid into the soft leather seats of his Jaguar and gave out a sigh of relief. Then he drove home and within thirty-five minutes he was nursing a large Jack Daniels.

CHAPTER TWENTY-THREE

Kenny Buxton, surrounded by his staff, sat his short fat balding fifty-eight year old self in his expensive leather padded chair at the head of the boardroom table and felt pleased.

On the second weekend in June he was planning to hold a two-day all singing all dancing, band playing, bunting flying, bubbly flowing, *One Day Wonders Ltd* debut for his new skydiving franchise at Redhill Aerodrome.

He was really excited about this one. Thousands of leaflets had been printed and distributed including newspaper and local radio advertising. For his promotion he had engaged a professional skydiving team with coloured smoke canisters, a fire-fighting exercise involving helicopters, a jazz band with a food marquee, rides for children, free T-shirts, badges, caps, the whole works. All with the possibility of being on the TV local news roundup.

Kenny Buxton had been shrewd. Guy Ericson had informed him about the film stunt scenes that were going to be carried out at Redhill Aerodrome for the Hollywood blockbuster that was being made. Kenny Buxton realised he could incorporate this into his two day promotion with a spectator viewing area at a safe distance.

It was a week before the big launch and Guy was seated next to the chairman, Kenny Buxton.

Now part of the team and newly promoted to business director, it was Guy's first board meeting since his own company had been incorporated into *One Day Wonders Ltd.*

At that moment he was flavour of the month, number one future son-in-law and a key cog in the company's decision making or so he would like to think.

Guy with his expertise would be in charge of the flying operation with a brief to build up new business at other airfields and outlets. Although he was excited with his new position he still delayed handing in his notice as flight chief to Bristow Helicopters Ltd. He wasn't going to tempt providence. He'd wait until he married Victoria, until he was part of the family. And then he'd tell Bristow's where to stick it.

Guy bathed in smiles and success although he knew it was his engagement to Vicky that made it all possible. He had to make sure his link to prosperity and the good-life was not jeopardised in any way.

The thing with Tina was just a distant memory. It had been two weeks. Local newspapers had called it a sad suicide. The note left in the diary confirmed it. Pregnant as well they hastened to add. However, there was just one thing that didn't add up. Why the Crimewatch appeal? Why did they want to know the last movements of a suicidal masseuse? For what reason? The Diary said it all. Guy felt secure in the knowledge that none of his friends or colleagues had seen them together.

Kenny Buxton glanced in annoyance at the empty chair and then at his watch. The chairman's team consisted of his PA, Beryl Knox, who always took the minutes at meetings and his daughter Victoria with her fiancé Guy. Then there was Graham Lumley the finance manager with Jim Dalton the events manager and Roger Brooks from sales.

Kenny Buxton asked dryly, 'Has anyone seen Graham?'

At that moment, the door opened and a flustered Graham Lumley carrying a buff folder entered the boardroom. 'Sorry I'm late, Sir. Just finished those figures you asked for.' He handed the paperwork to the chairmen and then took his place at the end of the table fumbling for his glasses and dropping the spectacle case with a clatter on the polished table.

'Thank you, Graham, if you could be more punctual it would be a help,' Kenny Buxton replied with a sarcastic bite.

Graham could see someone new sitting in his usual chair next to the chairman.

'As you were late, Graham, I'll briefly explain again. This is Guy Ericson who has joined us as business director.' The chairman beamed a smile at Guy and then he continued. 'Guy is bringing with him a wealth of knowledge and experience to help our company expand in the events sport of skydiving and parachute jumping. We will be using Guy's operation at Redhill Aerodrome to launch our new business location.'

Kenny Buxton beamed another smile at his daughter and Guy sitting together. 'And I would like to take this opportunity to add, that very soon, he is also going to be my future son-in-law.' At that news, everybody applauded and offered their congratulations to the couple.

Graham Lumley clapped half-heartedly with a sick expression. So that was the reason he'd lost his chair next to Kenny Buxton. Victoria's fiancé was filling it.

Graham cast a glance at her fiancé. He knew he'd seen him before somewhere but couldn't put his finger on it

'Now, let's get down to business.' The chairman was back to serious. 'As you all know, this weekend is our big opening at Redhill Aerodrome. I know I can count on you all to have everything in place so it runs smoothly.'

Everyone nodded in agreement.

'We've got a lot of local press with photographers coming down so it's important we get a good crowd attending.' The chairman picked up some leaflets with *FREE RIDES AND JUMPS* boldly written across them. He continued, 'Using Guy's suggestion,' he smiled at Guy, 'this Saturday and Sunday we wet the public's appetite so all the rides will be free. This includes helicopter, skydiving, parachuting and hot air ballooning. And for the kids we've got a bouncy castle, a carousel ride plus a helter-skelter.'

The chairman paused, fiddled with his notes and then continued. 'Now, where the parachuting is concerned, we've hired some extra instructors for the pre-jump training so

I expect all of you to have a go as well to encourage the members of your respective departments. Remember, in this company we lead from the front.'

Kenny Buxton picked up a clutch of leaflets and handed them out to everyone. 'Take these back to your offices and get your staff to sign up including friends and relations.' With a broad smile he added, 'Remember, it's a free weekend so there's no excuse.'

With around forty staff in the building including maintenance, Kenny Buxton was counting on most of them to book a parachute jump in case of a slow response from the public. Although it was free, he didn't want to be left with egg on his face. Even so, he wasn't unduly worried.

Guy took the floor and spoke as a man with experience and assured them all, 'It's not everybody's cup of tea to throw themselves out of an aeroplane. These things start slow and generally pick up as the day goes on.' He wanted to sound optimistic and finished off by telling them, 'Once word gets around on the Saturday they'll be coming in their droves on the Sunday.'

Graham Lumley had a sinking feeling. He hated heights but he didn't want to look a big sissy in front of sir, and especially Victoria and her grinning boyfriend. And there was something else. He just couldn't put his finger on it.

The board meeting had run on late until six-thirty. As everybody rose to get up, Kenny Buxton reminded them eagerly, 'Don't forget it's my birthday and I'm in the chair. I want to see you all at Harry's Wine Bar in the high street for a drink. I'm sure you can all manage one before you shoot off home.' He looked at them for confirmation.

They chanted back, 'Thanks, Mister Buxton.'

Most people knew from experience, it wasn't advisable to disregard an invite from the chairman. Kenny Buxton took things personally.

There'd been members of staff that hadn't bothered with the odd Christmas party in the boardroom or attend a choral evening with his wife performing when she was alive. And their positions were quickly filled with members of staff who did attend dull Christmas parties in the boardroom and clap enthusiastically at his wife's awful singing during a choral evening.

*

Harry's Wine Bar was the in place for suits that time in the evening. The happy hour from six-thirty helped as well.

The seven of them found the only available table near the big bulky television on the bar counter. Thankfully the volume was low on the news programme being shown, although it didn't matter. The noise from the bar was easily drowning it out.

While Kenny Buxton had the full attention of Beryl, Jim and Roger, telling them a lewd joke he'd heard from his golf club pals, Graham could only pretend he was listening. Finally, while grinning in earnest at the punchline, he was furtively glancing at Victoria and Guy. God, she was beautiful, he thought. If only it had worked out with her. However, the couple only had eyes for each other.

How he envied Guy. Victoria had her arm around his shoulder. Graham sneaked a look while she nibbled Guy's ear. If only that was his ear. That bastard had it all; on the board of directors, negotiating a healthy business merger with Kenny Buxton and soon to be marrying his daughter. What more could a man want he thought.

It wasn't fair. He'd worked for twelve loyal years at *One Day Wonders Ltd*. Couldn't remember having a day off sick. Started as an office junior and worked his way up. God knows how many evenings he'd stayed late for sir - finishing this off, finishing that off. Getting figures ready for an early morning meeting - and for what? To be passed over for the new kid on the block who hadn't been with the company for more than a couple of months.

His mother being a single parent wanted him to be a success. She'd worked for years at various cleaning jobs. Scrimping and scraping so he could get a decent education. Get to grammar school and then college. She still cleaned part time even now. She'd been on a crusade with her son, having had a drunk for a husband who died of liver failure when Graham was ten.

At thirty-six years old, Graham Lumley was a bit of a loner. In fact, he still lived with his mother. He wasn't proud of the fact. He'd rather have his own place with its independence. However, he'd never had many girlfriends and wearing thick glasses didn't help. Graham always felt it was a turnoff where women were concerned. So, with nobody to share and split the rent, there was no point in moving out, his mother would say. And mother was always right. Even telling him to set his cap at the governor's daughter.

Mother had smirked when he'd told her Victoria was getting married. That was his chance and now he'd blown it, she'd said. Told him he wasn't pushy enough.

Graham looked around the bar. He detected a heavy mix of aftershaves and perfumes coming off groups of people talking loudly over one another to make themselves heard.

Harry's Wine Bar in Reigate High Street was decorated in traditional Bodega style with lots of dark oak ceiling beams with a collection of wine barrels stacked up against one wall and Spanish carved tables and chairs sitting on rustic floor tiles.

Over the top of the service counter there were six attractive Art Nouveau leaded light shades of yellow and green that were spaced out its entire length. Although the décor tried to give a fashionable atmosphere, the chairs were hard. Graham wriggled with discomfort. He wanted to leave, he couldn't stand the place. If that wasn't bad enough, he was having to sit there and have his face rubbed in it with those two love birds all over each other while he was having to nurse an orange juice at the same time. Mother disapproved of drinking for obvious reasons and gave him a lecture if she smelt it on his breath.

Graham was bored. Everybody else was talking. He glanced at the dominating presence of the bulky television.

The news announcer's lips were moving but he couldn't hear a word. It switched to a block of flats with a close-up of a balcony. The headline on the screen: *New evidence. The Surrey Police Constabulary have just released new information concerning the death of Tina Warfield. Skin samples taken from under the victim's fingernails indicate she may have been murdered. These are believed to have come from her killer...*

Graham tried to read the rest of the news bulletin from where he was sitting but the print was too small. He pulled out his glasses and gave them a wipe. Now he had a clearer picture. Then a photo of a young woman appeared. At that moment, Guy stood up to leave. He kissed Victoria, told her he was off to his martial arts class but he'd see her later. They'd have dinner.

As Guy turned to go, he froze for a second at the television. Graham saw his face drain then he quickly composed himself. He shook Kenny Buxton's hand, waved to the others and was gone.

Graham looked at the woman's photo. Victoria was saying something to him. He glanced and saw her lips moving but his mind was on the television.

She leaned over and pulled his arm playfully. 'Sorry to interrupt, but have we been that boring,' she said with a smile.

He looked at her, God, she was gorgeous, that lucky bastard. 'Sorry, Vicky, I was miles away.'

'I'm only kidding.' She looked at the television, the woman's photo. 'Were you a witness to her car accident or something?' Victoria teased.

Then it came to him. At the traffic lights. That shit with the nutter, having a go at his wife or girlfriend whatever. The woman yelling at him, Gus or Guy something, calling him back. The big ape ignoring her, coming to sort him out. That was it. Jesus Christ, that's where he saw her and Guy.

She was waiting for an answer.

Graham turned to the television then back to Victoria. He leaned forward and held her arm. 'I...I was just.' What the hell should he do, tell her? 'Victoria, there's...there's something you should know.' She looked at his hand on her arm as though it was something alien. Graham withdrew it as though he'd been scalded. 'Vicky, it's about Guy. I saw him with that woman who hanged herself from the balcony,' he nodded to the screen. 'They were together in a car. Having a row or something.'

'What! What do you mean?' She looked at him in astonishment.

'Some time back at traffic lights. I pulled up alongside them. They were arguing. The window was down. It was all very quick. She was crying, upset. I said something and he got annoyed. He got out the car, a Jaguar I think. Started walking towards me. I didn't hang around, just drove off.'

'You're mad; it must have been someone else.'

'No I'm sure it was them.'

'Oh, you're sure now,' she said laughing.

'Seriously, Vicky, I'd swear it–'

'Was it dark?' She interrupted.

'Well...yes, but I got a clear–'

CHAPTER TWENTY-THREE

'Now, Graham, be honest with me,' she teased. 'Were you wearing your glasses?'

'Well, no…I don't when driving at night but—'

'Ah, people have been hung for less, Graham,' she teased him again.

'Vicky, I'm not joking, it was definitely Guy and that woman.'

'Graham, don't be ridicules.' Victoria had turned serious. 'What would my Guy be doing with a woman that's killed herself?'

'Look, should I go to the police or something, Vicky?' He said anxiously. 'They're looking for witnesses.'

'Graham, you're over reacting, calm down,' she said. 'It was dark, late at night, without your glasses,' she chided.

'I'm not a fool, Vicky, I know what I saw.' Graham leant towards her. 'I mean, be honest, Vicky, what do you know about this Guy?'

'Oh, so that's what this is,' Victoria scoffed. 'Lover boy, a bit jealous? Can't stand a bit of competition. Look, Graham, we went out a few times, you were keen I wasn't. That's life. We move on.'

'Don't be stupid, Vicky,' Graham said angrily. 'That's got nothing to do with it.' He stood up. 'It's my duty as a witness to at least report it and let the police sort it out.'

'Sit down, you idiot,' she shouted. A couple of people looked over and Victoria quickly smiled pretending to be joking. 'I said, sit down,' she spoke softly through clenched teeth while casting a furtive glance, left and right.

Graham did as he was told. She was still a director and the governor's daughter.

'Listen, Graham.' She leaned in. 'Whatever your ultimate reasons for all this, I don't know. But be warned. I'm getting married to Guy, whether you like it or not and the last thing we need, including this company, is bad publicity right now at our wedding and the new skydive launch. I can assure you my father wouldn't be too pleased. There's too much at stake riding on this, Graham.' She checked she wasn't being overheard and then carried on. 'If you cause a smear and damage our reputation with all this nonsense, we can always find ourselves a new finance manager. Do I make myself clear?'

He nodded and swallowed hard.

Victoria stood up to leave. 'You know, Graham, why I'm marrying Guy?' she said with a sneer.

He looked at her with frightened eyes.

'Because he's a man, not a mummy's boy like you.' She brushed passed him and then waved to the others and kissed her father goodbye.

CHAPTER TWENTY-FOUR

'Do you know what that four-eyed prat wanted to do?' She laughed. 'Go to the police.'

'You've got to be joking,' Guy replied, nuzzling Victoria's neck. 'Sounds like he wants to sour our day because he's jealous.'

'That's what I told him,' she said a little boisterous. 'And when I threatened him with dad, he shut up like a clam. I let him know I was marrying a man, not a mouse like him. If he mentions it again I'll tell him he's too afraid to leave his own mother, let alone parachute out of an aeroplane.'

'Well done, you Little Tiger.' Guy nuzzled her neck again. 'No one messes with our Vicky.'

She laughed and cuddled up to him.

They were sitting in a cosy booth at Botticelli's waiting for their table, each nursing a glass of Sancerre. As it was Guy's favourite Italian, he wanted to impress Victoria again and fortunately this was on his account with them. He could settle up later. He didn't mind laying out a few bob, considering what was going to fall into his lap after the wedding.

He looked at Victoria and couldn't believe his luck. She smiled back.

'Your table is ready, Mister Ericson.' The suited Maitre d' grinned and then beckoned a waiter to take them to a quiet corner position.

They started with fish soup and foie gras terrine accompanied by a 2007 Chablis from the Domaine Laroche. Then on to a grilled lobster each with a shared salad. The food looked beautiful set amongst glinting silverware and the romantic table candelabra.

Guy knew he was pushing the boat out, and why not; knowing he would soon have the new Mrs Victoria Ericson on his arm.

They toasted each other and as they held hands across the table, Guy winced as she squeezed.

'What's up?' She asked him, a little surprised.

'Oh nothing. You just grabbed my oven burn,' he joked.

Victoria saw the edge of a skin graze protruding out from under the cuff of his jacket.

'It's an occupational hazard for us bachelors.'

'It won't be for long,' she said, and kissed his hand with a big smile.

As the waiter approached with their chocolate tart and crème Brule desert, Guy excused himself to the men's washroom.

The elderly concierge looked up and greeted him. 'Good evening, Mister Ericson.'

'Good evening, Arthur.' Guy moved to a fancy green sink with gold taps and washed his sticky fingers - the down side of cracking lobster claws. He dried them on the towel and fussed with his new Louis Vuitton tie – a purchase from Harrods.

Arthur came up behind him and fussed over the shoulders of his jacket with a fine clothes brush. 'Hope you're enjoying your meal, Mister Ericson.'

'Yes, thank you, Arthur.'

Arthur continued brushing him down. 'Oh, by the way, Mister Ericson, please accept my condolences for your partner. I saw it on the news. Terrible...terrible tragedy, Sir, and one so young to commit suicide...' Arthur discretely tapered off his commiserations and continued with the brushing.

Guy stiffened in the mirror. He was about to deny all; tell him he had the wrong person. However, Arthur seemed very sure. Mustn't draw attention. Guy decided to probe. 'You'd a... You'd seen her before, Arthur?' He asked tentatively.

Arthur stopped brushing and looked at him in the mirror in surprise. 'Only with you, Sir, in the restaurant.'

Guy relaxed. 'Do you know what, Arthur,' he turned to him with a smile. 'You're the third person to tell me that. Even my sister was astonished when she saw the news and the likeness to herself with the picture that was shown on the television of the poor woman that killed herself.'

'Oh, my goodness, Sir...your sister?' Arthur was gobsmacked. 'I never realised. I'm so sorry to have alarmed you, Mister Ericson. You could have knocked me down with a feather, Sir. Your sister you say...The likeness is uncanny.'

'That's okay, Arthur. I saw the news myself and I must admit there is a likeness. My sister Jean even said, apart from height and hair colour they could have been twins.' Guy continued fussing with his tie in the mirror, then took out his comb and titivated with his dark wavy hair.

Arthur carried on brushing his shoulders. 'Yes of course, Sir, how silly of me to make such a mistake.' Arthur seemed flustered. 'Again, Sir, please accept my apologies.' Then he hesitated. 'I...I would be grateful, Mister Ericson, if you didn't mention my silly error to the Maître d.'

Guy took out his wallet and pulled a twenty-pound note. He thought for a moment and then said, 'It was a simple mistake to make, but I'll keep mum if you keep mum?' He laughed. 'And if you hear any staff mentioning the likeness you can put them right.' Guy patted Arthur on the shoulder and tucked the money into his breast pocket. 'If you could remember to tell anyone that asks, you saw me dining here with my sister on the evening of June the eighth, I'm sure the Maître d will never have to know.'

Arthur swallowed hard and said, 'Of course, Mister Ericson, anything you say, Sir.'

Guy gave him an affectionate hug. 'Now you treat yourself and your good lady to a nice fish and chip supper and a bottle of stout each,' he joked.

Arthur looked relieved and clutched Guy's hand. 'Thank you, Mister Ericson, God bless you, Sir.'

As Guy left the washroom, he stopped at the door, turned and put a finger to his lips.

CHAPTER TWENTY-FOUR

The old man grinned and did the same.

On his way back to the table he realised that was a near miss. Guy did in fact have a sister that lived locally, although they weren't in touch a great deal. Still, if push came to shove, she'd cover for him with an alibi for the night he got rid of Tina. He'd certainly make it worth her while just to get him out of a sticky situation. And of course she didn't have to know the real truth.

Arthur on the other hand wouldn't be giving him any more grief; he valued his job too much. However, what about that idiot Graham. Graham had seen them together. He was a witness to his involvement with Tina. He'd seen them arguing. He wasn't going to keep quiet. Then what?

He was thinking as he approached a smiling Victoria, what she had said. He was too afraid to leave his own mother, let alone parachute out of an aeroplane.

*

'She said that to you? And what did you say?' Graham's seventy-year old mother was on his back again.

'What could I say? She threatened me with her father,' Graham exclaimed.

They were having dinner in the kitchen and surrounded by bright yellow Formica tops and units with polystyrene ceiling tiles and fluorescent lighting.

His mother was a thin short sprightly woman with bobbed grey hair and flat features on a serious looking face. Wearing her floral apron she'd cooked him his favourite, shepherd's pie and chips, always on a Friday. 'She can't stop you going to the Police. It's your civil duty as a citizen,' she said. 'And what if this bloke she's marrying did kill that woman or something? What if he kills *her* later on? He could be a nutcase. Do you want that on your conscience?'

'I know but–'

'Ungrateful, Bitch,' his mother interrupted. 'You, trying to be helpful, warning her. You should've given her a mouthful there and then.'

'I know, Mother, but—'

'And after all the years you've worked there. That's what they think of you.' She was getting annoyed with him. 'You've got to tell her father, straight away. You've got to be forceful, Graham. Let them know they can't walk all over you.'

'I know but—'

'Listen to me, Graham.' His mother was on his case, well and truly. 'This is your big chance to shine. Have you spoken to this Guy person about it?'

'Well no I haven't, but he's only going to deny it all.'

'Okay, so we know for sure he's got something to hide.'

'Well yes, I saw his face when he saw the woman on the television. Like he'd seen a ghost. I certainly wouldn't like to tangle with him. Rumours have it he's into martial arts and all that.'

'Martial arts. My God,' his mother said astonished. 'He could be a trained assassin. They can kill people with a single chop.'

'Well that's another reason I don't want a confrontation,' Graham replied. 'I rather like being alive, thank you.'

'Look, you have to speak to her father,' she said again. 'It's the only way. Convince him his daughter could be in danger. Make it clear you have to go to the police. Then if this person she's marrying is guilty, he'll be indebted to you for ever for saving his daughter. There's nothing he wouldn't offer you including a directorship. Even his daughter might come round. See you in a different light. A real man, Graham. But you have to stand on your own two feet. Bang the fist on the table.' As she said it, she did just that, startling him and making the plates jump.

'OK, Mother,' Graham sighed, 'whatever you say.'

*

He knocked on the door with the fancy brass plaque that read KENNY BUXTON. (CHAIRMAN).

'Come in.'

'Sorry to disturb you, Sir, but there's something important I want to talk to you about.' Graham, while detecting the stale smell of cigar smoke, had plucked up courage and was standing in Kenny Buxton's spacious office in front of a huge expensive highly polished desk.

Sitting behind it in a reproduction leather studded swivel chair, Kenny Buxton was going over the final plans for the big launch day. On the wall behind was an enormous portrait of himself receiving the chain of office as one of the previous

Mayors' of Reigate. Looking up with a half-smile he said, 'Yes, Graham, what is it?'

'Well, Sir...it's about Guy Ericson.'

'What about him?' Kenny Buxton's face changed to serious. His daughter had told him about the exchange they'd had in Harry's Bar. Victoria had convinced her father it was all to do with Graham's jealousy at being passed over in love and her fiancé's promotion to the board. She'd also told him, Graham could be a spiteful bastard and should be watched.

Victoria had been to Harvard Business School and qualified with an MBA while her father had worked his way up with no frills or education. However, he valued his daughter's input and expertise in marketing and promoting a reputable brand image and the importance of a good reputation with customers. And Kenny Buxton wasn't going to have that reputation soured or put to the test, especially now at this critical launch stage by some love lost geek who wanted to get even with the new boyfriend.

'I know this Guy Ericson chap was involved with the girl on the news. The one that died, Sir. I saw them together having a quarrel the night before her death.'

'Yes - yes, Graham, I know. My daughter told me all about it.'

Kenny Buxton gave a reluctant sigh and slowly rose from his desk. He approached Graham and put a friendly arm around his shoulder. 'Look, Graham, old chap. I've had a word with Guy and he assured me it wasn't him. Guy confirmed on the evening of June 8th, the night you said you saw him, he and his sister were at Botticelli's in Banstead Village. It's a well-known Italian restaurant, I've used it myself. Guy has an independent witness to prove he was there until eleven-thirty - the concierge in the men's washroom. Last week I was dining there with my wife. I had a word with the elderly gentleman. He remembers seeing Guy coming in late to wash his hands. He confirmed the time.'

'I know what I saw, Sir.'

'You think you saw him.' Kenny Buxton smiled and hugged Graham's shoulders affectionately. 'The light can play funny tricks of a night-time.' He lapsed into thought for a second and then said, 'Many years ago I remember once on a train pulling out from Kings Cross. Just for a moment, I saw my father standing on the platform. I tell you, Graham, it was him. I would have put a month's wages on it. But it couldn't have been. He'd been dead some years before.' He patted Graham's shoulder to make him see reason. 'You see, it must have been his double, someone very much like him. Just like you saw on the night.'

Graham was adamant. 'Sir, for some reason that Guy Ericson is lying, and if he's got a witness then he's paid them to lie as well.'

Kenny Buxton quickly removed his arm from Graham's shoulder. 'Are you saying my daughter is lying as well, Lumley? She confirms Guy was with his sister that evening.'

'Well...Err, no Sir, but perhaps he forced her to lie. He might have a hold over her. Your daughter's life may be in danger, Sir.'

'Now listen, Lumley.' Kenny Buxton eyeballed him with a mean stare. 'I've been patient with you so far but these accusations have to stop. Enough is enough.' Then he lightened with a sweet smile. 'Of course, if this is a problem you can't work with, you can always leave. And we'll just have to find ourselves a new finance manager. Am I making myself understood, Lumley?'

Graham's Adam's apple twitched nervously. 'I do understand, Sir.'

'Good, it would be a shame to lose someone as yourself. We need you on the team, Graham.' He put his arm around his shoulder again. 'Look, Old Man, there's a saying, never bite the hand that feeds you.' He laughed and slapped Graham playfully on the back. 'I know I can count on you, Graham. Remember, we've got a big weekend coming up and the company has laid out a lot of capital. We want it to run as smooth as possible, don't we?'

Graham stared at the floor. He said dejectedly, 'Yes, Sir, of course, Sir.'

'Good man, that's the spirit.' Still with his arm around his shoulder he walked Graham to the door. 'Oh, by the way, while you're here, I've arranged a board meeting at three tomorrow afternoon for all heads of departments, just to finalise a few things for the big opening.'

'I'll be there, Sir.'

'Good, Man,' Kenny Buxton said closing his office door.

Graham stood outside for a while feeling frustrated, knowing his mother would have called him, "A big girls blouse."

CHAPTER TWENTY-FIVE

The boardroom was buzzing with personnel sitting around the long highly polished yew table, each of them clutching their agenda notes and instructions for the big day tomorrow.

Kenny Buxton as Chairman opened the meeting with, 'Good afternoon, All.'

They all replied back, 'Good afternoon, Sir.'

Graham made sure he wasn't late. Demoted to the far end of the table, he could only envy those people who filled the important chairs near the Chairman.

To Kenny Buxton's right, which should have been his place, sat Guy Ericson. To the left sat his daughter Victoria, looking as beautiful as ever. Next to her sat Beryl his PA taking the minutes and then Jim the events manager and Roger from sales. The remaining people around the table were made up of pilots, jump instructors, a hot air balloonist and a representative from a security company who would be providing staff in uniforms to control the public and monitor the no-go areas. There was also someone from the Saint John Ambulance Brigade who would be manning a tent in the middle of the airfield.

Graham fumbled for his glasses as he flicked through some papers and figures he'd prepared for sir.

Kenny Buxton looked down at his notes and said, 'Now, in accordance with BBC suggestions, I've prepared an itinerary for the jumps tomorrow that will tie-in with their outside broadcasting for the television news roundup. This will be shown on the television at six o'clock tomorrow evening and hopefully on Sunday as well. We need as much television coverage as possible, so it means an early start tomorrow morning for the sky dive and parachute training.'

The Chairman looked down at his notes again and picked up a pad. 'From the booking sheets you all returned it says here we've got forty-seven people signed for the tandem skydive and thirty-six for the parachute jumps. They've all been sent their schedule with times so that's amazing everyone, well done and many thanks for that. It gives us a bit of breathing space to know we've got people available when the TV cameras are rolling.' He smiled and put his hands together in prayer. 'Let's just hope the rest of Joe Public turns up tomorrow and Sunday and the weather stays good.'

All of them said, 'Here - here,' in agreement.

Kenny Buxton nodded to his new business director with a smile. 'Now I'll hand you over to Guy here who will go through tomorrow's timetable.'

Guy stood up and moved over to the large map pinned on the notice board. He pointed to the airfield plan and the area they had rented for the weekend activities. Like a sergeant major with his stick, he drew their attention to the key areas for take-off and landing where skydiving, parachuting and ballooning would operate. He also pointed out the location of the *One Day Wonders* reception for advance bookings.

Again, Guy went over the day's events and their times including the aerial skydiving display with coloured smoke and the filming of the action scenes for the ongoing Hollywood blockbuster.

Kenny Buxton was grateful that Guy had managed to get permission from the film director Dimitri Irwin to allow the action scenes for the Hollywood blockbuster that were being filmed, to be incorporated as part of his show. A roped off area had been designated at a safe distance for viewing. This was over at the fire-fighting area so the public could watch helicopters pour gasoline from dangling buckets onto seated mannequins and then see them set alight from dropped flares.

Guy continued. 'The instructors will take care of the tandem skydives while I'll take care of the parachute jumps. Now I've organised six teams of six with the department heads being a team leader.'

Graham swallowed. The last thing he wanted to do was jump out of an aeroplane. He wouldn't even go up a ladder. His mother nagged him once to give the bedroom windows a wipe over. He got to the ninth rung and froze. She had to get a neighbour to help him down.

Guy handed out the forms with the teams on, to each department head. As Graham received his, just for a second their eyes met and Guy gave him a sweet mocking smile.

Graham shuddered inside. The eyes he'd looked into were soulless eyes. Like a dead trout on a fishmonger's slab. Glassy and staring with that lifeless grin.

Guy carried on. 'Can team leaders make sure their members are at the reception marquee by nine-thirty sharp tomorrow morning please, so the jump kits and helmets can be issued according to size and then we'll proceed with training. Static line training will take up to about six-hours for your first jump, so please be patient. This will encompass familiarisation and fitting of parachute equipment, canopy control and flight drills, reserve chute drills, parachute landing fall, emergency landing procedures, malfunctions of reserve chute drills, abnormal landings procedure and finally a written test.' Guy paused, 'Any questions?'

Graham swallowed again. *What the fuck did he mean by abnormal landings? Hitting the ground at a hundred miles per hour?* Graham was too afraid to ask. He looked at the form he'd been handed. His name clearly written at the top in bold capitals as team leader with the names of his department subordinates underneath. How on earth was he going to get out of this and still show face? He could of course go sick. Just not turn up. Ring in to sir, coughing and spluttering over the phone with the twenty-four hour flu. Problem was he hadn't had a day off sick for the last twelve years. He'd made a rod for his own back. And it could be a bad career move for sure if Kenny Buxton smelt a rat on the eve of his big day. Probably think he was boycotting the show because of Guy and his daughter. Then it would be personal. He'd been warned at their private meeting.

Beryl the PA put up her hand.

'Yes, Beryl?'

'How high will we be jumping?'

Guy joked with her, 'High enough for a fantastic view, Beryl, weather permitting. And they say it's going to be warm and sunny tomorrow.'

A few titters went around the room while Graham was thinking, *shit, if only the weather could change. A severe gale force nine would do it with a hurricane thrown in. Just my luck it was going to be a nice weekend.*

'Joking aside, Beryl.' Guy put on his know-it-all hat again while Victoria gave him an admiring smile. 'The Static Line jump is performed at three and a half thousand feet above the ground from one of our Cessna aircraft. Once you exit the plane, a lanyard or static line, which is packed into your main parachute container, will extend its full length and aid in the opening of your main parachute. The free fall time you will experience is approximately seven seconds before your parachute begins deployment. Once your parachute is open you will enjoy your very own solo descent. On the ground, we will be in communication with you via a radio attached to your helmet. This is to guide you to the target area which you will clearly see coming down, and to make sure you enjoy every second of your parachute flight. Total time should be around three-minutes. Of course we will be going over these points in more detail tomorrow with your teams.'

Three minutes of pure hell, how lovely, Graham bitched in his mind, *and I just can't wait for you to go over the points in detail tomorrow, Guy, with your starry-eyed fiancé looking on.*

Kenny Buxton stood up. 'Many thanks for the presentation, Guy. Most informative.' Then he got serious. 'Now listen everyone, remember our company motto, management lead from the front. So I don't want anybody pulling a sickie tomorrow because they're not up to it. Bring all your friends and get them to skydive.'

Jim Dalton from events called out, 'We're all behind you, Sir, we'll be there.'

'That's the spirit, everyone,' Kenny Buxton smiled, 'I know I can count on you.'

As the meeting broke up, Guy, Victoria and Graham were the last to leave. To rub salt in, she pulled Guy towards her in an embrace and playfully ruffled his hair. He nuzzled her neck and they broke into giggles. Victoria joked, 'You're not wearing that flying jacket tonight are you? It's all I ever see you in.' She looked down. 'And you've got a button missing. Incorrectly dressed. You could be on a charge for that,' she laughed.

'You're beginning to sound like a nagging housewife already?' he teased, then he kissed her again.

As Graham passed by them, Guy looked over his shoulder and said sarcastically, 'See you tomorrow, Graham, don't be late.'

He looked up embarrassed, 'Err, yes…see you both tomorrow.' He heard their sniggering behind his back as he made his exit.

Guy muttered, 'What an utter Dickhead,' and they broke into laughter while he nuzzled her neck again.

Graham was angry with himself. He knew he should have confronted Guy about that evening he saw him with the woman.

No doubt Victoria had told Guy he stilled lived with his mother. Bet they'd had a few rib ticklers over that one. He imagined them thinking he was a big girl's blouse. A mummy's boy scared of his own shadow. But he'd show them tomorrow. He'd just have to bite the bullet and do the jump. Not let them see his fear.

Sitting in his car, he took off his glasses and switched on the ignition. Then a wave of panic came over him. He buried his head in his hands and started shaking. *The only thing to do is get plastered,* he thought.

His mother was away for the weekend, thank God. That's all he needed, her nagging in his ear. Gone to stay with her sister in Dorking - *That's it, stop off and take a decent bottle of malt whisky home.* Anything to dull the nerves so he could get some sleep through the night. Then have a few nips first thing in the morning before getting on the plane. No one would know. A little bit of Dutch courage didn't hurt anybody.

By ten-thirty that evening, Graham had only eaten half the chicken roast she'd left him in the oven. With the television on, he was on his third large one. Looking at a blurred picture of Shaw Taylor presenting Police 5, Graham topped up with some American Dry. He could hear what he was saying but wasn't taking it in. The picture flashed to a block of flats and then a balcony. After that, a photo of Tina Warfield appeared. Then a close-up of a metal button with a ruler at its side to give it scale. Underneath was a caption giving the button details: Mil-Spec USN G-1 Bronze engraved type – used on flight or military style jackets.

He gazed at the screen lost in thought - what could have been for him and Victoria. Meanwhile, Shaw Taylor appealed to viewers, 'The Surrey Police Constabulary have released new information concerning a uniform style metal button that was recently found at the scene of the crime. They are appealing to anyone who knows somebody out there with a missing button or recognises the button connected to a person with scratch marks on the face or hands. Your help would be most appreciated. Your calls will be treated in the strictest confidence, please telephone Police Five...'

Graham fumbled around for the remote and switched off the television. He took another large swig and put his glass down. He closed his eyes. He was thinking, if only mother could see him now. He'd certainly get it in the neck... Then he opened them. *What did he say? They'd found a brass button or something.* Then he remembered what Vicky had said. The missing button on Guy's flying jacket. *Oh my God it must have been him...*

Seeing double, Graham tried to focus. Should he ring the police and tell them what he knew? He raised himself from the sofa a bit unsteady and plodded to the telephone. He fumbled for his glasses and tried to dial 999. After the third misdial he began to have second thoughts. What if he was wrong? What if it had been a different woman he'd seen Guy with? It was at night and he wasn't wearing his glasses. Then what? He'd look more of an idiot, and more likely an idiot without a job.

Graham replaced the receiver and made his way back to the sofa.

Within minutes, he was snoring amongst some twitches and unintelligible mutterings about mother and nagging.

CHAPTER TWENTY-SIX

By four-thirty in the afternoon, Graham had finished his six-hour static line parachute training. A local television crew looked on and filmed while he queued with his office team and Roger's sales team to board the Cessna Caravan 208B. His harness with the deployment bag felt heavy on him, while the helmet with the radio attached made his head feel like a pendulum rocking back and forth.

With everyone on board, Guy Ericson closed the roll up door. He had delegated himself as the dispatcher - the man by the hatch.

Graham's nerves were jangling as he and eleven others sat on the long bench seat while Guy threaded the static line through the loop in their deployment bags. Graham made sure to sit at the end, to be the last man out. Like himself, he could detect the smell of stale nervous sweat coming off from people.

He didn't like flying. On the rare occasions he'd done so with his mother on economy class to Italy for holidays

- mother liked seeing the sights; coliseum, Vatican, Pisa, Venice and such like - he'd dosed himself up with tranquilizers and chosen an aisle seat away from the window. Even so, those seats had been comfortable with a headrest. Now he was scrunched up, hungry and aching from all that training, feeling like a scared paratrooper about to be dropped over occupied France on his first combat mission.

For his birthday last year his mother had given him a fifty-pence coin concealed in a stainless steel locket to wear around his neck. She'd bought it at a fair. The elderly fortune teller dressed as a gypsy told her it was lucky. It was a bit gaudy, but he wore it so as not to hurt her feelings; and Graham always did what mother wanted. However, now it took on some significance as he fingered it and closed his eyes and whispered a prayer.

With the co-pilot asking everybody to be seated, his colleague switched on the ignition and fired up the Pratt & Whitney single turboprop engine.

Graham with the others clung on to the overhead handrail as the Cessna Caravan bumped its way along the grass until it reached the tarmac of the runway. As it approached the yellow lines of the turn, the pilot radioed to the control tower asking permission for clearance and take off, while informing them the direction they would be taking.

After waiting a short time, to let a helicopter and a light aircraft pass over to land, Graham gritted his teeth as the pilot increased the engine revs to an ear splitting noise. Then the

Cessna accelerated along the tarmac and took off, climbing at a rate of nine-hundred-feet per minute.

Graham knew this was the point of no return. There was no backing out now, certainly not in front of the team passengers on-board. He could just imagine if he did, the behind the back sniggers from his own office or worse still, from Guy and Victoria.

After around four-minutes they levelled out at a height of three-thousand-five-hundred-feet. Graham couldn't relax, the slight turbulence making matters worse. He turned to look out of the passenger window. They were circling; the aerodrome was beneath them. He could see the small planes grouped on the ground.

At that moment, the engine noise increased along with a fierce ice-cold draft as Guy Ericson rolled up the hatch door. This was it.

Guy looked at everyone and gave the thumbs up.

Graham tried to smile, wanted to look brave.

All the jumpers as instructed moved along the bench seat, guiding their deployment bag loop until they were all lined up together by the hatch.

Holding the first jumper, Guy double-checked the harness and loop and then waited for a nod from the co-pilot to confirm they were over the right spot. When it came, Guy patted the jumpers back and with a push, they were gone.

Graham looked out the window and instantly saw their pilot chute inflate and then the main canopy, thrusting them back upwards with a tremendous force. Guy quickly hauled in the static line with the deployment bag attached and then got the next jumper ready. As they quickly shuffled along the bench seat, Graham knew his turn was only seconds away.

He began to feel sick as the queue thinned down. He was last man out. Now he was wishing he could have been the first. Then all of a sudden, it was his turn. He felt the harsh rush of wind on his faced as he stood by the gaping hatch.

Guy grabbed him to get into position.

Graham's head was spinning. It was so surreal. He looked down at the patchwork of green and brown fields separated by hedgerows. It instantly came to him; he remembered his grandfather wore a quilted dressing gown just like it when they visited him in the home.

Guy was saying something. Graham wasn't taking it in. He looked into cold blue lifeless eyes as Guy's face twisted with a cruel smirk. 'Have a nice fall, Graham.'

He looked down and swallowed. In those few seconds, he realised what he meant. *Have a nice fall, Graham.* 'No I don't want to jump, I've changed my mind.' Graham held back but Guy had other ideas. He clung on to Guy's arm, yelling at the pilots for their attention; but they didn't turn round, they couldn't hear with all the noise and the wind.

Guy was forcing him with a look of mean pleasure towards the gaping hatch.

With one hand on Guy's flight jacket lapel and the other clutching the side of the hatch he shouted in his face. 'What do you mean by have a nice fall? It was you, wasn't it? You killed her.'

Guy grinned, forcing him over the edge, 'Too late, you're never going to find out.'

'What do you mean, never going to find out?' Graham was wrestling with him, trying to hold on but it was useless.

Guy was taller and stronger. His fingers now on Graham's neck, trying for a karate pressure point.

Graham shouted again, 'What do you mean, never going to find out?' Then Graham stiffened. The penny suddenly dropped. In training, Guy had assured them all he was a qualified parachute rigger. He always packed his clients parachute. 'Oh, fuck! Oh, Shit!' Graham started screaming at the pilots for help but they still couldn't hear. Guy's thumb was digging into his neck. He was beginning to feel light headed. Graham's grip was slipping off the side of the hatch, the ice-cold wind cutting into his face.

Guy turned his head towards the pilots; he had to be quick in case they looked round. With his free hand, he started punching Graham in the stomach.

Graham coughed as he was winded, trying to fight back, holding on to Guy's jacket, hitting him with just his elbow.

Then Guy took an almighty swing and hit Graham square on the chin.

He felt brief pain with stars, together with a tremendous rush of cold air. Graham was falling, then an instant surge as the main canopy opened tugged him back up.

He felt groggy from the blow but the adrenalin racing through him was bringing him quickly round. He glanced up, 'Thank, God,' he cried out as the huge parachute loomed over his head.

Graham relaxed a little, whatever Guy had planned was not working; however, the sooner he was back on terra firma the better. Then he heard a voice, 'You're doing just great, from where we're looking you've dropped just over a thousand feet, well done. You need to pull your left steering toggle a little so as–'

'Jesus,' Graham shouted over him. He'd forgotten about the two-way radio fitted in his helmet. 'Listen to me, it was Guy Ericson all the time, he killed the—'

TWANG! Graham felt the kick and looked up. He saw one of the suspension lines was broken. *TWANG! TWANG!* Another two massive kicks, 'My God.' *TWANG!* 'Oh, fuck.'

Four suspension lines had snapped, he could see them spiralling into the air. *TWANG!* Then another one, 'Sweet Jesus, help me.' Craning his neck, he saw three quarters of the parachute had collapsed and he felt the increase in wind as he began to plummet.

In his panic, he could hear someone shouting over the radio, *'Pull the three-ring release! Pull the three-ring release!'*

Graham couldn't think straight, he'd gone over it in training how to cut away the main canopy if it was damaged, which automatically pulled out the reserve shoot, but now where the fuck was it. His mind was a puddle of confusion as he began to tumble down out of control - then he remembered, it was attached to his shoulder strap. He yanked at the handle and immediately felt a thump as it jettisoned away - then his armpits were wrenched upwards with another surge as the reserve chute opened. 'Oh Jesus, thank God,' Graham cried out.

CHAPTER TWENTY-SIX

The man on the radio was shouting, 'Well done, Old Chap.'

'Listen to me,' Graham yelled. 'It was Guy Ericson—' He was having a panic attack, gulping in lots of air and trying to compose himself. *'He killed that Tina Warfield. He must have sabotaged my chute'* Graham wasn't making sense.

'What did you say?' The man on the radio hesitated. 'Didn't quite get that, Old Chap. You can't guide the chute?'

'No, you idiot—' Graham swallowed taking deep breaths. 'I said it was…' He heard the rip and looked up. Graham could see blue sky through the reserve chute. Then another tear with a lot more blue sky. For a second Graham was spellbound as he saw the parachute collapse in on itself and elongate like a twisting cigar. The wind rush was increasing as he began to skydive out of control. The picturesque view from the Cessna, the patchwork of fields and their pretty colours was racing towards him now at approximately one-hundred and twenty-miles per hour.

Graham began screaming, *'Help me, mama, I don't want to die…please God save me…'* The last thing Graham heard was the radio man shouting something in his ear. He closed his eyes for the inevitable.

*

It was a warm clear Sunday morning as the silver E-Type Jaguar sped along the A25 amongst little traffic. With Victoria beside him listening to Stevie Wonder on Radio One, Kenny Buxton was touching eighty-miles per hour as he sped towards Redhill Aerodrome. He was grateful the media hadn't got hold of the accident yet. However, this being the second day he was still missing, that would be short lived if Graham Lumley was found dead. The only thing on his mind was how that idiot Lumley could have fucked up on a parachute jump and jeopardised the whole event. He'd spent a lot of money on financing the two day show. The main point being how safe parachuting and skydiving was for the public. Now it looked as though it was all about to go down the drain because of that four-eyed prat. He should have got rid of the jealous idiot there and then when he came snitching last week about Guy being mixed up with another woman.

Victoria had picked up a magazine and was idly flicking through the pages of Vogue when the car telephone bleeped.

Kenny Buxton looked down and saw the flashing red light on the Motorola Pulsar. 'Can you get that, Vicky? I don't want to stop.'

Victoria leant across and picked up the receiver.

The operator asked her, 'Would you like to take a call from London?'

'Yes that's fine,' Victoria replied.

After some crackle of background interference a distinguished voice said, 'Is that Victoria Buxton?'

'Yes, who's speaking?'

Commander Potting told her, 'Don't forget to tell your father, Kimberly will be coming for supper.'

Victoria Buxton stiffened. 'Kimberly? Thank you for reminding me.' She replaced the receiver with a faraway look in her eyes.

'Kimberly? Who's that?' Kenny Buxton glanced at Victoria with a puzzled expression.

'Oh, it's just a wine bar friend I'm meeting tonight.' She sat back and picked up the magazine again.

Ahead on the opposite side of the road, Victoria could see road work traffic lights and the rear end of a green Bedford flatbed truck parked with plant hire equipment on board. The single lane light was green. Victoria looked up and adjusted herself in the seat. She started counting to herself mentally. As the roadworks came nearer she flexed her fingers. All sound had disappeared from her hearing. It was as if she'd become tuned in.

Then at twenty-five feet, Victoria wrenched the steering wheel from her father.

'What're you doing?' he shouted. With the skid, the E-Type smashed sideways into the rear end of the truck. An enormous explosion of fire and black smoke shot upwards to thirty feet. The back half of the severed E-Type containing Victoria's head, flipped over on its roof and screeched along the concrete until it hit a lamppost and then slurred to a halt.

The little traffic had already stopped. They watched in horror as the plant hire driver who happened to be unloading his tarmac vehicle, kicked at his smouldering cab door and then flung himself out into the road partially on fire. He rolled and rolled until he'd extinguished most of the flames. A few motorists had left their cars and were edging cautiously towards the smouldering carnage. The road was a battlefield littered with glass, torn metal and the smell of burning rubber mixed with petrol fumes. Someone had got a blanket and was feverously patting out the charred clothing of the tarmac driver lying on the floor. Another man across the street peered into the remains of the E-Type rear half and then brought up his breakfast at the side of the road.

The E-Type front half containing the mangled body of Kenny Buxton, also decapitated, lay deep and embedded inside the rear end bowels of the Bedford flatbed truck. To the side of him amongst the twisted wreck, Victoria's headless torso had eventually finished up in a sitting position with her bloody magazine still open in front of her.

Amongst the traffic, now steadily backing up, a green Post Office Commer van was the first to telephone for the emergency services.

A few minutes later the distant bells of a fire-engine could be heard along with the wail of a police car siren. No doubt an ambulance was on its way, but only to attend to the tarmac driver who was now sitting on a wall shivering in shock with the blanket around his shoulders.

CHAPTER TWENTY-SEVEN

Graham Lumley awoke on his back looking up to a clear blue sky. He'd been unconscious for over twenty hours. He had a tingling sensation all over. It was very peaceful and quiet. *Oh dear God,* he thought. *This must be my funeral. Everybody has left. This is what happens now. Shed the coffin and come through to the other side.*

Graham tried to raise himself but a wrapped sheet pinned his arms to his side. He wrestled with it and then, with a sudden click from somewhere, it fell off him. Graham realised it must be his crinoline. As he tried to get up, the soft floor gave way and he stumbled and fell. Graham tried again and with difficulty managed to stand. He was in a pit of some kind. Of course he suddenly realised, it had been his grave. With legs apart to keep his balance, he trod his way carefully, stumbling again until he reached the wall. The surface was prickly as Graham hauled himself up, digging his feet into the side for grip until he rolled himself over the top edge.

Sitting there shading his eyes, he was surprised how bright it was. Graham felt in his breast pocket for his glasses. Pulling them out he saw they were in pieces. Broken beyond repair. 'Shit!' he cursed. 'Still, I wonder if I'll need them here?'

For some reason he was high up. He couldn't make it out. Graham felt dizzy. He looked back down into the pit and saw himself laying there - all dead and crumpled with the crinoline around him. Was he hallucinating or was it for real?

He tried to stand, still swaying a bit unsteady. Then he realised something was wrong, something was missing. Graham wriggled his ears. 'God, I'm deaf, stone deaf.' There was something else - no smell. He sniffed the air, but nothing. It was like having a bad cold. He wondered if being dead was the reason. Shock perhaps due to his accident. *It's got to come back*, he thought. *Now I'm in heaven.* Feeling a bit optimistic with himself he confirmed, *well it has too, no point in being in heaven otherwise.*

From where he was standing, he could see pastures and fields. At the edge of a distant fence, he could see a lane winding its way. Then Graham saw something he'd missed earlier. Over to his right the top of a ladder protruded.

With his feet sinking in with each step, Graham wobbled his way over to it. *Jesus* he thought as he looked over the edge. The drop was at least twenty-feet. He poked the ladder with his foot. It seemed steady enough. Graham had never been up this high on a ladder. Then he thought about it. *What the heck, I'm dead aren't I. It's got to be safe if this is heaven. They've laid this on for me, so I can get down. So I can go and see the Man himself. Perhaps this happens to people in accidents. You come on through where you've died. They make a route for you.*

Graham carefully manoeuvred himself on and then gingerly descended, step by step with his eyes closed. At the bottom he sighed with relief - *Never liked those bloody things at the best of times.*

From where he was he could still see the lane. More confident with solid ground under his feet, he made his way towards it, but it seemed as if he was walking in slow motion. Everything around him was just out of focus, blurry, as if looking through frosted glass. Graham rubbed his eyes but it was still the same.

Picking his way along a dirt track, he came to a fence with a stile. Climbing over, he stood and looked both ways along the lane. He saw to his left in a layby, what looked like a sheltered bus stop. Graham could make out two people queuing at the sign.

As he approached, he could see an elderly woman and a middle-aged man. Graham nodded an acknowledgement. Both of them ignored him.

Without his glasses, he couldn't read anything on the bus stop timetable. 'Excuse me.' It sounded strange, he couldn't hear himself. 'Would any of you know where the buses go to?' Graham made light of it with a laugh, 'I'm not too sure where I am...'

They didn't respond. He moved himself into their eye line and asked once more, but there was no reaction, not even a hint of recognition. Then it occurred to him. *Perhaps they can't hear or see me? What if I'm some sort of spirit or ghost come back? Is that how it is before you go to the other side? If you're not accepted, do you just wander about for ever in limbo land? Or maybe they're dead as well and we can't communicate until we've been accepted and allowed in.*

Still ignoring him, the two moved closer to the bus stop in anticipation. Graham followed their gaze and saw far off in the distance a single decker white bus approaching. He thought, *My God, this is it. This has come to pick me up. Take me to Him.* Graham felt nervous; his throat was dry.

Then he wondered. *What would He look like? Some sort of Jesus with sandals - like you see in the films. Would He actually sit on a cloud and play a harp? More to the point, what do you say to Him? Would you even get to speak to Him? Perhaps you're seen by an aide first, Saint Peter, whatever. Would He have your whole life documented? Good and bad form. Then weigh up whether to allow you through the Pearly Gates. The Pearly Gates, do they really exist?*

Graham wondered if he'd scored enough brownie points. *Must have, never done anything bad. Always been good to mum. What could they fail me on? Compared to evil bastards like Hitler or Stalin, even that Guy Ericson, I must be a saint? Surely, that bastard Ericson wouldn't be allowed in. Certainly have something to say if he was, especially if I was turned away.*

Then with a lump in his throat, he thought of his mother. When would he see her again?

As the bus drew nearer, his eyes became moist. *What she must have gone through? Seeing me at the undertakers in the coffin. The last goodbye. Crouched over, crying. Then the funeral; standing with all the relations at the edge of the grave. Uncle Stan with his arm around her shoulders as the local Reverend chanted through the service. At least she'd get a bit of my company pension, the life insurance part - three times my annual salary. With her own state pension, it would keep her going for a while.*

The company would have probably sent a nice wreath. Kenny Buxton could be a funny bastard sometimes but he was good like that. Hopefully, he'd have given mum a little handshake in my memory, a few hundred quid or so. Then Graham thought about it. *Should bloody hope so, I did get killed representing the company. More to the point, mum should be in line for some compensation award. Technically speaking, One Day Wonders Ltd were to blame. No doubt, Guy Ericson would have covered his arse. Made sure it looked like a freak accident.*

Can just see him standing there at the coroner's inquiry, holding bits of parachute. Showing where the lines had frayed and the reserve had torn. He'd have some story off pat. That slick type always did. And to think, he'd got away with murder twice, if not more, and got to marry the governor's daughter.

The bus slurred to a halt in front of him. Graham thought, *it's certainly a novel way to go around and collect everybody that's passed over.*

Immediately, the elderly woman and the middle-aged man made their way onto the platform and moved inside finding a seat each. Graham hovered. The man in the uniform looked at him expectantly with his hand on the cord. Graham stepped on hesitantly and made his way passed him to a seat. The overweight middle-aged bus conductor with ginger bushy eyebrows and matching thinning hair was staring at Graham.

He gave a nervous smile back.

With two dings on the bell, the bus pulled away. Graham checked out the passengers. They were mostly older than he was. *At least, most of this lot had lived a life, fifty or sixty years plus* he thought.

Graham pondered; *I wonder how long the ride takes. How many others do we pick up before we meet The Almighty, himself?*

The conductor proceeded to collect fares and after eight-minutes, the bus slowed and Graham could see a stop ahead. The conductor called out, 'Next stop, Ridge Green.'

A rather large elderly woman in a thick coat stepped on. She moved down the bus. Graham thought, *that big, she must have had a heart attack.*

As she brushed passed him to sit down, Graham felt an almighty pain *'ARGH!'* he yelled and clutched his left hand. Everybody turned round and looked at him. His finger, the little finger was bent backwards, broken, it had to be. Graham shouted at her, 'Jesus Christ, can't you be more careful.'

She looked over and fiddled with her hearing aid, 'I'm sorry, what did you say?'

Graham froze. *Pain, surely not supposed to feel pain up here.* Then he realised he could hear himself.

CHAPTER TWENTY-SEVEN

She leaned over and said again, 'I'm sorry young man, what did you say?'

Graham realised, he could hear everything.

The conductor moved towards him. Standing in front of Graham with a set of bushy eyebrows that looked like a couple of caterpillars about to have a fight, he said in a gruff tone, 'Excuse me, Sir, you 'aven't paid.'

'Paid, why should…how can I…I thought this was going to…' A slow blanket of realisation was beginning to wrap itself around Graham. His finger was throbbing badly. Not only that, his right ankle felt like someone was stabbing it with a knife. And suddenly the smell. The smell hit him, rising up from his shoes. He'd trod in a cow pat or manure.

'Listen Mate,' the two caterpillars on his forehead were now wrestling with one another, 'I'm not 'aving any fare dodgers on my bus, is that clear?'

'You mean…Oh dear God…you mean we're not…we're not…in heaven…'

'What 'eaven? What you on about? 'Ave you been drinking? I don't 'ave drunks on my bus and shouting at elderly people for no reason. You'd better get off now.' He grabbed Grahams arm and in the struggle knocked his finger.

'*ARGH!*' He yelled again. 'Be careful you idiot, can't you see it's broken.'

'Listen, Mate, I've no sympathy for drunks that fall over and 'urt themselves.'

'I didn't fall over, I fell out a bloody plane.' Graham's ankle was now throbbing more than the finger. 'Oh Jesus…I made it…The shock…the shock must have worn off…'

Graham grabbed the conductor's arm with excitement. 'I'm alive aren't I? I'm fucking alive,' he shouted to the whole bus.

'Now listen, Mate, enough of that swearing. I want you off the bus now.'

'No you don't…understand.' Graham doubled up in pain… 'Jesus, my ankle,' he gasped. 'I can't walk. Look, honestly, I was doing a parachute jump from Redhill Aerodrome and it failed to open. I thought I was dead…I survived the fall…you must believe me.' Graham crouched over in agony again.

The conductor looked at him as if he was mad. He could see the man was suffering. He glanced at his watch again. The other passengers were ignoring the commotion. Many heads were either buried in newspapers or looking out of the window. They didn't want to get involved. The bus driver was looking behind in his cabin, wondering why the holdup.

Graham straightened up gasping for air. Little white dots exploded in front of his eyes in time with the throbbing from his ankle and finger. Then Graham remembered his mother's locket around his neck containing the lucky fifty pence coin. He fumbled with one hand and managed to prise open the clasp. He offered it. 'I can pay you. How much is it?'

'Well,' the conductor hesitated and then he scratched his head. He slowly took it from Graham, still debating. 'It's fifty-pence all round up to Redhill Aerodrome. We don't pass any 'ospitals but there's a show at the airfield. They might 'ave a first aid tent there. I suggest you get yourself seen too.' He turned to go and then stopped. 'But listen, Mate. I don't want any more trouble from you. Is that clear?'

Graham let out a gasp. 'Yes, sure…sure…take me to Redhill.' Then he bent over again moaning with pain.

Two seats behind, a smartly dressed man rolled his eyes and said to his wife, 'Bloody drunks.'

The conductor rang the bell and the bus moved off.

The rest of Graham's journey around the outside perimeter road was uneventful. Passengers steered clear of him. People getting on at the following two stops just assumed Graham, who had collapsed in his seat mumbling gibberish while covered in bits of straw and dirt, smelling like a latrine in the hot sun, was a tramp or some vagrant and probably drunk.

Within fifteen minutes, although to Graham it seemed an eternity, and feeling as if someone was hitting his ankle and finger with a hammer, the bus pulled up at Redhill Aerodrome.

The conductor motioned for him to get off and thought - the sooner he was gone the better. The stench from his clothes was getting to the immediate passengers who were holding their noses.

Wincing, Graham raised himself and slowly limped his way to the platform, stopping once to take the weight off his foot. Eventually, holding on to the handrail, he gingerly stepped down, *'ARGH!'* He collapsed on one knee. Then taking deep breaths he hauled himself up.

With the conductor shaking his head in disgust and a *Ding-Ding* on the bell, the bus pulled away. A few people at the windows looked back at him with a blank stare.

There was no one at the stop, which wasn't surprising. Unbeknown to Graham it was late Sunday afternoon.

He looked at his wristwatch. The second hand was still moving. It was 6:10 p.m. *My God,* he thought. *I've been gone for three hours.*

He could see the airport entrance with the reception building some distance away.

It was going to be a walk. Graham gritted his teeth and started hobbling. Then he ducked as a police helicopter swept low over the airport buildings and hovered above him.

He looked up and shielded his eyes from the low sun. Even without his glasses, Graham could clearly see Reigate and Redhill Constabulary written on its side. A man leaned out with a megaphone. 'Are you Mister Graham Lumley? Please raise your hand, Sir, if you are.'

Graham looked up astonished, he slowly raised his arm.

'Stay right there, Sir, we'll get you help,' the co-pilot leaned inwards as the helicopter banked away.

It wasn't more than two minutes after, when Graham heard the wail and saw the flashing lights. As the car park barrier lifted, the aerodrome emergency services ambulance sped out from the airfield entrance and screeched to a halt by his side. Two paramedics dressed in green jumped out with a collapsible wheelchair and blankets. Wrapping them around Graham's shoulders, they helped him to sit down while one took his pulse.

'Give me an injection for the pain,' Graham pleaded with them. 'I think my finger's busted and I've done my ankle in.'

'Okay, Sir.' One of them tore open a cardboard packet and paused with a syringe containing a Methoxyflurane pain killer. 'Anything you're allergic to, Sir?'

'Nothing, apart from parachuting,' Graham grimaced.

The two paramedics laughed while one gave the injection. The other one shone a pencil torch in each eye to check for concussion. Then an oxygen mask was placed over his face as they began to wheel him to the ambulance.

Graham tore it off amongst their protests. In short excited gasps he shouted, *'I want to see that bastard. I want to see that Guy Ericson's face.'*

The Paramedic reassured him, 'Yes - yes, it's all in hand, Sir, now you just calm down and relax. The police are at the aerodrome. Do you know they've had a search party out for you, Sir? You've been missing for over twenty-four hours. I must say from the information we were given we never expected to find you...' The medic stopped himself and grinned. 'If you don't mind me asking, Sir, would you fill out my pools coupon for next Saturday?'

Graham looked at him confused, and then the penny dropped. For the first time in ages, he actually started to laugh. Then he got serious. The painkiller was kicking in. He threw off the blanket and raised himself up clambering out of the wheelchair.

'What are you doing,' they protested holding him back by the arms.

'Before I go to hospital I want to see that bastard's face. Let him know his plan didn't work.' He pulled himself free from their grasp and hobbled off in the direction of the aerodrome.

'You need to go to hospital, Sir, to be checked over,' one of them shouted after him. 'You've still got concussion.'

Graham wasn't taking any notice. He limped his way down the side of the airport building and onto the services road at the edge of the airfield. Even without his glasses, he could see lots of people milling around and a number of police alongside their cars looking over to the firefighting area where filming was taking place.

It was late Sunday afternoon and there were many still at the show for the second day. The hot air balloon was getting ready for another take off and the jazz band was in full swing with a long line of people at the barbeque. The bouncy castle with the carousel ride and the helter-skelter were busy with kids, and the professional skydiving team with the coloured smoke canisters were on their third jump coming down.

A Hollywood film crew had also got themselves into position over at the fire training area where a Wimbledon Centre Court seating mock-up had been built. Helicopters would be flying over two-thousand seated mannequins and dowsing them with gasoline and flares.

As Graham opened the door of the main aerodrome reception he heard the wail of a siren and then a Morris JU 250 police van screeched to a halt with its flashing blue light. Five police officers immediately jumped out followed by two detectives. The middle-aged detective wearing a dark pin striped suit approached him. In one hand, he held what looked like a flying jacket. In the other, he flashed his Detective Superintendent Warrant Card.

'Good God, Sir, is it Graham Lumley? I was told you'd had a terrible accident.'

Graham, still covered with stuck-on bits of straw and fowl smelling cow pat, nodded holding his arm, wincing with pain.

'I'm DS Clark and this is my colleague, DC Withers.'

Graham took a deep breath and gabbled excitedly. *'It was Guy…Guy Ericson…the man who organised the jump…He tried to kill me…he rigged the chute…he killed that woman… the one on TV who was…'*

'Yes we know, Sir. We have his flying jacket with the missing button. The button was found in Patricia Warfield's hand. His deceased girlfriend.'

At the reception door, forty-six year old Roger Boswell approached. Boswell at five-foot eight-inches tall with receding dark hair and puffy eyebrows had a stocky build and a flattish nose that was a left over from his RAF amateur boxing days.

He introduced himself to DS Clark. 'Assistant Chief Pilot Roger Boswell. It was me who you spoke to on the phone. I can take you to Guy Ericson. He's over at the fire training area where they're doing some filming.'

CHAPTER TWENTY-EIGHT

The film crew had erected two-thousand tiered seats with mannequins over in the fire training area of the aerodrome. Lorries had brought in large sections of scenery which were painted to represent higher rows of people and the overhanging roof of the Wimbledon Centre Court.

With the predicted good weather, film hands and sceneshifters went about dressing the mannequins and fixing them to seats. All the mannequins had been fitted with jumping jack flashes, so once alight they would hopefully move about and look realistic. It had been decided the flares should be thrown by the fire staff on duty and not the pilots overhead. This was to ensure combustion would take place at designated locations where the cameras were ideally placed.

The film director was pleased for once. Dimitri Irwin liked the backdrop of the Wimbledon set and told his assistant it looked as good as the sketches in fact.

The director sat himself behind one of the three cameras carefully positioned while a parked refuelling truck waited in readiness to fill the fibreglass helicopter bucket. For added safety, a bright red aerodrome fire engine stood on call.

Guy Ericson had earlier given the pilots a hand hooking the cumbersome bucket to the steel line attached to the heavy cargo hook. Then the bucket release cable with its hand control had been threaded through the cargo hook aperture into the cockpit and taped to the pilots cyclic. Finally, the mobile refuelling truck had filled the fibreglass container with twelve-hundred gallons of aviation fuel.

Fadil had organised himself and Jamal to pilot the twin turbine S-61N Sikorsky helicopter while Hashim would be the belly man - lying on the floor looking through a hole with his eye over the dangling bucket trying to guide the pilots over the target. Hashim was the best choice for this, being a short thin Palestinian and the lightest in the group with dark cropped hair and a chin full of black stubble. The sunglasses that he never took off made him look even more sinister.

Ericson had done his pre-check. Wind speed for the day was around fifteen knots so they would be using the fifty-foot recommended cable length. The forecast for June this week was warm at around seventy-two degrees with just a few white fluffy clouds.

With an all clear from the control tower, the helicopter had risen vertically while ground crew had steadied the bucket. At fifty-feet, after the cable slack was taken up, the container had begun to lift. Now the helicopter was at one-hundred and seventy-feet and levelling out.

Dimitri Irwin sucking on a fat cigar gave a thumbs up to the pilots and then lifted his megaphone and shouted, 'Okay let's do it,' Immediately followed by the snap of a clapperboard and someone shouting, 'Take-1, scene-36, action!'

Guy Ericson wearing headphones and a walkie-talkie was in a three way communication with the director and the pilots. With instructions from the director he told the pilots to keep to the same altitude and move another hundred feet to the east above the perimeter road and then swing in with an arc at a run of forty knots towards the seated mannequins.

As the Sikorsky approached, Hashim with his eye over the bucket raised his hand ready. The height, speed and drop point were critical to achieve maximum spread of fuel across the area.

With Fadil at the controls, Jamal was ready with the hand held bucket release. As Hashim dropped his hand, Jamal pressed the release button.

Nothing happened. Hashim looked puzzled and dropped his hand again. Jamal pressed hard, he pressed the button repeatedly.

Guy Ericson called them. 'What's up?' What happened with the fuel release?'

Jamal came over the frequency, 'I not know, Chief. It be stuck.'

With instructions from the director, Ericson told them, 'Come round and try again.'

To the sound of, 'Take-2 scene-36, action.' The twin turbine S-61N Sikorsky headed away and then circled round in the distance for the second run in attempt.

The Sikorsky approached while Hashim got himself ready with his arm raised just as before. Passing over the seated mannequins, Hashim dropped his hand and Jamal pressed the release. Again, nothing happened. Jamal shouted, 'Sweet Mohamed, it is jammed or something.'

Ericson adjusted his headset; he could hear Jamal and yelled over the turbine noise. 'Bring her round again and hover. Maybe the line is snagged somewhere.' As they circled, he moved himself in for a closer look.

The wind had increased to around twenty-five knots. Fadil was trying to keep the helicopter under control while being buffeted. It swayed above Ericson as he looked up shielding his eyes from the sun. He shouted to them through his headset, 'Bring her down another sixty feet and I'll take a closer look.'

The bucket swung like a pendulum. Ericson's head moved with it as if being hypnotised. It was drawing him in. Not looking down, he moved nearer the mannequins until he was directly underneath the swinging container. He screwed up his eyes. 'Looks okay from here,' he shouted.

Jamal tried again. He depressed the release button and this time the bucket valve opened.

As Ericson ducked, over eleven-hundred gallons of aviation fuel crashed down on to him with a roar. The mannequins shuffled and the seats groaned. A misty haze of fumes rose up blocking the director's view. Ericson collapsed with the impact and was knocked unconscious. As he lay amongst the seats, Dimitri Irwin, shouted through his walkie-talkie. 'You okay, Chief.'

Quick thinking, Fadil, impersonated Ericson. He called over the radio, 'Chief here, I'm Ok and got clear. You can throw the flares.'

Dimitri Irwin responded, 'That's great, we'll film the fire and shoot the flying scenes afterwards.'

Two of the scene-shifters watching from the side had spotted what had happened. They began waving frantically and shouting to the film director but their protests were lost over the noise of the helicopter.

The director knew he only had seconds to get this shot right before the fuel began to evaporate and soak away. He shouted through his megaphone, 'Throw the flares.'

On cue, half a dozen spiraled through the air like Roman Candles. As they disappeared amongst the mannequins there was silence. Everyone held their breath.

Suddenly it was like the gates of hell had opened. The explosive fireball was immense. It plumed up to over sixty-feet in height into a boiling cauldron of fire and black smoke. The burning mannequins jerk into motion from the fireworks placed inside them. The special effects had worked. Even behind the safety tape at the designated event seating area for the public, the searing heat made faces flinch back and put up arms for protection.

After a further five minutes of filming and then a thumbs up from the other two camera crews to show they'd had it all, the director signaled to the firemen who then sprang into action and began dowsing the flames using engine hoses.

As the helicopter moved off, the director waved his appreciation. He shouted in the megaphone, 'Well done everybody, we have a wrap.' A cheer rose up and everyone began to applaud. Dimitri Irwin looked around. 'Where's the Chief?'

Safety staff nearby, responded with a shrug. 'We thought he was with you,' replied a young fireman manhandling a hose off his engine.

*

The Coroner's inquest was a solemn affair. Guy Ericson's sister was there in tears with some immediate relations.

Mr David Stoughton, Coroner for the inquiry said, 'A post-mortem revealed, Chief Flying Officer Guy Ericson, after suffering an impact blow to the head rendering him unconscious, died from inhalation of poisonous fumes brought on by a combination of burning plastics and consumables together with ninety-degree burns from a gasoline related fire.' He looked down at his notes and then continued, 'Health and Safety for the Civil Aviation Authority had been called in to examine the release mechanism of the helicopter bucket. The collective lever manual release in the cockpit was found to be working satisfactory. However, the release valve on the end of the bucket was damaged. Close inspection of the mechanism had failed to determine if the damage occurred on impact with the ground or just rough handling with poor maintenance.'

In summing up, the Coroner had no issue with the fire and safety procedures of Redhill Aerodrome and therefore recorded a verdict of accidental death. He extended his condolences and that of the court to the grieving relations.

Fadil and Jamal sighed with relief. It had been a near call. The faulty bucket was like a dangling carrot to Ericson. Peening over a pin, giving the release mechanism the required stiffness was pure luck. There was no way they could test it beforehand. However, they were counting on Ericson to be the first to investigate if there was a malfunction, and it paid off. They had a backup though, in case the flares hadn't been thrown. Jamal above was ready with one if it had been required.

After an investigation to ensure no one else was involved with the murder of Tina Warfield and the attempted murder of Graham Lumley, and because their main suspect was now dead, the Director of Public Prosecutions decided to close the case against Guy Ericson.

*

'I told you to tell them earlier, but you wouldn't listen.'

'Yes, Mother.'

'I said you should have gone to the police, but you wouldn't listen.'

'Yes, Mother.'

That evening, Graham Lumley and his mother were having dinner in the kitchen. She'd cooked him his favourite again, Shepherd's pie and chips.

'Nearly, got yourself killed, because of it,'

'Yes - yes, I know Mother.'

'Now listen, Graham. Now the bank and shareholders have appointed you as the new Managing Director you've got to be more assertive.'

'Yes, Mother.'

 Show them you can do the job long term.'

'Yes, Mother.'

'What about the bank manager's daughter you met at the shareholders meeting last week? 'Lita or—'

Graham interrupted. 'Lisa, her name was Lisa.'

'Lisa that was it. You said she wasn't wearing a ring.'

'I know, Mother.'

She loaded some more Shepherd's pie onto her fork. 'You could let her know you're interested. No harm in asking her out on a date.'

'Yes, Mother.'

'That bank manager is going to be far more interested in having you as a permanent MD if you was engaged or married to his daughter.'

'I know, Mother.'

'You could take her somewhere nice. What about that restaurant, Botticelli's or something.'

'Okay, Mother.'

'And try not to wear those new glasses all the time.'

'Yes, Mother.'

'You don't want to put her off.'

Okay, Mother.'

*

Commander Gregory Potting stood by the window of his large office. From here he could look down on Whitehall. Across the road was Banqueting House while further down he still had a good view of the Cabinet Office. The traffic was moving well today. It was a sunny morning and he was in a good mood. He'd just come off the phone to the PM. He'd thanked him for getting it all sorted. It wasn't often he'd got a pat on the back from the governor himself. Mind you, that's all that was said. However, they both knew what was being referred too.

Catching his eye, he remembered his morning tea with a digestive. His private secretary Margaret, always there on the dot with his elevenses. Commander Potting walked over to his desk and sat down. He sipped his Darjeeling and broke the biscuit in half. He surveyed his new office. Promotion had brought forth many benefits as well as a salary increase; including thick Persian rugs as well as expensive mahogany bookcases, with matching boardroom table and chairs for his office. Then there were the walled art deco Tiffany lamps and the two huge ginger jars sitting either side of the Tudor stone fireplace; and not forgetting of course the two large magnificent chandeliers. He took another sip and pulled the drawer of his new Cromwell pedestal leather topped desk; one more little goody that went with the job.

Commander Potting withdrew a clutch of files. He sifted through them and then reached for his pad and stamp. With the folders of Martin Lavender, Kenny Buxton, Victoria Buxton, Tina Warfield and Guy Ericson, he thumped down in red letters EXPIRED on the buff covers. Then he picked up the file of Francis Hodder. He thought for a while and frowned. Then he reached for the special red telephone and dialled the number for Briar Lodge Manor. 'Give me Doctor Weise please.'

A few seconds later. 'Doctor Weise speaking.'

'Good morning, Doctor. Potting here. It's about your sleeper Francis Hodder.'

'What about him, Old Chap.'

The Commander asked him, 'I thought you programmed him to kill himself after his father was killed?'

A silent pause for a while and then the doctor said. 'The problem is, Old Chap, he's on the run. From his publicity as the Beauty Spot Butcher it looks like his Roxanne character has taken over and is out of control. We never removed it. Him being a schizophrenic it was already there at the time. The Roxanne part of his character never surfaced during his conditioning. The self-destruct trigger is for the Francis character. We think he's using the Roxanne alias as a prostitute. You know, for the punters that require something a bit special, if you know what I mean.' The doctor laughed but it wasn't reciprocated. He cleared his throat nervously.

'Without confronting him or phoning him to release the self-destruct trigger, he'll remain alive.'

'Is there anyway, Doctor, this can backfire on us? If there is I couldn't guarantee your safety.'

'No – no, Old Chap.' Doctor Weise swallowed hard. 'Even under extreme torture he wouldn't remember his masters. I promise you.'

'I hope you're right, Doctor Weise, for your sake. Good morning.'

Dr Weise replaced the receiver and slowly put his head in his hands.

CHAPTER TWENTY-NINE

Assistant Chief Pilot, Roger Boswell, was quickly appointed by Alan Bristow Helicopters to step in and take control of training operations. He would be carrying on with Ericson's workload, although not exactly the board's first choice.

Boswell, known to vacillate on decisions, while further advancement in the company seemed to have passed him by, was a sporty family man who was better at stripping down an engine rather than managerial responsibilities. His promotion from mechanic to a pilot and then to a warm office desk job was mostly down to his pushy wife wanting him to get on in the company. Her desire for the finer things in life included a detached four-bedroomed house and a villa in Spain. However, for the immediate moment, Boswell was in the frame. He would be the new man to liaise with the film company for the remaining flying scenes over the Wimbledon All England Club.

The next morning at the aerodrome, the pilots were summoned to Boswell's office. The strong smell of cigar smoke met them as they entered, which was supported by a Cuban stub smouldering in a heavy glass ashtray. Standing next to Boswell was film director Dimitri Irwin.

With the pilots seated and a nod from Boswell, the film director offered his commiserations for their Chief. 'Again I am lost for words over this tragic accident. Guy Ericson was a great man with a big heart. I know he was a friend and colleague to most of you and that he will be sorely missed.' He looked down with a pained expression and paused thoughtfully. 'Let me remind you, being involved in film stunts is not for the faint hearted. In most cases, no one gets hurt. However, the work can be dangerous with hidden pitfalls.' The director glanced sheepishly at the new Flight Chief and then continued. 'Of course I understand if some of you are reluctant to carry on working on the flying scenes as a mark of respect for your colleague. However, next Thursday and Friday are the last two days of filming before Wimbledon starts which is the following week, and so, Gentlemen, we need your help in finishing these scenes.'

The director waited for a response, but the pilots just stared at him. Assuming this could be very costly to the studio if they decided to pull out, the director quickly added, 'For every pilot that wants to continue, the studio will pay him a three-hundred pounds cash bonus!'

Fadil gave a low whistle of astonishment while the other faces lit up with fake interest.

Dimitri Irwin hesitated. He was counting on them. If this picture came in over budget or with delays, his reputation in Hollywood was at stake. 'Can I have a show of hands for finishing our schedule?'

All five pilots lifted their arms.

The director relaxed. That was an enormous weight of his mind. 'Okay, Gentlemen, just to remind you, shooting starts on Thursday at 11:00 a.m. sharp. This will involve water bombing four-thousand extras on the Wimbledon Centre court. We've allowed two days for this to get it right. For those two days we've hired at an enormous cost, part of Wimbledon Park. This will be to land and refuel including the use of their boating lake for the helicopters to water scoop. 'The Wimbledon Park Lake is adjacent to the All England Club. You'll see the markings for landing as you approach.'

Looking over to Boswell, the director reminded him, 'We'll need two of your large Sikorsky's for this scene and no more than five-hundred gallons of water in each bucket. This is the maximum load advised by the health and safety board. Anything heavier and we'll have extra's with broken necks on our hands.

'Just one more thing, we have to get the shots right because Wimbledon Tennis starts this Monday and we won't be allowed to fly over the club after that because of the enforced restricted air space.' He looked at the flight instructor for confirmation.

'That's right,' Roger Boswell added. 'The London Emergency Services Liaison Panel are on standby alert for real IRA attacks. Which means, anybody caught flying over The All England Club during the tennis tournament without a dam good excuse will be shot down by military helicopters from RAF Northolt. A sobering thought, gentlemen.'

*

The same evening, with the usual excuse for prayers at the Southfields Mosque, they left Redhill Aerodrome and headed to the flat to hold a meeting.

Fadil spread out the ordinance survey map of Wimbledon Common. He told them, 'Jamal, you fly one helicopter with Hirad as belly-man and Arif, you fly the other with Hashim as belly-man; is that clear?'

They nodded.

Hirad and Arif were brothers and the quietest of the group. Like the others, they had lost family in the Palestine wars. Brought up in a refugee orphanage after their parents were killed, they bore the scars mentally. They could have been mistaken for twins being tall, dark looking and in their late twenties with black frizzy hair and thick bushy beards that stretched from ear to ear.

Fadil explained to them, 'We have to get access to mobile refueling truck. They will use for fuel backup while they film. I will ask new flight chief if I hitch a lift when they take truck Thursday morning. Then somewhere convenient, I get rid of driver. Next, I drive to horse ring here on common.' Fadil pointed to it on the map. 'As I am only one that drives, I will steal getaway car and switch plates. We hide car here in garage that comes with flat. Then day before attack, I will take to pavilion near horse ring. I have NO ENTRY signs to hang around area. Hopefully will keep public away.

'When you fly to Wimbledon Park Lake but not scoop,' he pointed again to the map, 'you fly to me instead, then hover and position buckets in turn, so I can fill with fuel.' Fadil placed his finger on the map at the Wimbledon All England Club.

'Once you dumped fuel and flares *here* and burned infidel scum, you fly back to me and land in horse ring. We make our way down gravel track to getaway car. From there drive to Dover and catch ferry to Calais, from Calais to Genoa and then boat home.'

Jamal asked, 'What about flares?'

Fadil told him, 'I hide eight from last time, when they fuss around Ericson at his accident. I will light two on common to guide you to truck. You have six to drop on infidels.'

With that, he stood stiffly and punched the air with a clenched fist salute and shouted, 'We have six flares to drop on enemies of Allah. Death to infidels and Allah's enemies. Allah Akbar, Allah Akbar.'

The rest of them followed with a clenched fist salute and repeated, 'Death to infidels and Allah's enemies. Allah Akbar, Allah Akbar.'

Fadil shouted the Black September chant, 'We here to burn them. We here to burn infidels in the name of Allah.' He raised his hands to his shoulders in a submissive pose and the others followed. 'Believers, take neither Jews or Christians for friends while here in country of idolatry worship. We seek Zionist enemies relentlessly. Slay them wherever we find them. Make war on Zionist unbelievers and allies. Make war on them until Allah's religion reign supreme. Make war so Allah chastise them, humble them and grant us victory.'

Then all together, they punched the air in frenzied unison, 'Death to infidels and Allah's enemies. Allah Akbar, Allah Akbar.'

*

It was the 21st June, the Thursday before The All England Wimbledon Tournament and a perfectly clear warm sunny morning, however, Dimitri Irwin was nervous. Using his megaphone to organize over four-thousand film extras, he wanted them all seated quickly into the front rows nearest the grass on the Wimbledon Centre Court.

The director looked at his watch. It was ten o'clock. There was an hour to go before filming. It was going to be a tight schedule. 'Can you all be seated please?' He waited a few minutes until they were settled. 'I hope you've all brought a change of clothing as asked, because most of you are going to get very wet.' A light titter went around the crowd. 'Now, if you look across the grass you'll see a coloured light at each corner of the tennis court. As each light flashes, turn your head towards it. For the camera this will look like everyone is watching a tennis rally.'

As the lights came on, the heads turned but not in unison. 'Stop! - stop! You're not together,' said the director. 'Let's start again with everyone looking at the right flash first. Okay.'

This time was better. 'That's great, keep going, you're all in rhythm,' the director shouted. 'Now, when the idiot-boards are held up, I want you all to OOH and ARH as if you're watching a firework display.'

It was working well. Two cameras on tracks with men carrying sound booms moved along at the front edge of the grass capturing the scene.

Fadil had squared it with Boswell to get a lift from Harry who would be taking the mobile gasoline truck. It had been arranged for them to arrive early at Wimbledon Park to enable Fadil to set up an area where the helicopters could land and refuel. He would supervise ground operations and any maintenance that would be required.

Harry Symes, the truck driver, a balding heavy built middle-aged man, wasn't going to give Fadil too much trouble.

With an early morning start, the 1971 Ford F600 tanker was already onto the A217. After forty-minutes, mostly in rush-hour traffic, they were passing through Wimbledon village and approaching Church Road.

Fadil crossed his legs and moaned, 'I need relieve myself, badly. Too much coffees this morning.'

Harry Symes hesitated, he was about to turn right. 'Can't you wait, we're nearly there?'

'In the name of Allah I bursting, Harry.' He moaned again. 'Do me favour please and take left by memorial there.' Fadil pointed. 'I will pee amongst trees.'

As they swung into Southside Common Road, Fadil felt for his gun. It was quiet along here with little through traffic.

He indicated to park up by some bushes. 'Thank you, Harry, you real diamond as they say.' Checking the windows quickly, Fadil made for the door. 'I won't be moment.' Then he pulled the Walther P38. Without a moment's hesitation, he swung round and pumped two bullets into Harry Symes chest.

Like a sack of potatoes, he collapsed dead onto the steering wheel. Fadil was grateful for no ricochet. He had over three-thousand gallons of fuel behind him. Fadil sat for a moment with the gun ready. His heart was thumping. Someone must have heard the shots. After a minute he checked both side windows. Nothing looked suspicious. Now he knew there was no turning back.

Being careful, he half opened his door to give himself room and then hauled the body onto the passenger side. Then he pushed it into the foot dwell and covered it with a tartan travelling rug he'd packed in his mechanic bag.

Fadil nonchalantly got out and went around to the driver's side. With a last double check, back and front, he climbed in and composed himself. Taking his time, he started up the tanker and slowly pulled away.

Fadil continued at a steady pace along Southside until he reached Copse Hill; from there into Coombe Lane and then onto the A3. Driving at fifty-miles per hour he reached the Robin Hood Roundabout and then did a complete U turn and came back down the A3 common side. He kept to the inside lane and continued for half a mile and then turned into Robin Hood Road. It was quiet as he passed the pavilion and its car park.

The stolen tan coloured M3 Cortina with the false plates still looked inconspicuous tucked away over in the corner. He pulled up at the wooden gate that marked the entrance to Gravelly Hill. Fadil climbed out and took stock. It was quiet. He was glad it wasn't a popular part of the common unless you were a horse rider.

Delving into his bag he took out the wire and picked the padlock. To his relief it snapped open immediately. Then he got back in and drove forward a little. He climbed out and closed the gate snapping the padlock shut. After hanging the made up sign: NO ENTRY. WIMBLEDON BOROUGH PARKS GIVES NOTICE: NEW HORSE RING FLOOR BEING LAID BETWEEN 22nd June to 29th June, Fadil proceeded slowly, bumping along the gravel track for quarter of a mile until he reached the horse exercise ring. It was deserted as expected.

Nearby he spotted a clump of tall bushes. Fadil swung off the track and headed for them. Amidst the scratching and scraping of branches he stopped. When he climbed out he was more than satisfied. Well covered, the truck would be hard to detect from the sky.

Fadil was sweating. He spotted the drivers lunch satchel and found a can of orange drink. As the ring-pull hissed, he gulped and dribbled until it was all gone. He sat back, burped and rested for a minute. Then it was back to work.

He climbed out and moved round to the other door. Opening it, he took hold of the driver's feet and pulled the body clear. As the head and shoulders thumped to the ground, he stopped and listened. But only silence, broken by the odd rasp of a magpie and the creak of overhead branches.

Dragging the body with some exertion, he finally positioned it out of sight amongst thick undergrowth; the earthy smell from the disturbance rising up at Fadil's nostrils. Still he was pleased. The overhanging trees made it secluded. It was perfect.

Fadil checked his watch. It was 10:35 a.m. He moved swiftly into the centre of the horse ring and proceeded to ignite and position two red flares as a guide for the pilots.

CHAPTER THIRTY

The two-polished S-61N Sikorsky's sporting their red, white and blue stripes with the Bristow ribbon trademark, stood on the grass outside Hangar 6. They glistened as the sun winked off the bodywork while the pilots walked around the craft to do the first preflight checklist of the day. The fiberglass water buckets with their long lines attached to the cargo hook sat neatly by each helicopter.

With a brief inspection of all compartment doors and panels with no visual fluid leaks, the pilots climbed into their cockpits with one of them at the controls and the other taking up the position of the belly man. The flares had been smuggled onto the two Sikorsky's, three apiece and were well hidden.

After pre-start checks covering the usual: seat belts, pedals, collective, hydraulics, fuel, switches and instruments, both helicopter main rotors slowly began to turn as the ignition buttons were depressed. With the engine run-up checks underway for circuit breakers, fuel boost, lights, radio, throttle and governor; the pilots concentrated on critical gauges: TOT-turbine temp, torque and NI–gas turbine. With these stabilized, the pilots requested ATC for clearance to land away at Wimbledon SW19.

ATC came back to them, 'Start approved, lift – air taxi – line up on runway four to use, facing north. Wind speed twelve-knots.' The time was 10:40 a.m.

Confirming, permission given to take off on runway four and depart North Reigate, they lifted with their noses tilted and thudded off majestically trailing their buckets to a height of 1,500 feet. They would be taking the H7 route over Banstead to Morden and then veering right for Wimbledon.

Fadil had told them, although their flight had been logged by the London Emergency Services they would still be on high IRA alert. So expect to see military and police helicopters patrolling. In other words, don't draw suspicion. Keep to the route and maintain the correct flight levels on the approach path to Wimbledon.

With their navigation beams on, the pilots' journey would be plotted momentarily by Redhill ATC. Then North of Reigate, Heathrow specials ATC would monitor as they would be flying into London airspace. Both pilots communicated, 'Gulf – Uniform – Bravo – changing frequency to Heathrow Specials 125625.'

Redhill ATC confirmed, 'Frequency approved.'

Heathrow automatically notified RAF Northolt who had on standby, two WG 13 Lynx helicopters. They were kitted out with 7.62mm machine gun installations at the sides and

2.75in FFAR rockets mounted on stub-wings attached to the fuselage.

With the two Sikorsky's airborne, Jamal and Arif knew their journey was only going to take five-minutes at the outside. Then sure enough, just after they passed over Morden, Arif radioed to Jamal that he'd spotted an RAF WG 13 Lynx approaching his port side. The Lynx eased up at a distance and flew parallel with them for thirty-seconds then took off. Both pilots breathed a sigh of relief.

The Wimbledon Centre Court with its distinct roof was in sight now as they began to descend to five-hundred feet. To their left, Jamal and Arif could see the bunkers of Wimbledon golf course. Both helicopters began to throttle down and descend even further, passing over the golf clubhouse with players looking up shielding their eyes from the sun. Then just over Caesar's Camp, Robin Hood Road was visible and ahead the Kingston By-Pass.

Jamal, with the map on his knee, moved his finger across it while scanning the common from his cockpit window. All at once his heart leapt. He saw them, the red flares to his left. He radioed Arif with excitement.

As they descended, the tiny figure of Fadil frantically waving became clearer. The horse exercise ring loomed large before them, however, they realised in their excitement they had to watch the overhanging trees. There wasn't space to hover side by side. Jamal radioed to Arif, he'd move lower first.

With the bucket swinging towards him, Fadil grabbed at it and brought it under control. He steered it nearer the mobile truck and unhooked the fuel hose. Moving the release lever, the aviation fuel began to fill the bucket at a flow of three-hundred gallons per minute.

At twelve-hundred gallons, he switched off. Then gave Jamal the thumbs-up. The helicopter slowly rose then climbed away to a hovering position. Jamal knew this is where they'd be at their most vulnerable. To be spotted now by a patrolling RAF Lynx, off the registered flight route, meant they could be shot down immediately.

Such were the powers of the LESLP with their terrorist prevention policy.

As Arif manoeuvred into position, Jamal scanned the skyline with a knot in his stomach.

*

Wearing headphones and very irritated, Flight chief, Roger Boswell was in contact with Redhill Aerodrome fuel depot. 'So where's the fuel truck? It should have been here forty minutes ago.'

Dimitri Irwin stood on centre court and chewed his fat Cuban Cigar. The film director checked his watch for the third time. 'Why are the helicopters late? They should have arrived by now.' He turned in annoyance to the flight chief. 'I'm paying your outfit good money for this, Boswell!'

'I'll – I'll try and call them again, Mr Irwin,' he said nervously. Twiddling the frequency knob on his hand held transmitter, he said loudly, 'Gulf – Charlie – Delta – Uniform - Bravo QN11. Do you read me?'

After some crackles and a spell of interference, Jamal responded. 'Gulf – Charlie – Delta – Uniform - Bravo QN11, reading you loud and clear. We have both water scooped and are approaching the northeast side of the stadium as planned. We are beginning our first pass.'

The flight chief gave a thumbs-up to the director. 'I've got them, their ready for a first take!' He relaxed, then pondered with a puzzled expression. *The water scoop? They would've been seen over the stadium to water scoop in the Wimbledon Park Lake.* Shouting over the approaching noise, he turned to the director, 'That's funny, did you see them water...'

Dimitri Irwin wasn't listening.

As the unmistakeable thud of two large helicopters became louder and louder, the clapper boy shouted, 'Take-7, scene-36, Action!'

The director put the megaphone to his mouth and shouted, 'Thank, Christ, you're here at last.'

With two cameras on the extras and two pointing upwards, the helicopters swung into view. As Jamal's Sikorsky swooped over the centre court roof, the flight chief shouted into his transmitter for their cue. Hirad on his stomach, gave Jamal the thumbs-up to activate the hand-held water release trigger line.

Like a giant tidal wave, twelve-hundred gallons of aviation fuel thundered down onto the extras, knocking many out of their seats. Instantly, everywhere was engulfed in steam with a fine mist spreading.

Water didn't do that. Something was wrong. Roger Boswell knew the smell.

Then the shouts and cries from the extras as many held their necks in pain. Others clambered onto the grass court rubbing their stinging eyes. This was not as rehearsed.

As Jamal hovered, Arif thundered over and with a signal from Hashim, jettisoned his load. Instantly, another twelve-hundred gallons of aviation fuel crashed down onto the scattering crowd.

Dimitri Irwin was hysterical, shouting in his megaphone, 'Keep rolling - keep rolling, this is absolutely great.' He turned to Dave, his assistant director, 'Tell the stunt coach he's done a fantastic job with them.'

Roger Boswell shouted into his transmitter, 'You idiots, you've used fuel instead of—' He saw the first two flares drop onto the grass well away from the seating. They burned on their own like red Roman candles. The flight chief froze; the glow was hypnotic. Spell bound for a few seconds, he managed to turn his head away and look up at both helicopters hovering. Then the full realization hit him. *The missing truck? Using fuel instead of water? Stores asking about the unaccounted flares?* Then to his horror, his fears were justified. Two more flares were spiralling downwards.

Boswell shouted to the director. 'Get them out of there for Christ's sake; they're going to kill—'

It was like an atomic eruption. A huge boiling cauldron of orange and black fire exploded upwards into a raging inferno. The fireball rose above the top of the stadium roof.

The director, shielding his face from the heat, watched hundreds of extras screaming and writhing as the flames engulfed them. The grass court was smouldering with people. They ran around on fire like headless chickens. Some rolled on the floor leaving a path of charred grass.

Dimitri Irwin shouted through his megaphone, 'Keep them rolling, this is great stuff.' His assistant director approached with a dazed expression. He looked slightly comical with his trousers in shreds. 'Dave, this is unbelievable, well done. Where the hell did you get all the fire proof clothing? I know I should be pleased, Dave, but I'm the one who authorises the action scenes. You should have told me you changed...' He trailed off.

Smoke was coming from behind Dave's back. He had a faraway look as he managed to say, 'You know, Mr Irwin, I feel very cold.' Then he fell flat on his face like a logged tree.

Dimitri Irwin put a hand to his mouth in shock. The whole of his assistant's back and trousers were burned away. All that remained was smoking charred flesh. He stood there, not quite able to comprehend. Then someone was pulling him, shouting in his face amongst the bedlam of screams and sirens.

'Move, you Stupid Bastard,' yelled Roger Boswell. 'Do you want to get killed?' As he dragged the director by the arm across the grass, they stumbled over dead and smouldering bodies.

A man with his face and hair alight grabbed blindly at Boswell's leg, moaning, 'Help me.'

Boswell with a grunt shook him off. They had to get undercover in case the pilots planned to kamikaze or were blown out of the sky by the military. Either way, it was dangerous to be out in the open. It looked like gangway D on the west stand was their best hope. Gangway B, the nearest escape exit was blocked by panicking extras. They had run blindly, on fire, and now a mass of burning bodies blocked the entrance.

As the director was pulled along in a state of shock, he looked back. The whole of the east stand was ablaze with flames towering above the roof. The air was filled with the sweet smell of charred flesh and burning seats, with many people still trapped in the front rows. The director mumbled, 'What went wrong, Chief? Was it the special effects?'

Boswell shouted, 'Hurry, You Idiot, while we've still got time.' The chaos was horrific as they jostled their way through. Like disorientated blackened zombies, people reached out with burnt skinless arms and moaned in despair as Boswell pushed them away to reach the gangway.

Hovering side by side over the stadium, Arif and Jamal could see two WG 13 Lynx helicopters approaching in the distance, no doubt from RAF Northolt. One of them was moving in from the Wimbledon Common side. That meant they were cut off. There was no point in running. Using flight binoculars, Arif could see they were armed with 2.75in FFAR rockets.

Sensing they knew their time had come, Arif signaled to Jamal through the cockpit window using a cut-throat gesture. Immediately they switched of their ignitions.

As the helicopters spiraled out of control onto the centre court, the crews shouted their last Arabic prayer, *'Adab arz hai! Astaghfirullah Inna lillahi wa inna ilayhi rajiun!'*

Just before they entered gangway D, the blast and searing heat from the two explosions knocked them to the ground. Boswell and the director winced as two massive fireballs plumed upwards with bits of rotor blade whistling over them like bullets. Others were not so lucky. Decapitated heads and limbs fell about amongst high-pitched screams.

CHAPTER THIRTY-ONE

From where he was waiting, he could see the smoke and hear the sirens. Fadil sat in the truck with the Walther P38 resting on his knee. They'd been too long. He knew of course they'd gone to Allah. That was the alternative. Now he was on his own. It was everyman for himself.

Gathering up what he could from the truck, including a small medical kit and the remains of Harry's lunch, Fadil walked quickly down the gravel track until he reached the stolen car.

The Ford key, from the set that were left in the ignition while the man had popped into the paper shop to buy cigarettes, turned in the door lock to let him in.

Fadil sat still. He did a complete sweep of the car park. It could be a trap. They'd found the car and were waiting for him. But nothing. It all looked quiet and peaceful. He started the engine and then hesitated. There was no point now in trying for a ferry. As well as airports, all the Chanel ports would be covered. He'd have to lie low and change his appearance. He had the new passport Salah Khalaf had sent. It just needed a new photo.

He'd have to find a cheap hotel somewhere local. No doubt, all the South coast hotels and B&B's would be under scrutiny. First thing was to get back to the flat and clear out everything. He had some remaining money hidden there and small firearms that could be useful. Then dump the car as soon as possible.

*

Fadil lay on the bed looking at the television. Although the attack was six-days old, it still headed the news. Probably due to the heavy loss of life. Over thirteen-hundred dead and still counting with more than seven-hundred injured, ranging from near-deaths-door to walking-wounded.

Reporters close to the scene were still giving out the latest up-dates. Initially, it was thought to have been the IRA. Then within a few hours, the Redhill Aerodrome conspiracy began to materialise. Finally, a cable sent to the BBC by Salah Khalaf from his secret headquarters in Beirut, confirmed it was Black September.

Salah Khalaf would be pleased with him, even more so if he got back alive. Back in Palestine, he would be hailed as a hero. Fadil had more than once imagined himself sitting next to Khalaf and Yasser Arafat in an open topped limo slowly cruising the streets of Beirut with mobs of people shouting and waving, throwing flowers at them.

The contents of a half-eaten TV dinner littered the bedside table. The room he'd booked for two weeks at the St Georges Hotel in Shepherd's Bush just off the Uxbridge Road was old and basic and smelt mostly of mothballs with a hint of stewed cabbage that seemed to seep under the door at certain times of the day. However, it had clean sheets and he felt safe. Even more so with the Walther P38 pistol in its holster near at hand. The plan was to lie low for a fortnight until the initial heat was off.

Fadil moved himself off the bed and looked again in the dressing table mirror. His own mother wouldn't have recognized him. A blonde crew-cut and a smooth shaven face replaced the beard and the head of thick black hair. The pink shirt with the giant lapels along with the leather waistcoat and flares, was typical seventies fashion. The John Lennon cap finished it off with the over the top white sunglasses. Fadil looked a cool dude. He'd also learnt to snap his fingers like a soul man.

Checking in, he'd put singer in the register after giving the false name of Sal Rodrigues. The Shepherds Bush Empire were holding gigs every week, so it wasn't uncommon to have artists passing through.

With a record player from the market, Wilson Picket and Otis Reading could be heard outside his door. Not too loud to annoy, but enough to justify his musical involvement. To cement the image, he always passed hotel reception holding a saxophone case. It was early days but the deception seemed to be working.

Now he was feeling randy. He wanted to screw. Fadil perused the card that had been left in the hotel lobby phone booth. *International Escorts for Hire, contact Francis on 01-943 0238 between 10:0 p.m. to 10:30 p.m.*

*

The wrist had a small plaster cast, however, hidden by the long sleeves of the cool tight fitting raincoat, it didn't show. The black Cleopatra style wig with the tanned make up, set against a heavy red outline of lipstick and green eye shadow together with the black fishnet stockings, suggested a walking siren. Still, it was the oldest profession in the world some people would say.

At reception, the piece of paper with a scribbled name was shown with a one-pound note discreetly folded underneath. The portly old man in braces with bad breath and wearing holed slippers, smiled as he pocketed his commission. He knew Brass when it called.

Glancing at the register, he looked up. 'First floor on the right, number eight.'

Francis took the stairs. At the door, the index knuckle knocked twice and then waited. As it opened, a face cagily appeared. Francis breathed in sharply. It was a split second decision to do a runner. However, Fadil never recognised him. And why would he. He'd been reported as committing suicide. MI5 had told the police to keep the autopsy incident under wraps.

CHAPTER THIRTY-ONE

He hesitated and then smiled. 'Is it Francis?'

Francis grinned. 'Well, it's not the fucking Pope, Handsome.'

Fadil laughed at the quip. 'Come in.'

He entered and seductively took off the cream coloured raincoat and stood there. It was then Francis realised the Roxanne tattoo on his arm. He subtly turned so Fadil couldn't see it.

Fadil cupped his hands with delight. 'Allah be praised.'

Francis's shiny black leather crotch pouch matched the suspenders and garter belt. The red brassiere stuffed with cotton wool was giving Fadil an erection.

'Francis, I would be grateful for consideration. First, I have to take Salat al-'isha,' informed Fadil.

Francis responded, 'You're paying for the time, Honey.'

He withdrew his prayer matt from underneath the bed and then orientated himself to face Mecca. As he dropped to his knees, he looked up at Francis. 'You see, to fuck a man is against the beliefs of Islam. I have to pray for forgiveness first.'

'You take all the time in the world, honey. I'll just sit and watch.'

As Fadil crouched and started mumbling, Francis's fingers with the painted nails felt for the shiny plastic handbag and flipped the gold clasp. The grip of the bone handle knife felt good, like a hard dick.

CHAPTER THIRTY-TWO

The card in the stationer's window drew his attention. **£22 per week. Self-contained fully furnished flat facing Nonsuch Park. Ideal for a professional couple or single man or woman. For address apply within.**

With the information scribbled down, Francis made his way through the park. It was a mid-August warm morning. He took the perimeter trail where the woodland smells of oak, cedar and birch mixed with dry earth leeched into his senses. Although a walk, it was quieter. Public transport he could do without. Only if it was a necessity. He had to be careful.

The rear of the houses were shielded by high fences. As he came out through the side footpath into a select quiet road he suddenly realised. The stupid Bitch schoolgirl with her diary. This was where she lived.

Her diary had always worried him in case it was found. It had been eight years and although a man had been mistakenly sentenced for the crime, nothing else had been mentioned in the news. The diary had probably been burnt to ashes in the house fire. However, there was still a possibility it could be found.

Francis took out the slip of paper. Number twenty-eight he had to find. As he counted down, he stopped in front of a recognisable door. Jesus. This was the same house. It had to be.

He looked around. It was quiet. Pressing the doorbell he waited. Francis pressed again and then he saw a shape through the thick glass. The door opened a little, restricted by a chain.

A short middle-aged lady with greying hair that was pulled back into a bun with a worried looking lined face, wearing a multi-coloured stained smock and holding an artists' paint brush, poked her head around. 'Yes.'

'Oh, good morning, sorry to disturb you but I've come about the flat. Is it still vacant?'

The lady looked him up and down and said, 'Err yes. Would you mind telling me where you saw it advertised?'

Francis replied with an agreeable smile. 'The card in the stationers on the Broadway.'

She closed the door and he heard the chain withdrawn and then she opened it and invited him in.

The large hall with the black mottled marble tiles had an African theme. Tribal masks and spears adorned the white walls while two huge elephant tusks set into mahogany bases sat majestically under a balcony framing a leopard skin rug complete with its head, feet and tail. 'My husband and I loved to go on Safaris to Kruger Park,' she informed him.

Francis thought the rug would have looked better on the animal, however, he thought twice of saying something as he hadn't got the room yet.

After introducing himself as Derek Smith, he followed the landlady, Mrs Julia Potting, up the stairs to the second door on the landing. For a second the memories came flooding back. Francis recognised the hall and stairs.

Mrs Potting informed him, 'We've lived here since 1967. My husband died last year, so as there was only the two of us it was either downsize or keep the house and convert it into flats. I live in the ground floor flat and this second floor one is to rent.' She gave him a smile, 'You're my first prospective tenant.'

She escorted Francis through the rooms. It all looked maintenance free with white emulsion walls, woodblock flooring and a white tiled bathroom suite. After some payment negotiations for water, gas, electricity and rates, they shook hands and it was agreed he'd move in on the coming Monday. Francis immediately payed cash up front for the first two months' rent. He wanted her to feel secure in the knowledge that money would not be an issue and he wasn't going to do a runner owing rent.

Francis was pleased. The plan was to lie low for a while and then move abroad to Fire Island. He still had the blackmail money from his father.

Francis and his former boyfriend, Isaac Constantine, had been on holiday once to the seaside resort on Fire Island, about sixty miles east of New York. It was a gay mans' paradise of bars, clubs, restaurants and hotels where anything goes. One could dress as a drag queen. Parade as a transvestite or just walk arm in arm with your lover just wearing a tight fitting pair of swimming trunks and smooch openly without being arrested. Before the singer was killed he had talked of buying a summer home there for themselves.

*

It was the third day of his tenancy and one morning as Francis made his way down the stairs he heard the postman deliver the mail. Three letters were on the doormat. Francis nonchalantly picked them up to leave on the telephone table for Mrs Potting. One of them grabbed his attention. It was covered in postage marks with many redirected addresses.

It appeared to have lost its way getting to this one. Some of the faded postage dates were eight years old. It was the name on the envelope that made him freeze. Annabel was clearly written in neat handwriting. That was the girl he'd killed. Francis glanced over his shoulder. He hadn't been heard so he pocketed the letter.

Upstairs in the safety of his flat he carefully steamed open the envelope. At the top was an Australian address. At the bottom it was signed Twigs. The letter explained she was sorry she hadn't written earlier but had so much going on as one could imagine, emigrating with her parents. The college in Brisbane was great but she missed her friends. The letter went on to say she was having similar problems with her nosey mum. Her dad was okay but mum wanted to know who her new friends were? Who was she telephoning? No doubt checking out her bedroom for drugs and contraceptive pills while she was at her new college.

Twigs highlighted that she took her advice and hid her own diary in the wall vent. Then came other news about a boy she was keen on and they'd studied together at the college library.

Francis reread the passage concerning the diary in the wall vent. Could it be? He wondered.

He proceeded to check out all the rooms in his flat. None had air vents.

Later in the morning from his upstairs window he watched Mrs Potting go shopping. Now he had a chance to check out the other walls without being heard.

Using the end of a broom, Francis tried every room, knocking along the walls high up for a hollow sound, just in case they'd been covered up during the house renovation. No such luck, it all sounded solid behind the wall plaster. Then he remembered the other door on the opposite side of the balcony landing. Mrs Potting had informed him that was her painting studio. She'd dabbled all her life painting wildlife scenes but had concentrated more on the hobby since her husband had died.

Double checking through the window in case she was on her way back, he moved over to the other landing door. Francis tried the handle but it was locked. He looked through the keyhole and could see some paintings and an easel.

Two days later on the Friday morning, with the diary still clawing at his mind, he got a bit of luck. Mrs Potting informed him she was off to see her sister in Daventry for the weekend and wouldn't be back until the Monday. Francis smiled, and responded he hoped she had a nice time and a safe journey. When Friday evening came he couldn't contain himself. Alone in the house at last, the world was his oyster. Overhead he heard the rumble of a summer storm brooding and his curtains flickered with lightning.

By eleven o'clock, and quite sure Mrs Potting was safely on her way, Francis softly and purposefully made his way across the balcony landing. The storm was overhead now and rain continually lashed the large landing window.

Using a hairgrip he'd found on the downstairs hallway carpet, Francis picked at the lock and cursed under his breath. It always looked so easy in films and television. Then just as he was about to give up and perhaps call a locksmith in the morning under the pretence that he'd lost the key, he jiggled it once more and a heavy click was heard. Francis turned the doorknob in anticipation and the door swung inwards.

The room smelt of lacquer and turpentine. Hung paintings danced into life as white lightning strobed them into movement while thunder rolled and shook the house. He closed the bedroom door carefully, holding a torch. He'd rather use a torch. Best thing in case a neighbour spotted a light and told Mrs Potting when she got back.

Playing the pencil torch, Francis could see canvasses propped against white painted walls. An easel stood on sentry by the window. Now he recognised the bedroom. It had been Annabel's bedroom. The pencilled spotlight searched the walls high up until, it finally rested on an air brick.

Positioning a small set of steps that she probably used for her extra-large paintings, Francis with the aid of the palette knife stuck the blade in one of the vent holes and tried to lever the brick. It was loose. He tried levering again. This time after some cursing the airbrick pulled away.

Francis couldn't control his excitement. He swept away the remaining bits of rubble and shone the torch into the gaping hole. Instantly he felt elated, as if he'd discovered a fresh seam of gold or like Carter with the treasures of Tutankhamun.

There in the dusty cavity lay a diary. Francis clutched it feverishly. He stepped down from the ladder and using the torch he flicked through the pages to the last entry. The message, ***I knew it was you, Francis Hodder***, stared back at him. For a second he couldn't quite comprehend. The date on the page was wrong. It stated this year's date August 1973. It should have been August 1965.

At that moment, on cue with a tremendous thunderclap, the bedroom illuminated with Mrs Potting's hand on the light switch. Francis spun round in shock.

'Is *this* what you're looking for, Francis? *Oh my God.*' She cut off and shrunk back in shock.

Francis was wearing his favourite. A black Cleopatra wig with tanned make up, set against a heavy red outline of lipstick and green eye shadow together with fishnet stockings and high heels. A shiny black leather crotch pouch complimented the matching suspenders and garter belt. The red brassiere stuffed with cotton wool stood out against his hairy chest. He sneered at her. 'The name's Roxanne, you nosy Bitch.'

Just then a white flash lit up the hallway behind her and a roll of thunder boomed. Mrs Potting flinched but she wasn't going to be phased. She said defiantly, 'The letter you found was fake. I wrote and planted it after I saw your Roxanne tattoo. Annabel mentioned it in her diary. There was no point in going to the police first as I had to be sure. And now I know.' She held up the diary. 'It's all in here, you pervert. This is her real diary. How she saw you in the bushes on the day she disappeared. How you chased her. She named *you*, Francis, and the Roxanne tattoo. All her secrets in that wall, and nobody knew until I found it three months ago while decorating.'

Francis reached into his brassiere for the letter. *'Before that letter arrived. Before that bloody letter came, everything was fine.'* The veins in his neck bulged with anger as he started tearing it up, ripping it into shreds symbolically.

Holding her gaze with a vicious sneer he said, 'We can work this out, Mrs Potting. No one has to know. I can pay you. I have money.' Francis advanced slowly towards her holding the palette knife.

Mrs Potting stepped backwards clutching the diary.

'I have too much to lose, Mrs Potting. My whole life is before me. I can't have it ruined by the petty diary scribble of some snooping college girl. Give me the diary, Mrs Potting.' Francis came nearer brandishing the palette knife.

She edged out of the bedroom onto the balcony landing. Her back rested on the rail. It was dark apart from the continuous flashes of white lightening that flickered through the landing window and lit up the white walls as thunder echoed and shook the house.

Francis slowly approached. *One little push* he thought, *and then I'm free.* He moved quickly to the side to cut off the stairs. She was trapped. The other end of the balcony was a walled dead end.

Francis's lips were pulled back into a sickly grin. Spit shone on his teeth as his face lit up momentarily with a flash followed by a roll of thunder. Like a Zombie in an old horror movie, he came steadily nearer with the palette knife raised.

Mrs Potting screamed and lunged at him grabbing his arm, both her hands now wrestling for the palette knife.

Suddenly, the huge oak tree in the back garden was struck by a lightning bolt. Both of them ducked at the massive explosion. Then came splintering and more cracking sounds until, the landing window caved inwards with the tree crashing through and finally coming to rest on the balcony rail amongst brick and rubble.

Francis froze, spellbound. He stared in disbelief. Then the rail gave way under the weight. He lost his balance skidding on the slippery leaves. His arms were waving, flailing, trying to grab a hold of something, anything to save himself.

Just in time, he clutched one of the balustrades. He screamed, *'Help me! Please, Mrs Potting.'* His body dangled over the edge of the balcony. One of his high heel shoes dropped off and cluttered as it hit the hall floor below. Francis was beginning to lose his grip. *'Please, help me. I'll do whatever you say. I'll tell them it was me. Just help me up. Please!'*

Mrs Potting picked up a piece of broken balustrade.

Francis looked up at her. His pleading eyes followed what she was holding.

She raised the splintered balustrade. She held it aloft for a few seconds and smiled at Francis. And then she smashed it down on his head.

He screamed and then was gone. A dull thud echoed below, quickly followed by a muffled scream.

Mrs Potting walked slowly down the stairs, as if in a trance. Her face was white, deathly white. The storm was moving away. The hall was now lit with faint pulsating flashes, as if illuminated from a dyeing neon sign.

Francis was still moving, impaled on one of the ornamental elephant tusks. It had gone through his spine. He was twitching in spasms like a maggot on a hook. His mouth was open, all bloody with red lipstick. With staring eyes he grinned like a dead carp.

She knelt and stroked the Roxanne tattoo on Francis's arm. If it hadn't been mentioned in the diary she might have never known. Fortunately being short sleeve weather, she'd spotted it when he first called.

Mrs Potting nonchalantly picked up the remains of Annabel's diary and flicked through the pages. Then she said to no one, 'She may have been a snooping college girl, but she happened to be *my* daughter.'

CHAPTER THIRTY-THREE

At 1:15 a.m. the six bedroom house in Virginia Water amongst the gated privileged residents of an exclusive cul-de-sac was quiet. Commander Gregory Potting this early Saturday morning, after three large twelve year old malts, was snoring away much to the annoyance of his wife. The duvet had been pulled backwards and forwards between them. Finally with one fierce tug his wife had major ownership at the moment. It was then the telephone rang.

Mrs Potting from years of experience had let it ring until her other half, fumbled and searched until the feel of a receiver silenced the annoying telephone shrill.

Commander Potting cursed, snorted and coughed and then clearly annoyed said, 'Yes, who's this?'

Julia Potting said shakily, 'Sorry to call you at this time but I thought I'd check with you first before I ring the police.'

'Julia,' what is it?' He sat bolt upright clutching the phone.

'Remember when I found the diary and you told me to hold fire, not to alert the police just yet. Well you'll never guess. Like you said. One day the killer might return and he did. It's a pity my husband isn't alive to see it. Your brother would have had some satisfaction before he passed away.'

'What! You mean you caught him?'

'Francis Hodder is in my hallway now dressed as…as some transvestite and very dead.'

'Dear, Christ, what happened?'

'He tried to kill me when I recognised him. He admitted killing her. The storm saved my life. We had a tree crash through a window and collapse the balcony we were standing on. He fell down onto one of those elephant tusks.' Julia added, 'Very messy.'

He said concerned, 'Julia, are you okay?'

Julia Potting gulped and said shakily, 'I'm okay, just wondered what I should do?'

'You said a tree crashed through. Have any neighbours called on you?'

'Not yet. It was at the back facing the park. With the storm no one probably heard.'

Commander Potting slid from his bed cupping the receiver. He wanted to be out of earshot from his wife. Shielding the phone he whispered, 'Now listen, Julia, we have to keep this under wraps. What's done is done. No point in calling the police. If any neighbours call don't let them in. Just say you've got the fire service on the way. Is that clear?'

'Yes…yes okay.' She hesitated and then said, 'Greg, what about that Reginald Stanton, the man they put away for Annabel's murder?'

'Too bad about him. He was a known villain anyway.' The Commander paused. 'Look, Julia, this could prove very embarrassing for the Home office for putting away the wrong man and for my department. We used Francis Hodder a while back. I can't say anymore, it's classified. Then he went into hiding. We've been after him sometime. If it all came out we had links with a known killer, was shielding this killer. Then the press would have a field day and my head would be on the block.' Commander Potting pulled his cigarettes and lit one. He'd been trying to give up and had since stopped smoking at work. He inhaled deeply. 'Stay where you are, Julia, and I'll get some people over to you immediately to get rid of him.'

She replied nervously. 'Okay, Greg, I'll do as you say.'

'Julia, it's no consolation, but at least we got the bastard that killed your daughter. What happens to him after that is of no concern. So not a word to anyone. Is that clear?'

'Yes…yes of course, Greg. I understand.'

'I'll call a cab and be with you in about an hour. Don't worry.'

Commander Potting finished the call and then dialled the clean-up number. 'Need to take away, right now, one basket of dirty linen and a spring clean afterwards at twenty-eight Fairfax Avenue, Ewell, near Nonsuch Park.'

He replaced the receiver deep in thought.

It was his wife who jolted him back. She turned over and sleepily said, 'Who the Christ was that at this hour?'

'Oh it was Julia. Ringing to say she'd had some storm damage. Tree had crashed through her window. She was worried being on her own. Wanted me to come over and deal with it. I won't be long.'

*

Commander Gregory Potting stood by the window of his large office. From here as always he could look down on Whitehall. Across the road was Banqueting House with the Cabinet Office further down. The traffic was moving well. Again it was a sunny morning and he was in a good mood.

Catching his eye, he remembered his morning tea with a digestive. His private secretary, Margaret, always there on the dot with his elevenses. Commander Potting walked over to his desk and sat down. He sipped his Darjeeling and broke the biscuit in half. He took another sip and pulled the drawer of his new Cromwell pedestal leather topped desk. He withdrew the file marked Francis Hodder with (Roxanne) in brackets. With his usual lopsided smile he rolled the stamp on the pad and thumped down in red letters EXPIRED on the buff cover.

www.ingramcontent.com/pod-product-compliance
Lightning Source LLC
Chambersburg PA
CBHW070747190726
48292CB00002B/447